TRANSCENDENT 2

TRANSCENDENT 2

The Year's Best Transgender Speculative Fiction

Edited by Bogi Takács

Lethe Press
Amherst, MA

Published in 2017 by Lethe Press, Inc.
6 University Drive, Suite 206 / PMB #223, Amherst, MA 01002
www.lethepressbooks.com • lethepress@aol.com isbn: 978-1-59021-662-0 / 1-59021-662-8

Set in Agmena, Truesdell, and Charlemagne.
Interior design: Alex Jeffers.
Cover art: Ari Utria.
Cover design: Inkspiral Design.

CONTENTS

INTRODUCTION

◄ Bogi Takács ►

The new trans revolution is here.

It is everywhere: in the streets, on the evening breaking news, and in speculative fiction. Trans people are no longer abstract talking points or "flavor" to spice up a story. We have been speaking for a very long time, and now the world is listening and engaging with us.

Trans characters and themes have been appearing in fantasy, science fiction, horror and all the myriad speculative subgenres. *Transcendent 2* samples from the best short-form work from the previous year, just like its predecessor *Transcendent* (edited by Kellan Szpara) did. The majority of the contributors to this anthology are transgender authors, though the project was very much open to cisgender authors writing about trans characters and themes respectfully. My goal was to showcase the best that trans SFF literature had to offer, and in so doing, reflect the multifaceted nature of current work.

Transcendent 2 has been a group effort. I asked my trans communities for help, and the stories poured in. People reposted the call for submissions, recommended their friends, sent me story leads, told me about potential stories for potential future anthologies too. I found and considered eighty-eight pieces from 2016, and purchased sixteen of them for reprinting. The quality of the submissions was very high, and I had many hard decisions to make. If you passed along the news or sent a story for consideration, you contributed to this anthology seeing the light of day, and I'd like to thank you right at the beginning.

Work reprinted in *Transcendent 2* had originally appeared in all kinds of venues, from self-publishing to the large online SFF professional magazines to small press publications to both traditionally published and Kickstarted anthologies. We are experiencing an explosion in trans literature, and speculative fiction is at the forefront of it.

There are so many trans writers that several large, separate circles have emerged that are currently engaging with SFF. There is often little crosstalk between these groups. Therefore, I sought out submissions as widely as I could, sending out over thirty solicitations to trans writers who otherwise might have missed such a call. I am happy to say that these solicitations resulted in many wonderful submissions and several purchases.

Trans writing communities are diverse in multiple senses of the term, and this is hopefully reflected in *Transcendent 2*. Many of the contributors are trans people of color, disabled trans people, and they are also positioned all over the trans spectrum — trans women, trans men, non-binary people with all kinds of gender IDs. This variety of perspectives is reflected in the characters, plots and settings of the stories as well.

The work in this anthology also has a wide range of emotional and thematic diversity. There are some very heavy stories in the collection, examining topics like the suicide of a partner in "The Pigeon Summer," or bullying in "The Nothing Spots Where Nobody Wants to Stay." But there is also plenty of hope and reassurance. In "The Way You Say Good-Night," a mortal who hasn't "found a gender that fits" rooms with a goddess and finds love despite difficulties. In "Happy REGARDS," everyone gets together to celebrate the birthday of a trans woman singer who is a key figure in her queer community, in the dystopian future.

Writers engage with all sorts of topics from classic SFF tropes in "This Is Not a Wardrobe Door" to Indigenous cultural traditions in "Transitions." These stories can be elaborately poetic like "Skerry-Bride," dynamic and explosive like "Three Points Masculine," mind-bendingly experimental like "Rhizomatic Diplomacy." There is the near future hard SF of "The L7 Gene" and the secondary-world musical fantasy of "Sky and Dew," alongside the newest, hottest approaches in SFF like the solarpunk elements in "Because Change Was the Ocean."

Transness can be more or less explicit — it can be brutally foregrounded, like in "Lisa's Story: Zombie Apocalypse," where a trans woman faces as much, if not more threat from human survivors as from the undead. But in *Transcendent* there is also room for more metaphorical transformations, like changing species in "Her Sacred Spirit Soars." While most of the included stories deal with transgender topics, I did not want to shut out work about nonhuman or posthuman transformations informed by real-world transgender perspectives, either.

Transness also manifests in relationship to others, and these stories showcase the place of trans people in the wider social fabric — sometimes in a very speculative sense. There is support between people of different ages in a post-apocalyptic rural future, like in "About a Woman and a Kid." There is gentle love between young people, even in a land of giant traveling monsters, as in "The Road, the Valley and the Beasts." There is collaboration and strife, kindness and fervor. Stories are in dialog with each other, like their authors.

Yet there are still gaps to fill. As a migrant from a non-Western country, I was on the lookout for stories by non-Western authors, but I found much fewer than I'd hoped for. I also wanted to include at least one translation, but sadly none of the translations I could locate worked for the purposes of the anthology. Translations seem increasingly common in English-language SFF, so I have high hopes for the following years.

I mentioned in the call for submissions that I'd be happy to consider intersex stories too — while these are thematically distinct, they are also both related and chronically underpromoted. I sadly couldn't find much intersex work to consider. A.J. Odasso had some powerful intersex-themed speculative poetry in 2016, some of which was also nominated for the Rhysling Award, but no related fiction in the past year.

While I could not include novels in the anthology, I want to mention some standout SFF novels in trans literature in 2016. Gabrielle Squailia's *Viscera* (published as Gabriel Squailia) was wildly inventive and still eminently readable dark fantasy. Yoon Ha Lee's military space opera *Ninefox Gambit* approached transness from an oblique angle of body-sharing, and at the time of writing this is up for several major SFF awards. RoAnna Sylver's superhero dystopian fantasy *Chameleon Moon* saw a new, updated second edition. And the list goes on and on, with each new story and book filling a longstanding gap in speculative literature.

Acknowledgments

I worked on this anthology in the traditional lands of the Kanza and Osage people, who were forcibly removed from their homes in the late nineteenth century. Today this land is still a home to people from many Indigenous nations, and I would like to acknowledge their presence and express my gratitude toward them.

TRANSCENDENT 2

Bogi Takács ▶

I would like to express my thanks to the following people for their story rec-ommendations, writer referrals and all manner of kind help (in alphabetic order by first name): Amy Jo Cousins, Everett Maroon, Jamie Berrout, Jeanne Thorn-ton, M. Eighteen Téllez and Shira Glassman. I owe story recommendations to D Libris and MamaDeb — I hope this anthology will serve as an entire bundle of recommendations! Thank you also to Kellan Szpara, who graciously shared his experience of editing the first *Transcendent* anthology, and Steve Berman for providing a home for the project. I am also grateful to my wonderful Spouseper-son Rose Lemberg for all their support, and Mati the Child, who kept my spirits up by childing.

G ood reading, and may the stories in *Transcendent* 2 resonate with you.

BECAUSE CHANGE WAS THE OCEAN AND WE LIVED BY HER MERCY

◄ Charlie Jane Anders ►

1. This was sacred, this was stolen

We stood naked on the shore of Bernal and watched the candles float across the bay, swept by a lazy current off to the north, in the direction of Potrero Island. A dozen or so candles stayed afloat and alight after half a league, their tiny flames bobbing up and down, casting long yellow reflections on the dark water alongside the streaks of moonlight. At times I fancied the candlelight could filter down onto streets and buildings, the old automobiles and houses full of children's toys, all the waterlogged treasures of long-gone people. We held hands, twenty or thirty of us, and watched the little candle-boats we'd made as they floated away. Joconda was humming an old reconstructed song about the wild road, hir beard full of flowers. We all just about held our breath. I felt my bare skin go electric with the intensity of the moment, like this could be the good time we'd all remember in the bad times to come. This was sacred, this was stolen. And then someone — probably Miranda — farted, and then we were all laughing, and the grown-up seriousness was gone. We were all busting up and falling over each other on the rocky ground, in a nude heap, scraping our knees and giggling into each other's limbs. When we got our breath back and looked up, the candles were all gone.

2. I felt like I had always been Wrong Headed

I couldn't deal with life in Fairbanks anymore. I grew up at the same time as the town, watched it go from regular city to mega-city as I hit my early twenties. I lived in an old decommissioned solar power station with five other kids, and we tried to make the loudest, most uncomforting music we could, with a beat as relentless and merciless as the tides. We wanted to shake our cinderblock walls and make people dance until their feet bled. But we sucked. We were bad at music, and not quite dumb enough not to know it. We all wore big hoods and spiky shoes and tried to make our own drums out of drycloth and cracked wood, and we read our poetry on Friday nights. There were bookhouses, along with stinktanks where you could drink up and listen to awful poetry about extinct animals. People came from all over, because everybody heard that Fairbanks was becoming the most civilized place on Earth, and that's when I decided to leave town. I had this moment of looking around at my musician friends and my restaurant job and our cool little scene, and feeling like there had to be more to life than this.

I hitched a ride down south and ended up in Olympia, at a house where they were growing their own food and drugs, and doing a way better job with the drugs than the food. We were all staring upwards at the first cloud anybody had seen in weeks, trying to identify what it could mean. When you hardly ever saw them, clouds had to be omens.

We were all complaining about our dumb families, still watching that cloud warp and contort, and I found myself talking about how my parents only liked to listen to that boring boo-pop music with the same three or four major chords and that cruddy AAA/BBB/CDE/CDE rhyme scheme, and how my mother insisted on saving every scrap of organic material we used, and collecting every drop of rainwater. "It's fucking pathetic, is what it is. They act like we're still living in the Great Decimation."

"They're just super traumatized," said this skinny genderfreak named Juya, who stood nearby holding the bong. "It's hard to even imagine. I mean, we're the first generation that just takes it for granted we're going to survive, as like a species. Our parents, our grandparents, and their grandparents, they were all living like every day could be the day the planet finally got done with us. They didn't grow up having moisture condensers and mycoprotein rinses and skinsus."

"Yeah, whatever," I said. But what Juya said stuck with me, because I had never thought of my parents as traumatized. I'd always thought they were just tightly wound and judgy. Juya had two cones of dark twisty hair on zir head and a red pajamzoot, and zi was only a year or two older than me but seemed a lot wiser.

"I want to find all the music we used to have," I said. "You know, the weird, noisy shit that made people's clothes fall off and their hair light on fire. The rock 'n' roll that just listening to it turned girls into boys, the songs that took away the fear of god. I've read about it, but I've never heard any of it, and I don't even know how to play it."

"Yeah, all the recordings and notations got lost in the Dataclysm," Juya said. "They were in formats that nobody can read, or they got corrupted, or they were printed on disks made from petroleum. Those songs are gone forever."

"I think they're under the ocean," I said. "I think they're down there somewhere."

Something about the way I said that helped Juya reach a decision. "Hey, I'm heading back down to the San Francisco archipelago in the morning. I got room in my car if you wanna come with."

Juya's car was an older solar model that had to stop every couple hours to recharge, and the self-driving module didn't work so great. My legs were resting in a pile of old headmods and biofills, plus those costooms that everybody used a few summers earlier that made your skin turn into snakeskin that you could shed in one piece. So the upshot was, we had a lot of time to talk and hold hands and look at the endless golden landscape stretching off to the east. Juya had these big bright eyes that laughed when the rest of zir face was stone serious, and strong tentative hands to hold me in place as zi tied me to the car seat with fronds of algae. I had never felt as safe and dangerous as when I crossed the wasteland with Juya. We talked for hours about how the world needed new communities, new ways to breathe life back into the ocean, new ways to be people.

By the time we got to Bernal Island and the Wrong Headed community, I was in love with Juya, deeper than I'd ever felt with anyone before.

Juya up and left Bernal a week and a half later, because zi got bored again, and I barely noticed that zi was gone. By then, I was in love with a hundred other people, and they were all in love with me.

Bernal Island was only accessible from one direction, from the big island in the middle, and only at a couple times of day when they let the bridge down and turned off the moat. After a few days on Bernal, I stopped even noticing the other islands on our horizon, let alone paying attention to my friends on social media talking about all the fancy new restaurants Fairbanks was getting. I was constantly having these intense, heartfelt moments with people in the Wrong Headed crew.

"The ocean is our lover, you can hear it laughing at us." Joconda was sort of the leader here. Sie sometimes had a beard and sometimes a smooth round face covered with perfect bright makeup. Hir eyes were as gray as the sea and just as unpredictable. For decades, San Francisco and other places like it had been abandoned, because the combination of seismic instability and a voracious dead ocean made them too scary and risky. But that city down there, under the waves, had been the place everybody came to, from all over the world, to find freedom. That legacy was ours now.

And those people had brought music from their native countries and their own cultures, and all those sounds had crashed together in those streets, night after night. Joconda's own ancestors had come from China and Peru, and hir great-grandparents had played nine-stringed guitars, melodies and rhythms that Joconda barely recalled now. Listening to hir, I almost fancied I could put my ear to the surface of the ocean and hear all the sounds from generations past, still reverberating. We sat all night, Joconda, some of the others and myself, and I got to play on an old-school drum made of cowhide or something. I felt like I had always been Wrong Headed, and I'd just never had the word for it before.

Juya sent me an email a month or two after zi left Bernal: "The moment I met you, I knew you needed to be with the rest of those maniacs. I've never been able to resist delivering lost children to their rightful homes. It's almost the only thing I'm good at, other than the things you already knew about." I never saw zir again.

3. "I'm so glad I found a group of people I would risk drowning in dead water for."

Back in the twenty-first century, everybody had theories about how to make the ocean breathe again. Fill her with quicklime, to neutralize the acid. Split the water molecules into hydrogen and oxygen, and bond the hydrogen with the surplus carbon in the water to create a clean-burning hydrocarbon fuel. Release genetically engineered fish, with special gills. Grow special algae that was designed to commit suicide after a while. Spray billions of nanotech balls into her. And a few other things. Now, we had to clean up the after-effects of all those failed solutions, while also helping the sea to let go of all that CO_2 from before.

The only way was the slow way. We pumped ocean water through our special enzyme store and then through a series of filters, until what came out the other end was clear and oxygen-rich. The waste, we separated out and disposed of. Some of it became raw materials for shoe soles and roof tiles. Some of it, the pure organic residue, we used as fertilizer or food for our mycoprotein.

I got used to staying up all night playing music with some of the other Wrong Headed kids, sometimes on the drum and sometimes on an old stringed instrument that was made of stained wood and had a leering cat face under its fret. Sometimes I thought I could hear something in the way our halting beats and scratchy notes bounced off the walls and the water beyond, like we were really conjuring a lost soundtrack. Sometimes it all just seemed like a waste.

What did it mean to be a real authentic person, in an era when everything great from the past was twenty feet underwater? Would you embrace prefab newness, or try to copy the images you can see from the handful of docs we'd scrounged from the Dataclysm? When we got tired of playing music, an hour before dawn, we would sit around arguing, and inevitably you got to that moment where you were looking straight into someone else's eyes and arguing about the past, and whether the past could ever be on land, or the past was doomed to be deep underwater forever.

I felt like I was just drunk all the time, on that cheap-ass vodka that everybody chugged in Fairbanks, or maybe on nitrous. My head was evaporating, but my heart just got more and more solid. I woke up every day on my bunk, or sometimes tangled up in someone else's arms and legs on the daybed, and felt actually jazzed to get up and go clean the scrubbers or churn the mycoprotein vats.

Every time we put down the bridge to the big island and turned off our moat, I felt everything go sour inside me, and my heart went funnel-shaped. People sometimes just wandered away from the Wrong Headed community without much in the way of goodbye — that was how Juya had gone — but meanwhile, new people showed up and got the exact same welcome that everyone had given to me. I got freaked out thinking of my perfect home being overrun by new selfish loud fuckers. Joconda had to sit me down, at the big table where sie did all the official business, and tell me to get over myself because change was the ocean and we lived on her mercy. "Seriously, Pris. I ever see that look on your face, I'm going to throw you into the myco vat myself." Joconda stared at me until I started laughing and promised to get with the program.

And then one day I was sitting at our big table, overlooking the straits between us and the big island. Staring at Sutro Tower and the tops of the skyscrapers poking out of the water here and there. And this obnoxious skinny bitch sat down next to me, chewing in my ear and talking about the impudence of impermanence or some similar. "Miranda," she introduced herself. "I just came up from Anaheim-Diego. Jeez, what a mess. They actually think they can build nanomechs and make it scalable. Whatta bunch of poutines."

"Stop chewing in my ear," I muttered. But then I found myself following her around everywhere she went.

Miranda was the one who convinced me to dive into the chasm of Fillmore Street in search of a souvenir from the old Church of John Coltrane, as a present for Joconda. I strapped on some goggles and a big apparatus that fed me oxygen while also helping me to navigate a little bit, and then we went out in a dinghy that looked old enough that someone had actually used it for fishing. Miranda gave me one of her crooked grins and studied a wrinkled old map. "I thinnnnnk it's right around here." She laughed. "Either that or the Korean barbecue restaurant where the mayor got assassinated that one time. Not super clear which is which."

I gave her a murderous look and jumped into the water, letting myself fall into the street at the speed of water resistance. Those sunken buildings turned into doorways and windows facing me, but they stayed blurry as the bilge flowed around them. I could barely find my feet, let alone identify a building on sight. One of these places had been a restaurant, I was pretty sure. Ancient automobiles lurched back and forth, like maybe even their brakes had rusted away. I figured the Church of John Coltrane would have a spire like a saxophone? Maybe? But all of the buildings looked exactly the same. I stumbled down the street, until I saw something that looked like a church, but it was a caved-in old McDonald's restaurant. Then I tripped over something, a downed pole or whatever, and my face mask cracked as I went down. The water was going down my throat, tasting like dirt, and my vision went all pale and wavy.

I almost just went under, but then I thought I could see a light up there, way above the street, and I kicked. I kicked and chopped and made myself float. I churned up there until I broke the surface. My arms were thrashing above the water and then I started to go back down, but Miranda had my neck and one shoulder. She hauled me up and out of the water and threw me into the dinghy. I was gasping and heaving up water, and she just sat and laughed at me.

"You managed to scavenge something after all." She pointed to something I'd clutched at on my way up out of the water: a rusted, barbed old piece of a car. "I'm sure Joconda will love it."

"Ugh," I said. "Fuck Old San Francisco. It's gross and corroded and there's nothing left of whatever used to be cool. But hey. I'm glad I found a group of people I would risk drowning in dead water for."

4. I chose to see that as a special status

Miranda had the kind of long-limbed, snaggle-toothed beauty that made you think she was born to make trouble. She loved to roughhouse, and usually ended up with her elbow on the back of my neck as she pushed me onto the dry dirt. She loved to invent cute insulting nicknames for me, like "Dolly-pris" or "Pris Ridiculous." She never got tired of reminding me that I might be a ninth level genderfreak, but I had all kinds of privilege, because I grew up in Fairbanks and never had to wonder how we were going to eat.

Miranda had this way of making me laugh even when the news got scary, when the government back in Fairbanks was trying to reestablish control over the whole West Coast, and extinction rose up like the shadows at the bottom of the sea. I would start to feel that scab inside my stomach, like the whole ugly unforgiving world could come down on us and our tiny island sanctuary at any moment, Miranda would suddenly start making up a weird dance or inventing a motto for a team of superhero mosquitos, and then I would be laughing so hard it was like I was squeezing the fear out of my insides. Her hands were a mass of scar tissue but they were as gentle as dried-up blades of grass on my thighs.

Miranda had five other lovers, but I was the only one she made fun of. I chose to see that as a special status.

5. "What are you people even about"

Falling in love with a community is always going to be more real that any love for a single human being could ever be. People will let you down, shatter your image of them, or try to melt down the wall between your self-image and theirs. People, one at a time, are too messy. Miranda was my hero and the lover I'd pretty much dreamed of since both puberties, but I also saved pieces of my heart for a bunch of other Wrong Headed people. I loved Joconda's totally random inspirations and perversions, like all of the art projects sie started getting me to build out of scraps from the sunken city after I brought back that car piece from Fillmore Street. Zell was this hyperactive kid with wild half-braids, who had this whole theory about digging up buried hard drives full of music files from the digital age, so we could reconstruct the actual sounds of Marvin Gaye and the Jenga Priests. Weo used to sit with me and watch the sunset going down over the islands, we didn't talk a lot except that Weo would suddenly whisper some weird beautiful notion about what it would be like to live at sea, one day when the sea was alive again. But it wasn't any individual, it was the whole group, we had gotten in a rhythm together and we all believed the same stuff. The love of the ocean, and her resilience in the face of whatever we had done to her, and the power of silliness to make you believe in abundance again. Openness, and a kind of generosity that is the opposite of monogamy.

But then one day I looked up, and some of the faces were different again. A few of my favorite people in the community had bugged out without saying anything, and one or two of the newcomers started seriously getting on my nerves. One person, Mage, just had a nasty temper, going off at anyone who crossed hir path whenever xie was in one of those moods, and you could usually tell from the unruly condition of Mage's bleach-blond hair and the broke-toothed scowl. Mage became one of Miranda's lovers right off the bat, of course.

I was just sitting on my hands and biting my tongue, reminding myself that I always hated change and then I always got used to it after a little while. This would be fine: change was the ocean and she took care of us.

Then we discovered the spoilage. We had been filtering the ocean water, removing toxic waste, filtering out excess gunk, and putting some of the organic byproducts into our mycoprotein vats as a feedstock. But one day, we opened the biggest vat and the stench was so powerful we all started to cry and retch, and we kept crying even after the puking stopped. Shit, that was half our food supply. It looked like our whole filtration system was off, there were remnants of buckystructures in the residue that we'd been feeding to our fungus, and the fungus was choking on them. Even the fungus that wasn't spoiled would have minimal protein yield. And this also meant that our filtration system wasn't doing anything to help clean the ocean, at all, because it was still letting the dead pieces of buckycrap through.

Joconda just stared at the mess and finally shook hir head and told us to bury it under the big hillside.

We didn't have enough food for the winter after that, so a bunch of us had to make the trip up north to Marin, by boat and on foot, to barter with some gun-crazy farmers in the hills. And they wanted free labor in exchange for food, so we left Weo and a few others behind to work in their fields. Trudging back down the hill pulling the first batch of produce in a cart, I kept looking over my shoulder to see our friends staring after us, as we left them surrounded by old dudes with rifles.

TRANSCENDENT 2

I couldn't look at the community the same way after that. Joconda fell into a depression that made hir unable to speak or look anyone in the eye for days at a time, and we were all staring at the walls of our poorly repaired dormitory buildings, which looked as though a strong wind could bring them down. I kept remembering myself walking away from those farmers, the way I told Weo it would be fine, we'd be back before anyone knew anything, this would be a funny story later. I tried to imagine myself doing something different. Putting my foot down maybe, or saying fuck this, we don't leave our own behind. It didn't seem like something I would ever do, though. I had always been someone who went along with what everybody else wanted. My one big act of rebellion was coming here to Bernal Island, and I wouldn't have ever come if Juya hadn't already been coming.

Miranda saw me coming and walked the other way. That happened a couple of times. She and I were supposed to have a fancy evening together, I was going to give her a bath even if it used up half my water allowance, but she canceled. We were on a tiny island but I kept only seeing her off in the distance, in a group of others, but whenever I got closer she was gone. At last I saw her walking on the big hill, and I followed her up there, until we were almost at eye level with the Transamerica Pyramid coming up out of the flat water. She turned and grabbed at the collar of my shirt and part of my collarbone. "You gotta let me have my day," she hissed. "You can't be in my face all the time. Giving me that look. You need to get out of my face."

"You blame me," I said, "for Weo and the others. For what happened."

"I blame you for being a clingy wet blanket. Just leave me alone for a while. Jeez." And then I kept walking behind her, and she turned and either made a gesture that connected with my chest, or else intentionally shoved me. I fell on my butt. I nearly tumbled head over heels down the rocky slope into the water, but then I got a handhold on a dead root.

"Oh fuck. Are you okay?" Miranda reached down to help me up, but I shook her off. I trudged down the hill alone.

I kept replaying that moment in my head, when I wasn't replaying the moment when I walked away with a ton of food and left Weo and the others at gunpoint. I had thought that being here, on this island, meant that the only past that mattered was the grand, mysterious, rebellious history that was down there under the water, in the wreckage of San Francisco. All of the wild music submerged between its walls. I had thought my own personal past no longer mattered at all.

TRANSCENDENT 2

Until suddenly, I had no mental energy for anything but replaying those two memories. Uglier each time around.

And then someone came up to me at lunch, as I sat and ate some of the proceeds from Weo's indenture: Kris, or Jamie, I forget which. And he whispered, "I'm on your side." A few other people said the same thing later that day. They had my back, Miranda was a bitch, she had assaulted me. I saw other people hanging around Miranda and staring at me, talking in her ear, telling her that I was a problem and they were with her.

I felt like crying, except that I couldn't find enough moisture inside me. I didn't know what to say to the people who were on my side. I was too scared to speak. I wished Joconda would wake up and tell everybody to quit it, to just get back to work and play and stop fomenting.

The next day, I went to the dining area, sitting at the other end of the long table from Miranda and her group of supporters. Miranda stood up so fast she knocked her own food on the floor, and she shouted at Yozni, "Just leave me the fuck alone. I don't want you on 'my side,' or anybody else. There are no sides. This is none of your business. You people. You goddamn people. What are you people even about?" She got up and left, kicking the wall on her way out.

After that, everybody was on my side.

6. The honeymoon was over, but the marriage was just starting

I rediscovered social media. I'd let my friendships with people back in Fairbanks and elsewhere run to seed, during all of this weird, but now I reconnected with people I hadn't talked to in a year or so. Everybody kept saying that Olympia had gotten really cool since I left, there was a vibrant music scene now and people were publishing zootbooks and having storytelling slams and stuff. And meanwhile, the government in Fairbanks had decided to cool it on trying to make the coast fall into line, though there was talk about some kind of loose articles of confederation at some point. Meanwhile, we'd even made some serious inroads against the warlords of Nevada.

I started looking around the dormitory buildings and kitchens and communal playspaces of Bernal, and at our ocean reclamation machines, as if I was trying to commit them to memory. One minute, I was looking at all of it as if this could be the last time I would see any of it, but then the next minute, I was just making peace with it so I could stay forever. I could just imagine how this moment could be the beginning of a new, more mature relationship with the Wrong Headed crew, where I wouldn't have any more illusions, but that would make my commitment even stronger.

I sat with Joconda and a few others, on that same stretch of shore where we'd all stood naked and launched candles, and we held hands after a while. Joconda smiled, and I felt like sie was coming back to us, so it was like the heart of our community was restored. "Decay is part of the process. Decay keeps the ocean warm." Today Joconda had wild hair with some bright colors in it, and a single strand of beard. I nodded.

Instead of the guilt or fear or selfish anxiety that I had been so aware of having inside me, I felt a weird feeling of acceptance. We were strong. We would get through this. We were Wrong Headed.

I went out in a dinghy and sailed around the big island, went up towards the ruins of Telegraph. I sailed right past the Newsom Spire, watching its carbon-fiber cladding flake away like shiny confetti. The water looked so opaque, it was like sailing on milk. I sat there in the middle of the city, a few miles from anyone, and felt totally peaceful. I had a kick of guilt at being so selfish, going off on my own when the others could probably use another pair of hands. But then I decided it was okay. I needed this time to myself. It would make me a better member of the community.

When I got back to Bernal, I felt calmer than I had in ages, and I was able to look at all the others — even Mage, who still gave me the murder eye from time to time — with patience and love. They were all my people. I was lucky to be among them.

I had this beautiful moment, that night, standing by a big bonfire with the rest of the crew, half of us some level of naked, and everybody looked radiant and free. I started to hum to myself, and it turned into a song, one of the old songs that Zell had supposedly brought back from digital extinction. It had this chorus about the wild kids and the wardance, and a bridge that doubled back on itself, and I had this feeling, like maybe the honeymoon is over, but the marriage is just beginning.

Then I found myself next to Miranda, who kicked at some embers with her boot. "I'm glad things calmed down," I whispered. "I didn't mean for everyone to get so crazy. We were all just on edge, and it was a bad time."

"Huh," Miranda said. "I noticed that you never told your peeps to cool it, even after I told the people defending me to shut their faces."

"Oh," I said. "But I actually," and then I didn't know what to say. I felt the feeling of helplessness, trapped in the grip of the past, coming back again. "I mean, I tried. I'm really sorry."

"Whatever," Miranda said. "I'm leaving soon. Probably going back to Anaheim-Diego. I heard they made some progress with the nanomechs after all."

"Oh." I looked into the fire, until my retinas were all blotchy. "I'll miss you."

"Whatever." Miranda slipped away. I tried to mourn her going, but then I realized I was just relieved. I wasn't going to be able to deal with her hanging around, like a bruise, when I was trying to move forward. With Miranda gone, I could maybe get back to feeling happy here.

Joconda came along when we went back up into Marin to get the rest of the food from those farmers, and collect Weo and the two others we had left there. We climbed up the steep path from the water, and Joconda kept needing to rest. Close to the water, everything was the kind of salty and moist that I'd gotten used to, but after a few miles, everything got dry and dusty. By the time we got to the farm, we were thirsty and we'd used up all our water, and the farmers saw us coming and got their rifles out.

Our friends had run away, the farmers said. Weo and the others. A few weeks earlier, and they didn't know where. They just ran off, left the work half done. So, too bad, we weren't going to get all the food we had been promised. Nothing personal, the lead farmer said. He had sunburnt cheeks, even though he wore a big straw hat. I watched Joconda's face pass through shock, anger, misery and resignation, without a single word coming out. The farmers had their guns slung over their shoulders, enough of a threat without even needing to aim. We took the cart, half full of food instead of all the way full, back down the hill to our boat.

We never found out what actually happened to Weo and the others.

7. "That's such an inappropriate line of inquiry I don't even know how to deal"

I spent a few weeks pretending I was in it for the long haul on Bernal Island, after we got back from Marin. This was my home, I had formed an identity here that meant the world to me, and these people were my family. Of course I was staying.

Then one day, I realized I was just trying to make up my mind whether to go back to Olympia, or all the way back to Fairbanks. In Fairbanks, they knew how to make thick-cut toast with egg smeared across it, you could go out dancing in

TRANSCENDENT 2

half a dozen different speakeasies that stayed open until dawn. I missed being in a real city, kind of. I realized I'd already decided to leave San Francisco a while ago, without ever consciously making the decision.

Everyone I had ever had a crush on, I had hooked up with already. Some of them, I still hooked up with sometimes, but it was nostalgia sex rather than anything else. I was actually happier sleeping alone, I didn't want anybody else's knees cramping my thighs in the middle of the night. I couldn't forgive the people who sided with Miranda against me, and I was even less able to forgive the people who sided with me against Miranda. I didn't like to dwell on stuff, but there were a lot of people I had obscure, unspoken grudges against, all around me. And then occasionally I would stand in a spot where I'd watched Weo sit and build a tiny raft out of sticks, and would feel the anger rise up all over again. At myself, mostly.

I wondered about what Miranda was doing now, and whether we would ever be able to face each other again. I had been so happy to see her go, but now I couldn't stop thinking about her.

The only time I even wondered about my decision was when I looked at the ocean, and the traces of the dead city underneath it, the amazing heritage that we were carrying on here. Sometimes I stared into the waves for hours, trying to hear the sound waves trapped in them, but then I started to feel like maybe the ocean had told me everything it was ever going to. The ocean always sang the same notes, it always passed over the same streets and came back with the same sad laughter. And staring down at the ocean only reminded me of how we'd thought we could help to heal her, with our enzyme treatments, a little at a time. I couldn't see why I had ever believed in that fairy tale. The ocean was going to heal on her own, sooner or later, but in the meantime we were just giving her meaningless therapy that made us feel better more than it actually helped. I got up every day and did my chores. I helped to repair the walls and tend the gardens and stuff. But I felt like I was just turning wheels to keep a giant machine going, so that I would be able to keep turning the wheels tomorrow.

I looked down at my own body, at the loose kelp-and-hemp garments I'd started wearing since I'd moved here. I looked at my hands and forearms, which were thicker, callused, and more veiny with all the hard work I'd been doing here — but also, the thousands of rhinestones in my fingernails glittered in the sunlight, and I felt like I moved differently than I used to. Even with all everything shitty that had happened, I'd learned something here, and wherever I went from now on, I would always be Wrong Headed.

TRANSCENDENT 2

I left without saying anything to anybody, the same way everyone else had.

A few years later, I had drinks with Miranda on that new floating platform that hovered over the wasteland of North America. Somehow we floated half a mile above the desert and the mountaintops — don't ask me how, but it was carbon neutral and all that good stuff. From up here, the hundreds of miles of parched earth looked like piles of gold.

"It's funny, right?" Miranda seemed to have guessed what I was thinking. "All that time, we were going on about the ocean and how it was our lover and our history and all that jazz. But look at that desert down there. It's all beautiful, too. It's another wounded environment, sure, but it's also a lovely fragment of the past. People sweated and died for that land, and maybe one day it'll come back. You know?" Miranda was, I guess, in her early thirties, and she looked amazing. She'd gotten the snaggle taken out of her teeth, and her hair was a perfect wave. She wore a crisp suit and she seemed powerful and relaxed. She'd become an important person in the world of nanomechs.

I stopped staring at Miranda and looked over the railing, down at the dunes. We'd made some pretty major progress at rooting out the warlords, but still nobody wanted to live there, in the vast majority of the continent. The desert was beautiful from up here, but maybe not so much up close.

"I heard Joconda killed hirself," Miranda said. "A while ago. Not because of anything in particular that had happened. Just the depression, it caught up with hir." She shook her head. "God. Sie was such an amazing leader. But hey, the Wrong Headed community is twice the size it was when you and I lived there, and they expanded onto the big island. I even heard they got a seat at the table of the confederation talks. Sucks that Joconda won't see what sie built get that recognition."

I was still dressed like a Wrong Headed person, even after a few years. I had the loose flowy garments, the smudgy paint on my face that helped obscure my gender rather than serving as a guide to it, the straight-line thin eyebrows and sparkly earrings and nails. I hadn't lived on Bernal in years, but it was still a huge part of who I was. Miranda looked like this whole other person, and I didn't know whether to feel ashamed that I hadn't moved on, or contemptuous of her for selling out, or some combination. I didn't know anybody who dressed the way Miranda was dressed, because I was still in Olympia where we were being radical artists.

I wanted to say something. An apology, or something sentimental about the amazing time we had shared, or I don't even know what. I didn't actually know what I wanted to say, and I had no words to put it into. So after a while I just raised my glass and we toasted to Wrong Headedness. Miranda laughed, that same old wild laugh, as our glasses touched. Then we went back to staring down at the wasteland, trying to imagine how many generations it would take before something green came out of it.

Thanks to Burrito Justice for the map, and Terry Johnson for the biotech insight true color of her eyes is the blue-black you see more often than not, licking like frostbite at your flesh; she is a stranger and you open the door to her every time, knowing someday there will be nothing to recognize.

You knew from the first, when a man with the wind-tightened face of a traveler and hair as pale as the drifting limbs of drowned men called you by the name you had not told him and you were not, instantly, afraid. It was summer then and he looked cool enough to lay like a nurse's wrist against your forehead, ice just melting to press against your lips. His bones were not boulders, he had only the usual number of heads; you saw two movies and a concert together, argued about representation in popular culture and ransacked your liquor cabinet for an experiment in obsolete cocktails, and when you woke that first morning beside a round-chinned woman whose hair coiled down between your skins as slipperily as shoreweed, it was no surprise. You did not try to guess her name, like a kenning riddle; she gave it before she left, quick as a flick of spray or the shiver-making skim of her mouth against yours one last time before she pulled on the T-shirt she had not been wearing last night and disappeared before she had even crossed the street. Only in the shower did you find the marks like port-wine spills or the press of great heat or cold, coming out under the slither of soap and water wherever his hands, hers, had rested for more than a moment on hip, shoulder, thigh, throat. They faded within the day, flared up tingling like pins and needles when a sharp-wristed girl with bilberries crushed around her mouth rapped two weeks later on the window where only oak leaves in their late-curling green had tossed a moment before. It is not an infallible sign. She has surprised you — squirrel, busker, shadow at the edge of the streetlight — before.

She will drown you, perhaps, one day, although you have never read that Ægir's daughters were sirens. You carry a gold coin in your pocket for her mother just in case, bought from the antique shop where the two of you lingered one afternoon over fin-de-siècle inkwells and memoirs of the merchant marine. She does not speak of Ragnarök or the Æsir, of Jötunheimr if she misses it or her father's cauldron-brewing hall, hung with the skins of sea-monsters and the nets of Rán. You joke about backpacking around Iceland or Norway, but not with your job as poor as it is, not with the strange nagging fear that Dröfn among her sisters might be something even less easily loved than the shape-changer she is now. Her kind are frost and fire and you cannot hold her safely or for long, no matter the shape she assumes to feel it. Your breath flashes white from kissing her, your fingers inside her ache like winter iron; she moves within you like a frozen sea, whitecaps above and the breathless abyss below. He lies afterward with his head in the hollow of your shoulder, winding the places over your still-trembling skin where his tattoos would twine like the bow of a dragon ship. When you begin to unbutton her hunter's shirt, the weight of her wave-rolling hair will blind you.

You touch her cheek, stark-boned as the failing season; you breathe her scent, this time of trampled rowan and rime. You watch her eyes shift color, the storm-light of St. Elmo's fire playing about church spires and mast-tops. You do not ask if she loves you, because she returns, any more that you tell her she does not, because she never returns the same. She leans into your touch, your warmth, everything she might be holding still for you; she is the stranger you know best and you draw the door shut behind her, this time as every other. You know what is true.

TRANSCENDENT 2

TRANSITIONS

◄ Gwen Benaway ►

I am late. Crossing subway lines, zigzagging through the city's underground, takes more time than I have. My Blackberry blinks red with twenty-five unread messages from work. My second phone, the one which links me to my other life, is also blinking with unread notifications. There is nothing for it but to rush to my appointment and hope there isn't anything urgent to deal with when I return to the office.

I push into the final train which will take me to the row of medical buildings and hospitals perched along University Avenue. All the seats are taken so I grab one of the metal poles near the door and hold on. I see my face in the train glass, highlighted by the reflected lights of the subway tunnel. My foundation is too heavy. I look whiter than usual, a combination of my half-breed skin tone and the mattifying powder I use to set my face. Half of transitioning from a man to a woman is learning to blend. The other half is hair removal.

I finished the first stage of my transition last fall. Now I'm working on the second stage, hormones and living full time as my chosen gender. This is why I'm heading to University Avenue in the middle of my work week, frantic and looking like a transgender ghost. They are running a new drug study on hormone therapy and need transgender guinea pigs. I signed up because they promised fewer side effects, lower cancer risks, and ongoing medical monitoring. I already have a doctor in the overworked clinic in the Village but since more support is better than less, I volunteered.

The train lurches every time it reaches a stop, pushing me off balance on my heels and forcing me to grip tighter onto the railing. I feel the glances from my fellow riders. Some days, in low light and when I've had time to work at it, I can pass if I don't speak. On days like today, behind schedule and plastering my foundation on between cups of coffee at work, I'm an obvious transwoman. I tell myself I don't care what people think. If looking like a supermodel was my primary motivation for transitioning, I'd have backed out after the first painful electrolysis session.

A man on the right side of the train keeps looking at my face. He is caught between fascination and disgust. He stares at my face, drops his eyes over my body like appraising artwork, and then looks back at my face again. I know the look. It means he thinks I'm a man but he isn't sure. He is searching me for some sign to confirm whatever assumptions he has created in his mind. I keep my eyes averted, focusing on the narrow billboards running along the top of the train. Let him think what he wants. I'm too late to care.

People think hormones are a magic pill which transform you into Tyra Banks. It doesn't work like that. They can soften your skin, shift your fat storage, but at the end of day, it's makeup and lasers which help you pass as a woman. Not that passing is my goal, but it makes you safer in public if no one can tell. I'd like to walk out of my condo and not feel like I was going to end up on the news for wearing my favourite dress, the one which shows off my arms and pushes up my tits like a platter of heaven. So here I am, departing the train at Museum station in downtown Toronto, heading into a research laboratory connected to Mount Sinai Hospital. Praying they haven't cancelled my appointment and don't put me into the control group that get a sugar pill. I need estrogen like a desert caravan needs a well.

Somehow I navigate the building maze and end up in the waiting room two minutes before my appointment is scheduled to begin. The letter they mailed me along with my legal waiver said to be fifteen minutes early, but the bored admin just waves me into one of the offices behind her desk and tells me to fill out my intake forms when my meeting with the research lead is done. I walk into the office, feeling like a shaved mouse about to be injected with bladder-cancer cells. It looks like every office on TV, beige and cluttered with file folders and sad spider plants.

The research lead is a polite woman in her late forties. Her glasses are heavy purple resin, suggesting a glamorous artistic personality. Her brown cashmere sweater, crumb laden and smudged with makeup, suggests a life of PBS documentaries and CBC Radio 1 interviews. The contrast is striking. As she leads me through a series of questions about my gender history, I find myself cataloguing the various inconsistencies in her appearance. Sensible flat black shoes imply a practical nature. A photo next to her desktop computer shows her in a tropical location with an oversized margarita and a leopard-print bikini. I wonder if she has an undisclosed drinking problem, one which encouraged her to pick out the glasses and buy the swimsuit when her real personality was safely saturated into incoherence.

My friends would tell me my focus on her appearance is patriarchy in action. I imagine my non-binary friend, Sten, scolding me by saying "women judging other women is how men police our bodies when they aren't present." I agree, but in this moment, listening to her list the long line of possible effects and downstream impacts to my biology, picking out the most banal parts of the interaction is the only way I can keep my skinny latte down. When I first came out of the Trans closet, announced my transition, and started the long process of hair removal, I felt an immediate and persistent urge to vomit. I feel the same rush of energy to my stomach now.

I interrupt, coughing to push down the bile in my throat. "Look, I know about the risks. I've read the forms and research." This wasn't lying, because I had used my workplace subscription to Pubmed to scour all research related to hormone therapy from the last twenty years. "Can I just sign whatever I need to sign and start?"

She blinks at me once, mentally turning off her script and moving back to real conversation. "Yes, I'm sure you have." She pauses to purse her lips and pushes her glasses up higher on her nose. "But there are unique risks with this drug. Its bioavailability is much higher than older treatments. We're not sure how it will work in human trials."

I resist the urge to roll my eyes. I smile, tight around the corners. "Sure, but the study was approved which means it's been reviewed and the animal trials had a tolerable side-effect profile. So please, if we can move on, I'd appreciate it."

She shrugs and spreads her hands. "Fine. Just stick to the dosing schedule and make sure you don't miss any of your blood-work appointments." She passes me a legal waiver to initial and date. I sign it. She files it into a blue folder and passes me another form to sign, this one confirming we went through the risks and she answered any questions I might have. I sign it as well.

Once the papers are signed, she hands me a schedule of blood-work appointments, a small plastic bag with pill bottles and a paper handout with dosage times and amounts labelled in red letters. I take the pills and the appointment schedule, stuffing them into my bag, and back out of her office while thanking her for her time. She has returned to staring at her computer screen, absent-mindedly waving me off and muttering about my contribution to the advancement of medical science. Screw that noise, I think, as I rush out of the research building and towards the subway. I don't care about science. I just want to get through the next stage of my transition without any more problems.

Then what, my mind asks, as I pass through the toll-collector station and return to the subway tunnels. I don't know, I answer. The seats are all taken again so I stand by the doors, metal pole in the hand while people gawk at me. I don't know at all. I can only take one step at a time towards another life in another body. I will still be me, but not the me that I've known. Closer to myself, farther away from the world and its pervasive expectations. I hope the hormones kick in quickly. I want to feel the calm which some transwomen have told me about, the slowing of testosterone and the influx of estrogen bringing peace. Almost there, I tell myself, almost at my stop for work and almost to the life I've been waiting for. I pop one of the pills into my mouth and swallow with a swig of water from the thermos in my bag. Womanhood, here I am.

Work is a slow hell. Pointless meetings with midlevel managers who will never go any further, jockeying over positions and influence like drunk coeds trying to get served next at the bar. By three p.m., I'm nauseous and my makeup feels like Saran Wrap on my face. My final meeting of the day isn't a meeting at all. It's an Elder's Teaching with an old wizened Anishinaabe woman from Serpent River First Nation. It's supposed to be on the Seven Grandfather/Grandmother teachings, but she's a real old-time Elder. She took twenty minutes to open up the teaching, smudging and thanking all the ancestors in Anishinaabemowin. The white office workers looked bored and uncomfortable which she spoke in Ojibwe. The other Indigenous staff looked euphoric at her words, as if she was the Pope blessing them at high mass and they were Jesuits. I doubt anyone else can follow anything she's saying, given how few of us have kept our language.

I know some, enough to understand her prayers, so I follow along in my head. The hormone pill is burning in my stomach. I didn't check the information booklet to see if I needed to take it with food. The Elder is talking about responsibilities in communities now, male roles and female roles. She looks over at me whenever she speaks about female roles, smiling a wide Anishinaabe smile

TRANSCENDENT 2

and nodding her head a little. It's comforting to know there are still traditional people who know the place of Two-Spirit people.

My family was Anishinaabe and Métis on both of my father's sides, but we weren't raised with the culture and language. Bushcraft, living off the land in Northern Michigan, was part of my grandparent's lives, but they weren't on reserve and didn't practice any obvious culture. The most obvious sign of their heritage was the stereotypical Indian crap around their dilapidated farm house. There were dreamcatchers in the windows, little creepy Indian maiden ceramic statues, and a mantel clock with the famous "lone brave" artwork painted on the clock face. That was their contribution to keeping tradition alive.

I liked the teaching though, despite the vomit feeling and the fact that it was running over its allotted time. People kept leaving the meeting room, saying "Sorry, I have another meeting" as they slipped out the door. The Elder just nod-ded at them in the unspoken disapproval style of all Elders everywhere and kept on speaking. When she reached the end of the teaching, the Elder lit up more sage and started another long prayer. This time, having reached the end of my mental reserves, I phased out and let her words flow over me.

That's the moment it started, the barely audible voices on the edge of my skin singing. They were singing a traditional song, the kind women's hand-drum groups across the city sing, but I didn't recognize it. It was like when my co-worker turned on the radio in her cubicle on the lowest volume setting to escape the detection of our bosses. The Elder prayed on and the other people in the room didn't seem to notice anything, so it was definitely only happening to me. Something with the hormone pill, I reasoned, some weird acid-like side effect. I tried to ignore and look normal for the rest of the session.

It got worse through the day. By the time I'd taken my second dose, I was having full-on visual hallucinations. While walking down Bloor Street, I saw a woman in a jingle dress at the intersection with Yonge Street. She stood on the corner, staring into the distance. At first, I thought it was a contemporary art piece by one of the Indigenous activists I know. There is an old burial ground at the intersection, so it would be the ideal place for a reclaiming piece. When a business-suited man strode through her without any effect, I knew it was the damn pills.

I dreamed the strangest dreams that night. In one dream, I was spinning just above the tree line in the bush. All I could see was a grove of winter birches be-neath me and a flat, grey skyline. The singing was there as well. If I was another kind of half-breed, more traditional or a ceremonialist, I would have put down tobacco. As it was, I just wanted it to stop. After the last dream of a rummaging bear in low brush, I promised myself I would call the research study lead in the morning. Girl has no time for this bullshit, I told myself, I'm just trying to become myself, not get into any mystical drug-fuelled cultural stuff.

W hen I called from my office at work, ten minutes past nine a.m., the research lead wasn't in. The admin passed me to her voicemail. I left a message explaining I was having unusual symptoms and gave her my office line. I went to work, routing emails and filtering the endless stream of drivel from my co-workers. When my phone rang an hour later, I rushed to grab the receiver. It wasn't the research leader, but the Elder from the other day. She wanted to ask if I had heard any feedback from the session and when her honorarium cheque would be mailed out. I answered her questions politely but tried to get her off the phone. I didn't want to miss when the research lead called back. The singing was still present and was getting on my nerves.

After winding down about her honorarium and the teaching, the Elder suddenly switched gears and asked me what I thought of the teachings about the roles of women. I froze on the phone, letting out a long "ummmm" while my mind frantically tried to make up a neutral response. "It was interesting. Very informative?" My voice trailed up on the last word, making it a question. I hoped she would jump in and go off on a new "sacred teaching."

Instead, she went right for the jugular. "You know, it's important for you as an Anishinaabe kwe to know your teachings. And the medicines and all that." She paused at the end of her statement, waiting for me to respond.

"Yes, it is important. I'm not really a very traditional kind of woman," I said, certain this would finally end the conversation. In my mind, I imagined hundreds of missed call notifications from the research lead. The Elder didn't leave it there.

"Really? You seemed like one of the only ones who was listening to me yesterday. I could tell you knew some Anishinaabemowin by how you paid attention when I was praying. Where are your people from?" Great. She is one of those Elders, the kind that get off on reconnecting people to their roots.

"Yeah, I know a little bit. We're half-breeds from Lake St. Clair." I used the word *half-breed*, not the more politically correct word of "Métis," because I figured it would throw her off.

"Well, that's good then." She paused for a second before adding, "I am conducting a sweat next Saturday up at Anishinaabe Health. You should come."

Time to end this conversation. I had been as polite as I could and I sure as hell was not going to anyone's sweat. "Thanks for the offer, but like I said, I don't really do ceremony anymore. I have a lot of other priorities going on my life right now."

"You don't need to go to ceremony to be in ceremony," she snorted. "I know what you are. What do they call it now, a transition?" She didn't wait for me to answer before continuing onward, "You know, back when we all had our language and culture, we had our own ceremonies for becoming a woman. There was a way we went about bringing you into the world as a woman. Not all the drugs and surgeries they use now."

"I'm sorry, but I'm expecting another call. I'm really glad you came out and provided your teaching yesterday. Hopefully we can have you back soon." I willed myself to hang up if she didn't accept this final closing sentence.

The Elder sighed on the line. "Girlie, you aren't listening to me. You must be Bear clan, so stubborn. Being a woman isn't about your body. It's about your spirit. You need ceremony to help with that, not pills." She sighed a second time, this time a little tired. "Look, your ancestors are going to find you, one way or another. Call me when you are ready to talk to them again."

"Okay, thanks. Goodbye!" I clicked the phone down and stared out the window. Everyone was an expert in my transition and wanted to tell me how to do things right. They would tell me the right shoes to wear, the perfect lipstick, skirt length, stockings, and where the best place to get my nails done was. It was helpful and supportive, but incredibly frustrating. No one seemed to understand that this was my body and my journey. I didn't need constant reminders of what I was doing wrong, especially from an Elder who knew nothing of my family or me.

The phone rang again. I stared at the call display, worried it was the Elder calling me back. It was the research lead. I grabbed it on the second ring and after dispensing with the politeness of the "Hello, how are you?" launched into a description of my symptoms. The research lead listened patiently but then cut me off as I started describing more of the visual side effects.

"Look, maybe you aren't a good match for this study. I'm not supposed to tell you this, but you aren't in the estrogen control group. You are in the placebo control group, so whatever is happening is not related to this study. Maybe you should contact your primary-care physician or some mental health supports?" She said the last words like I was the most insane person she had ever encountered.

TRANSCENDENT 2

"Oh. All right. Thanks for letting me know." I wasn't sure what to say next, so I just hung up. When the phone clicked down, the sound felt like it echoed through my office. I reached up and touched the space above my upper lip where a few hairs of my beard still resisted permanent removal. Outside my window, I could see a falcon dive and twist between office towers. Every day I watch the falcon hunt for pigeons in the parking lot, but today, it felt different. As if it was a messenger from the universe or my long dead grandmother.

The Elder's words came back into my mind. *Your ancestors will find you, one way or another.* I hate predestiny but what choice do I have? If I wasn't in the hormone study, I'd have to go on the older drugs with the higher side effects. I was not going to tell my primary doctor about the hallucinations or I'd end up having to delay my transition even further when they made me do psych evaluations. But the last thing I wanted to do was to hang out with a bunch of traditional people talking about the way things used to be.

The singing chose this moment to return. The same low voices as before, but the feeling of familiarity was stronger. I knew these voices even if I didn't understand them. I looked at the phone, still sitting silently from when I had hung up. My eyes ran across my bulletin board until I found the Post-It note with the Elder's contact information. I reached for the phone receiver and moved my hand over to the keypad to dial. Womanhood, here I am. Again.

THIS IS NOT A WARDROBE DOOR

◄ A. Merc Rustad ►

D ear Gatekeeper,
   Hi my name is Ellie and I'm six years old and my closet door is broken. My best friend Zera lives in your world and I visited her all the time, and sometimes I got older but turned six again when I came back, but that's okay. Can you please fix the door so I can play with Zera?
   Love,
   Ellie

Z era packs lightly for her journey: rose-petal rope and dewdrop boots, a jacket spun from bee song and buttoned with industrial-strength cricket clicks. She secures her belt (spun from the cloud memories, of course) and picks up her satchel. It has food for her and oil for Misu.
   Her best friend is missing and she must find out why.
   Misu, the palm-sized mechanical microraptor, perches on her seaweed braids, its glossy raindrop-colored feathers ruffled in concern.
   Misu says, *But what if the door is locked?*
   Zera smiles. "I'll find a key."
   But secretly, she's worried. What if there isn't one?

Dear Gatekeeper,
  I hope you got my last couple letters. I haven't heard back from you yet, and the closet door still doesn't work. Mommy says I'm wasting paper when I use too much crayon, so I'm using markers this time. Is Zera okay? Tell her I miss playing with the sea monsters and flying to the moon on the dragons most of all.

  Please open the door again.

  Ellie, age 7

Zera leaves the treehouse and climbs up the one thousand five hundred three rungs of the polka-dot ladder, each step a perfect note in a symphony. When she reaches the falcon aerie above, she bows to the Falcon Queen and asks if she may have a ride to the Land of Doors.

  The Falcon Queen tilts her magnificent head. "Have you not heard?" asks the queen in a voice like spring lightning and winter calm. "All the doors have gone quiet. There is a disease rotting wood and rusting hinges, and no one can find a cure."

  Misu shivers on Zera's shoulder. *It is like the dreams,* Misu says. *When everything is silent.*

  Zera frowns. "Hasn't the empress sent scientists to investigate?"

  The Falcon Queen nods. "They haven't returned. I dare not send my people into the cursed air until we know what is happening."

  Zera squares her shoulders. She needs answers, and quickly. Time passes differently (faster) on Ellie's home planet, because their worlds are so far apart, and a lag develops in the space-time continuum.

  "Then I will speak to the Forgotten Book," Zera says, hiding the tremor in her voice.

  The falcons ruffle their feathers in anxiety. Not even the empress sends envoys without the Forgotten Book's approval.

  "You are always brave," says the Falcon Queen. "Very well then, I will take you as far as the Island of Stars."

Hi Gatekeeper,
  Are you even there? It's been almost a year for me and still nothing. Did the ice elves get you? I hope not. Zera and I trapped them in the core of the passing comet so they'd go away, but you never know.

Why can't I get through anymore? I'm not too old, I promise. That was those Narnia books that had that rule (and they were stupid, we read them in class).

Please say something,

Ellie, age 8

Zera hops off the Falcon Queen's back and looks at the Island of Stars. It glows from the dim silver bubbles that hang thick in the air like tapioca pudding.

She sets off through the jungle of broken wire bed frames and abandoned armchairs; she steps around rusting toys and rotting books. There are memories curled everywhere — sad and lonely things, falling to pieces at the seams.

She looks around in horror. "What happened?"

Misu points with a tiny claw. *Look.*

In the middle of the island stands the Forgotten Book, its glass case shattered and anger radiating off its pages.

LEAVE, says the book. BEFORE MY CURSE DEVOURS YOU.

Gatekeeper,

I tried to tell Mom we can't move, but she won't listen. So now I'm three hundred miles away and I don't know anybody and all I want to do is scream and punch things, but I don't want Mom to get upset. This isn't the same closet door. Zera explained that the physical location wasn't as fixed like normal doors in our world, but I'm still freaking out.

I found my other letters. Stacks of notebook paper scribbled in crayon and marker and finger paint — all stacked in a box in Mom's bedroom.

"What are you doing with this?" I screamed at Mom, and she had tears in her eyes. "Why did you take the letters? They were supposed to get to Zera!"

Mom said she was sorry, she didn't want to tell me to stop since it seemed so important, but she kept finding them in her closet.

I said I'd never put them there, but she didn't believe me.

"We can't go there again," Mom said, "no one ever gets to go back!" and she stomped out of the kitchen and into the rain.

Has my mom been there? Why didn't she ever tell me? Why did you banish her too?

What did we do so wrong we can't come back?

Ellie

TRANSCENDENT 2

Zera's knees feel about to shatter.

"Why are you doing this?" Zera grips an old, warped rocking chair. "You've blacked out the Land of Doors, haven't you?"

YES, says the Book. ALL WHO GO THERE WILL SLEEP, UNDREAMING, UNTIL THE END.

Zera blinks hard, her head dizzy from the pressure in the air. "You can't take away everyone's happiness like this."

NO? says the Book. WHY NOT? NO ONE EVER REMEMBERS US THERE. THEY FORGET AND GROW OLD AND ABANDON US.

"That's not true," Zera says. "Ellie remembers. There are others."

Misu nods.

Zera pushes through the heavy air, reaching out a hand to the Book. "They tell stories of us there," Zera says, because Ellie used to bring stacks of novels with her instead of PBJ sandwiches in her backpack. "There are people who believe. But there won't be if we close all the doors. Stories in their world will dry up. We'll start to forget them, too."

WE MEAN NOTHING TO THEM.

Zera shakes her head. "That's not true. I don't want my best friend to disappear forever."

Gatekeeper,

I don't know why I bother anymore. You're not listening. I don't even know if you exist.

It's been a while, huh? Life got busy for me. High school, mostly. Mom got a better job and now we won't have to move again. Also I met this awesome girl named LaShawna and we've been dating for a month. God, I'm so in love with her. She's funny and smart and tough and kind — and she really gets me.

Sometimes she reminds me of Zera.

I asked Mom why she kept my letters.

She didn't avoid me this time. "I had a door when I was younger," she said, and she looked so awfully sad. "I was your age. I met the person I wanted to stay with forever." She let out her breath in a whoosh. "But then the door just…it broke, or something. I tried dating here. Met your father, but it just wasn't the same. Then he ran off and it was like losing it all again."

I told LaShawna about Zera's world. She said she didn't want to talk about it. I think maybe she had a door, too.

I was so angry growing up, feeling trapped. You know the best thing about Zera? She *got* me. I could be a girl, I could be a boy, and I could be neither — because that's how I feel a lot of the time. Shifting around between genders. I want that to be okay, but here? I don't know.

The thing is, I don't want to live in Zera's world forever. I love things here, too. I want to be able to go back and forth and have friends everywhere, and date LaShawna and get my degree and just *live*.

This will be my last letter to you, Gatekeeper.

If there was one thing Zera and I learned, it's that you have to build your own doors sometimes.

So I'm going to make my own. I'll construct it out of salvaged lumber; I'll take a metalworking class and forge my own hinges. I'll paper it with all my letters and all my memories. I'll set it up somewhere safe, and here's the thing — I'll make sure it never locks.

My door will be open for anyone who needs it: my mom, LaShawna, myself.

— Ell

The Book is silent.

"Please," Zera says. "Remove the curse. Let us all try again."

And she lays her hand gently on the Forgotten Book and lets the Book see all the happy memories she shared with Ellie, once, and how Ellie's mom Loraine once came here and met Vasha, who has waited by the door since the curse fell, and Misu, who befriended the lonely girl LaShawna and longs to see her again — and so many, many others that Zera has collected, her heart overfilled with joy and loss and grief and hope.

In return, she sees through space and time, right into Ell's world, where Ell has built a door and has her hand on the knob.

"Ell," Zera calls.

Ell looks up, eyes wide. "Zera?"

"Yes," Zera says, and knows her voice will sound dull behind the door. "I'm here."

Ell grins. "I can see your reflection in the door! Is that the Book with you?"

The Book trembles. SHE REMEMBERS.

Zera nods. The air is thinning, easing in her lungs. "I told you. Not everyone forgets."

I would like to see LaShawna again, says Misu.

VERY WELL, says the book. THE CURSE WILL BE REMOVED.

TRANSCENDENT 2

Ell turns the handle.

Bright lights beams into the Island of Stars, and Ell stands there in a doorway, arms spread wide. Zera leaps forward and hugs her best friend.

"You came back," Zera says.

"I brought some people with me, too," Ell says, and waves behind her, where two other women wait.

Loraine steps through the light with tears in her eyes. "I never thought I could come back…"

Misu squeaks in delight and flies to LaShawna.

Zera smiles at her friends. Things will be all right.

"We have a lot of work to do to repair this place," Zera says. She clasps Ell's hands. "The curse is gone, but we have to fix the doors and wake the sleepers. Are you ready?"

Ell grins and waves her mom and girlfriend to join her. "Yes. Let's do this."

THREE POINTS MASCULINE

◄ An Owomoyela ►

I was serving in Baxon just north of Hescher, guard-dogging a queue of first responders heading into the riot zones, and John caught my eye. Her beard caught my eye. Some troublemaker flaunting the rules, I thought, or a guy sneaking in under cover of audacity, thinking the Women's Volunteer Corps was a good place to get laid. If that was the case, *he* was looking to get roughed up, and it was my job to oblige. I pulled her out of the line.

"License."

Roughing someone up would've made my day, and my day needed making. Go figure that John stepped aside and said "Of course" in that tone people use at police, all placid and *don't shoot me*. She pulled her license and handed it over — and yeah, there it was: non-transitioned male sex, last Gender Assessment Test no more than two years ago, certified female register — certified female enough for government work, right — all of it signed by a state assessor I didn't just recognize as legit, I knew personally. The grainy photo even had her damn beard.

I thought about roughing her up for making me look a damn fool. I told myself I was better than that; even kinda believed it. "Get back in line."

In a fair world, that'd be that.

Isaac was walking the queue, giving the pep talk, getting everyone comfy with the bulletproofs and white flags. "All our pretty little heads will be back behind our boys in uniform," he said, and I kept my fingers on my rifle. "There's a chance our zone might go hot; if it does, we'll get plenty of warning, just get back on the buses and we'll peel rubber back here. Lickety-split. Time for dinner."

I caught up to him as we boarded the bus. For the sixteen women there were only four of us from City Guard, me looking plastic and the rest looking pale and greeny under the florescent lights. "Counting four boys in uniform right here," I said.

Isaac looked surprised, then looked at the insignia on his chest. He grinned. "Way wrong uniform, man."

I grunted, and pointed at John. "What's the story here?"

"What, him? — her," Isaac corrected. Takes more than a test and a license for some people to learn. Hand to God I don't think Isaac believes the GATs if he looks at someone and gets his own opinion, but like the rest of us, he'll play along because it's law. Least, like the rest of most people, he'll play along because it's law. "Hell if I know. Uh, hometown somewhere up north, been working with the WVC going on six years. Career, right? Just your type."

"Shove off," I said, and elbowed him. He cackled and headed for his seat. I took a seat near the front and decided it didn't matter. 'Sides, I could see or guess most of it: lily-white, unlike me. College-educated, unlike me. A girl, too, unlike me. Though half the bastards would've argued that, had they known.

Hescher was a hellhole. We smelled the smoke when we rolled in, and the moment they opened the doors, it was all white tents, Corps flags, antiseptic stench, and people moaning on the ground. A guy almost shoved a handful of red-yellow-green-black triage tags into my chest before deciding I wouldn't know a sucking chest wound from a bump on the head and shoving them at the ladies behind me.

They'd cleared out one of the big bargain stores for a medical center, and its parking lot was playing support. Place was peppered with City Guard, and one came over as soon as we led our girls off the bus. "Hey. I'm Ben Kessler, managing day dispatch and logistics here. Welcome to Camp Save Big. Any two of you got a moment?"

"I got one," I said, and Isaac came up beside me.

"So, what've you got going?" Isaac asked.

Ben groaned. "Cluster attacks." He hiked a thumb over his shoulder, and Isaac and I followed him across the lot. "We go three weeks without anyone blowing anything up and now we've had four bombings yesterday and today."

"Christos," I said, and Ben hoisted up the flap of the registration tent. We went inside.

Ben went over to the sat-fax and tapped his finger on a pile of papers. I went up and said, "What's up?"

"Your gals signed a pretty permissive contract," Ben said. "'Area of greatest need,' 'discretionary redeployment,' y'know."

"So where's our area of greatest need?" Isaac asked.

Ben pistoled a finger at him. "Here, go figure. But if it's not too much trouble, we need someone to back up the folks at the hospital. Triage and first response. They got slammed."

Isaac looked at me. "Hell, if that's it, we can walk our girls over."

"Be a dear?" Ben said, and pressed his hands together.

I crossed my arms over my chest, habit-like. Isaac whacked me on the shoulder. "We're your angels. C'mon, we'll pull our teams."

Isaac turned and walked back to the buses, and Ben held out a map for me. "You'll need this. A bunch of main roads are impassable."

I took the map, and looked over the scrawled edits. "You're going to make me regret wearing the injury-prev helmet instead of the smart display, aren't you?"

"Oh, there's a lot of regret here in Hescher," Ben said. "If that's all you've got, you're coming out ahead."

John was in Isaac's group. She didn't look at me when we rounded our eight up, and I mostly ignored her. We just got in line and marched into the evacuation zone. I did notice she didn't walk like a girl learned to, didn't hold herself like a girl learned to. She might've had the GAT, but she was off.

Shit like that makes me check how I'm walking. Out here, no one was gonna come up and check my license, but still, it's habit, like.

The evac zone was quiet. All these buildings, still as death — no one even looting, anymore. Plenty of people were probably displaced and angry somewhere easterly, keeping their mouths shut because you didn't bitch at the hand that fed you and rounded you up onto government buses, and that just left this place all creeped-out empty like a ghost town. Isaac and I didn't talk. We had our hands on our rifles, watching for revs, and the girls didn't talk because they knew you don't distract the guys with automatics. We went in past the empty houses, past the bombed-out school, over the recent debris that made driving impossible and walking a chore and, hand to God, but I didn't know what the revs thought they were getting by blowing up all the empty places. With all the rubble, though, I pitied the girls and their uniform skirts. Damn glad I didn't wear one.

We were maybe halfway to the hospital and passing office buildings when Isaac held up a hand, and we stopped and ducked down. Someone was running at us down the road.

He was yelling. "Get outta there! Get outta there!"

I took aim. I was just good enough for a hipshot — not being military I couldn't gun the guy down, not when he was waving his hands and not a gun, but for all I knew, he had three pounds of plastic on his chest. I thumbed my rifle over to single-shot, and yelled, "Do not come closer!"

Then the office behind us blew.

I was on my face like *that*. This chunk of concrete hit the pavement two feet from my shoulder and crap rained down, drifting on my uniform, drumming my helmet. A lot of it was glass. A rock the size of my fist caught me in the back, another almost took a chunk out of my hand. My head was ringing when I picked myself up.

First thing that crossed my mind was *That's okay, I can go home now, 'cause that was a bomb.*

Ten seconds later that didn't make sense to me, and it still doesn't. It's just what I thought.

I don't remember how I got to my feet. The place was quiet. Crap wasn't falling. The guy I'd been aiming at wasn't running at us any more, wasn't anywhere any more, and I looked around. The color was off. Everything was yellower, and I kept blinking and blinking, trying to make it go away, and then I caught this light coming through the buildings off west. I thought, *The bastards set the city on fire.*

Wasn't any smoke, though. It was the sun.

Then I thought, *Shit.* I'd thought no time had passed. No, I'd been down for half an hour, and my helmet fit odd — pressure and suction — like I had a head injury, and the automated aid kicked on.

And where the hell were my girls?

Ten minutes later I worked out that my helmet radio had given up the ghost and wasn't coming home for Christ's Mass. The tips of my fingers were numb and I couldn't pull the helmet for fear that I'd open up a wound, so poking at the buttons was the best I could do to fix it. My maps were safe and I should've headed back to drum up a search, but I had a chip on my shoulder for the guy who blew me up and I wasn't trotting home with my tail between my legs. Mama always said pride would get me killed.

So I went deeper into the evac zone.

Sure enough, before long I started seeing people, and I had to crouch down and sneak behind dumpsters and burnt-out cars and roadblocks. I could hear them yelling to each other, pick out the ones walking with rifles — and damn, some of those rifles were better than mine.

I found the supermarket easy. It was big, with people going in and out. The entire street in front was busy with revs, six or eight at a shot, walking around on important rev business. Someone came out with a big bag of something, and they gathered up and walked away. That was an opening if I ever saw one.

The supermarket was big, the kind with doors at both ends and checkout lanes lined up all across the front. Big, and stocked enough to be Rev HQ. That made walking into it a stupid idea, and of course that's what I did anyway. I snuck around, trying to avoid the automatic doors until I remembered there was no power to this neighborhood. The doors couldn't give me away. I picked one, poked it to see it didn't creak, and pushed it open.

And that's when I decided, you know, gloves off, shoot to kill. 'Cause that's when I saw Isaac slumped against a checkout stand, helmet off and eyes staring open, with an ugly dark gunshot blown out half his head.

I don't know why I didn't throw up then. I guess it didn't feel real, between the fuzz in my hearing and the hurt in my skull and the way I'd jumped from afternoon to evening earlier. Think I thought I was dreaming.

I saw the head rev right away, when I stopped staring at dead Isaac. At least, I saw the guy acting it up. Put his name on a bullet. He was up on one of the far stands hollering like a ringleader, and there was no way I'd be able to pick him off from the doorway I'd come in. It's hard to get sharpshooter training when you can't meet the army requirements for infantry. Hard to shoot with a pounding headache and blood loss, too.

They don't teach you much in City Guard, but I got on my stomach and did an army crawl like I'd seen in the comics and practiced, back home, back in that misspent youth of mine. Went creeping back into the supermarket until I found cover, with my head pounding and everything right of my pelvis one screaming mass of ache. The guy was up on the register counter, pacing back and forth, waving his gun around like that was the only way he could make a point.

TRANSCENDENT 2

"A state which controls right and wrong, which *legislates* right and wrong, a state which tells us what we can and can't do, can and can't *be*, can and can't *think*, is a state that has legislated our humanity!" he said.

Something like that. I got the gist: usual rev talk. Blah blah this, blah blah overthrow the government, 'cause the guys with the guns and the anger will for sure be the better choice. I crept past the shelves of cereal and the display of spoiled pears and came nearer.

"Look at this guy!"

I was close enough that I could see him reach down and grab John by the collar.

He hauled John up. "This guy is a mockery of a man!" he yelled, shaking her like a rattle. "If he decided one day to put on this dress, he would be sent to jail! It's only when the state tells him to that he can. There is no difference! The state has fabricated right and wrong!"

I lined up my shot.

And the first shot went so wild I was lucky it didn't take out the front door. The guy spun around and almost lost his footing, but he stayed up enough to swing his pistol and take a shot that came a lot closer to target than mine had. I ducked behind a display of Corn Crunch that wouldn't stop a ping-pong ball, but instinct said go for cover and I did. I flipped my rifle onto automatic, 'cause it's hard to miss on automatic, and thanked God the girls knew enough to get down.

You know. Blood splattered. Girls gasped, one of them screamed before another clapped a hand over her mouth, and I looked at John, white as a sheet and bloody. One of Isaac's girls, but I bet they all knew what happened to Isaac. They'd been looking shell-shocked before I took out that rev. I pushed off up the floor and ran to them, then dropped and just barely caught myself in a crouch. God, my head hurt. Christos, I didn't feel right. John touched my shoulder and I shoved her away.

The sensible one, the one who stopped the other girl from screaming, said, "We need to get away from the doors." I nodded. If no revs outside had heard us exchanging bullets, that'd be one miracle. To keep any from coming back, we'd need another.

"Yeah," I said. "Come on. Back through." My heart was pounding. Made my ears hurt, it was so loud, and I could feel it on my stomach. I stood up, and the store yanked sideways and shook like a dog toy. Then I was on the ground.

I was on the ground, and I was back farther in the store. I was leaning against a pile of budget toilet paper. All I could hear was my own blood.

The sensible one was crouched over me, like a bad flashback to post-op. I looked around, trying to get my bearings, saw a scatter of broken glass from a freezer case, a crumpled wrapper from a snack cake, a bottle of blackstrap molasses with its top off. Nothing made any sense. The sensible woman was pushing a water bottle to my lips. "Here. Drink this, if you can."

I caught a glance at her name tag: Agatha, with a low service number that meant she'd signed up early. That seemed important: signed up early. She was practically shoving the bottle up my nose, so I drank. The water was warm and sugary and made my headache ten times worse, but Agatha held it through two good gulps.

"Listen," she said. "I'm concerned that you're losing blood. Your helmet's gone red."

I guess I was lucky to have the injury-prev helmet instead of the HUD.

"We have to get out of here, but I don't think you're going to make a walk down Main Street," Agatha said. "Not before anyone comes by."

"There was a fire escape from the second floor down into the alley. I saw it when we were being brought in," John said. Of course John said. I should've said; I'd seen the damn thing when I was sneaking past, watching for revs hiding in the alleys. But I was messed up, and John and her damn beard were the ones taking charge.

God, I wished Isaac was there. But that gunshot crossed my mind, and I wanted to spew. Isaac was dead. I was the guardsman left, and I was being babied by a bunch of girls.

"Then that's where we'll go," Agatha said. "Come on; everyone back this way. Move it, all of you. John..."

John stepped up and got me under the arm to hold me up, and I yanked away. Shoved her and stumbled right into the toilet paper. Real smooth. But I didn't want her hands on me.

"I can stand up," I said, when they looked at me. My face was burning, but the rest of me was cold.

Agatha looked at me. Probably going to ask if I had a problem with the gender-reassigned, but I just took my rifle, pushed myself up, and concentrated on keeping steady. Were it that easy.

"I can walk," I told her again, and turned around and started walking.

The second floor was offices and a break room, and that's where we headed. Longest stair climb of my life. But with the shooting over and the adrenaline quieting down, it wasn't as bad — about as bad as sneaking to the store in the first place. We went into the break room, where the revs had left bags of trash and bowls from instant meals, empty bottles of alcohol, and a map of the city tacked up on the walls. Agatha turned up her nose. "Well, I suppose we know where they've been spending their time."

John went to the window and pushed it open. I went up to take a look, see if I needed to secure the alley below.

We weren't far up, and the fire escape was a good one — wasn't rickety or anything. But I looked and I heard myself say "Shit," and then I was back inside the window, on my knees, spewing lunch and molasses water into a trash can full of old receipts. Even after everything came up, I kept heaving until the vise in my head let go. My heart started pounding again.

I wasn't going to get out of there.

I swallowed, and wished I hadn't. Looked back at the girls, and saw John and Agatha kneeling near me. Before they could say anything I told them, "Look, it's about five blocks to the barricades, and none of you look like revs. Just get down the side and go for it. Keep your hands up and no one's gonna shoot you. Can you do that?"

"I'll see them through," Agatha said, then frowned. "Here; you'd better give me your sidearm."

"What?" I squinted until she focused back into one solid person instead of two blurry ones. "I will get my ass raked over the coals if I hand a pistol to someone who's never had gun training. There must be ten different laws against that."

"Tell them I stole it off you while you were throwing up," Agatha said. "Or do you want us just to sing if a rioter comes by?"

I squinted at her. "What?"

"It's what you do for bears," John said.

Fancy educated bastard. I groaned and put my head back. "Fine. Take it." I was just gonna close my eyes. And then I felt myself falling, in the back of my head, like all that darkness under my eyelids was some river, with an undertow, and I'd sink down through. Then I felt hot hands on my face and John pried open my eyes.

There she was, staring me in the face and yammering on about a concussion and hyposomething. I tried to wave her off like a horsefly. Then she said, "We talked it over. I'm going to stay with you."

No idea when they'd had time to *talk it over*. I laughed in John's face. "Why, 'cause you're the butch?"

"Because Agatha has more important things to do," John said, and I thought, *Yeah, like my job.*

"Lemme up," I said.

"Agatha's going to get everyone back to base," John said. "She's going to tell the rest of City Guard where we are, and they should be able to get someone in here to bring you out."

What I should've done in the first place. "I can make it," I said. "In my own time, yeah?"

Agatha did just what she should have: came over and crouched down and said, "Don't be an idiot. I'll break both your knees if you think you're going to crawl out, pass out, and make us carry you."

I liked her. Kinda wished she would stay with me. Not just that John torqued me, but I had a feeling Agatha could take on the entire rev mob with guts to spare.

The girls filed out the window, and I heard their feet going down the metal stairs. John went and closed the door, and turned all the lights off. Better for my head, at least. Then she came and sat by me.

"You don't like me much," she said.

I rubbed a sleeve across my mouth. "Does it matter?"

John sighed. "I have been accused of not playing to the spirit of the GAT."

Were it that fucking simple.

"Give me your hand," John said. I squinted.

"Why?"

"Medical reasons."

I squinted a bit more, and gave her my hand.

She took it and squeezed my thumbnail. Then she took my pulse. "Well, you haven't lost much more blood," she said, and let go of me. "Capillary refill's no worse than it was, and heart rate is good, considering." She shook her head. "You really shouldn't have come after us."

I tried to think of something sharp to say. I was angry — angrier than I had any right to be. Tried to blame my head.

"But thank you," John said.

Given the way the rev had been going after her — well, I know how these things go. Gender assessment gets people angry, anger gets people nasty. That's why most of us keep our dirty little secrets under our belts and our vests. Why most of us don't go wearing a damn beard.

That just got me feeling sick.

TRANSCENDENT 2

"What is it with you?" I asked, and looked at her. "Get a shave, put on some makeup, grow out your hair. You walk into a war zone and you come looking like that?"

"Not my style," John said.

I looked her up and down. "How the hell did you test female?" I asked.

John sighed. "Is this the conversation we're going to have?" she asked, like she'd had this one before.

Probably had. Probably every time someone had to talk to her. Make small talk. *So, John, what's up with your genitals? So, John, why you wanna be a girl?*

Didn't want to be a proper girl, though.

"You scored, what, a fifty-one fem, fifty masc on the GAT?" I asked. "Just enough to scrape through?"

John looked at me. "Sounds like you're familiar with the GAT."

"Yeah, familiar," I said. "Took it. Tried to go army. But I got eighty-two masculine, and the goddamn military is eighty-five, min." I flipped the convo around again, back at her. "You think you're a man, don't you?"

She hedged. "I don't think it's useful to pay too much attention to — "

"Bullshit. You think you're a man?"

John hesitated. Looking for any way not to answer the damn question, then answered it anyway. "Yeah, I do."

I sneered. "Thought so. Why the hell'd you do this? Getting some girls?"

She gave me this long-suffering look. "I wanted to serve. I wanted to go into care. I didn't have the stomach for armed service. I've thought a lot about why it was so important, and I don't know how to explain it — "

"So you're a man," I said. "You're not just playing queer, you're a man."

More hedging. "Well, legally I — "

"You're playing!" I almost shouted. I almost didn't care who heard me. I was shaking, I couldn't see straight. "You're a fucking — yeah, you know what? I grew *up* in this. I was playing with — fuck you. *Fuck* you! You want to know what it's really like?"

John got a look like she'd worked something out.

I hated that look. Straight up hated it.

"I know what — " John said, or started to say.

I ran right over her. Couldn't stop, and Christos, I wanted to. "Ever since I was a kid. Sold my dolls on my parents' net accounts. Thought I'd be able to get this toy gun — they forced me into a dress once and I nearly tore their eyes out, clawed up my mom's face so bad, and every day I was *sick* when someone looked at my chugs or called me ma'am, and you're fucking — "

You're a pretender, some sick trans-v playing in women's clothing. I wanted to say that. Didn't even care it was the same shit people used to fling at me.

"I was a boy," I spat out. "I had some chromosome problem but I knew what I was. This isn't a joke."

"It's not a joke for me," John said.

"No, it's a goddamn disguise," I said, leaned over, and puked again.

John put her hand on my back and I shoved her away. I didn't want to be touched. I spent my whole life up until the GAT and the surgery and the moving halfway across the country to Baxon having people say I'd grow out of this, like I'd grow out of my skin, be a normal girl, settle down with a normal guy, take those hands all over me, take him crawling on top of me, take him feeling better than me, stronger than me, like I'd take the whole five-course meal of what my life was supposed to look like and feel like and *be* shoved down my mouth the moment I was spewed out into the world, when some doctor looked between my legs and laid down the law on me. John's little card with her GAT score meant nothing on all that.

There's a word for that. Dysphoria. I got my chugs lopped off, got my own little card that got me into the City Guard with the rest of the boys, got a good haircut and remedial hormones and that all helped, but not enough. The damn rev had a point: I got to be a guy because I took a test and it said I got into enough fights, played enough sports, had enough right interests and few enough wrong ones. I got to be a guy because some white-collar jackhole stamped and signed a form. I never would've got to be a guy just *because* I was a guy.

John was quiet when I was done spewing. Then she said, "The only way I could've gotten this job was by acting, every day, like I was something I wasn't."

The only way I got this job was by arguing my whole life I was who I was.

"Do you think it makes sense?" John asked.

"Yeah, funny thing is, no one ever asked me."

John was quiet. Then she said, "I hate it."

I looked at her. Didn't know what she meant.

"You can feel it," John said. "How they look at you."

I grimaced. "Yeah," I agreed. "How it goes sliding over you. Like they just look, and — "

"And it's not even — it's a look that says 'I know what you are,'" John said. "Like they've figured you out."

TRANSCENDENT 2

"And you can't say no. You can't — "

"You just want to say, *that's not me!*"

I turned my head to look at her. Him. I looked at him. "Why do you put up with this shit?" I said. "Just get another goddamn job."

He watched me with blank hazel eyes. "Why didn't you just wear the goddamn dress?"

I twisted around and punched him.

I split his lip on his teeth. If I hadn't been wearing gloves I'd've split my knuckle on his teeth. He jerked back and spat blood, and gave me the kind of look people give bad wiring.

After a while, I said, "Sorry."

John wiped a glob of blood off his lips. "I had brothers," he said. "I'll survive."

"I meant — " I waved a hand. "Sorry for the other stuff. Pulling you out of the queue."

John was quiet for a moment. "You were just doing your job."

"So was the guy who said I wasn't man enough to be in the army." I ground my fingernails into my fist. "I just — this is shit, what they make us do."

Wasn't much to say, after that.

I closed my eyes and tried to keep the headache down. John got up and walked to the window, looked out at the alley and the street. Then I heard him take breath in.

"Someone's coming."

I opened my eyes. "That our boys?"

John was standing way too still, and his shoulders came up toward his ears. "No," he said.

Revs.

I pulled myself up on the windowsill, and John grabbed my arm to keep me standing. I couldn't see — headache made it hard — but John said, "There. Three, coming for the front entrance."

Where they'd find Isaac. They'd find that dead rev. They'd look and wonder where their hostages got to, and they'd come up here to plan. I cussed and reached for the window, and John stopped my hand.

"Are you going to make it down?"

I didn't look out. Figured that if I went with my eyes closed, I wouldn't lose it. "We have a choice?"

"You get sick on the stairs and they'll hear you," John said. "We'll be easy marks in that alley. We can find somewhere to hide, let the guard flush them out."

I groaned. "Where, like the girls' bathroom?"

John shrugged. "Good as anywhere."

He got me under the arm and we went to the door, quiet as possible. We slipped through, just as quiet, and someone yelled "Hey!" from the stairs.

John hadn't seen the *first* bunch of revs to come home.

There was maybe a second where the rev just saw John's dress, and most people leave medical types alone. Never know when one might save your bacon, even if you are on the wrong side. Then he saw me, though, and the one thing the revs hated as much as appointed officials was City Guard.

He probably put together who'd shot his pal, too.

Pride might get me killed, but twitchy kept me alive. I shot from the hip, literally, didn't kill the guy but came close, and the other revs started shouting downstairs.

I remember thinking something about high ground. I remember my helmet fitting too tight, watching myself like a live-action movie, like I was outside my head, stumbling down the stairs and crashing down under cover behind the pulp books. I shot one guy in the chest because I don't think he believed what was happening — damn revs talk big, but most are just city boys, low on the masc score, lower than me — and then it was on.

By the time I hit the registers I was skidding on adrenaline. Yeah, so I had stupid ideas about action and heroism, like every kid who wanted to be in the army. Thought I'd be a big hero, mowing down hostiles and never taking a hit, lighting up a cig with a big grin. Instead I was sick to my stomach and my heart was pounding too fast; I thought I'd wig out any second. The way my hands were shaking, I can't believe I shot anyone, but I must've, sometime in between the shelves knocking over and the displays getting torn apart over me. I fought those revs until my magazine was empty, not that it took more than a minute at that, and that's when the boys in uniform came and rescued me.

I can't remember the trip back to Camp Save Big. I know I didn't make it on my own power. Mostly I remember the bit before I woke up, swimming in that big back-of-the-eyelid river, up and down until I broke the surface.

Didn't wake in any proper hospital. This was where they put the special projects, I guess. I could feel a catheter in, and my stomach dropped three feet. All I could think was *Shit*. All I could think was, *Cover blown*. People aren't in the habit of asking after your privates unless they knew you took a reassessment, and I'd been liking that no one here knew. No one asks to see your license if you pass yourself off. If you don't have chugs or a damn beard. Or a goddamn head injury that makes them stick a catheter in.

I bit down hard, and made fists hard, and held on to nothing until I heard a door open and guy's voice say "Hey," beside me.

Look up and there was John, and he reached over to take my pulse. "Don't worry," he said. "I'm your attending. I told them you might like a private room, and they gave you this one — you being the hero of the hour."

I looked around at shelves shoved into a corner, a few warehouse pallets stacked in another corner, and decided it had been a crappy back room before becoming my crappy suite. Then what he said hit me. "Wait there. Hero?"

"Hero of the battle of Fresh Food Mart," John said. "Save the day. Get the girl. You know, if you want her."

I gave him a funny look, and he burst out laughing. "Christos, not *me!*"

I laughed, too. "Think I'm Agatha's type?"

He reached down and patted my shoulder, and the funny thing was, I didn't mind. Like, maybe it didn't matter to his thinking that I got no bits — just like he got no girliness. We both had our dirty little secrets.

"Tell you what, though. That's got to be worth three points masculine on the GAT."

"Not unless they hand me a medal over it." I groaned. Don't get me wrong, I'd rather get treatment than none and I was glad that my head didn't hurt, but I wanted out of that bed, out of that hospital gown that fell down between my legs, out of just lying there helpless and feeling exposed to the world. John looked at his fingers.

"Not fair, is it?"

Yeah, and we both knew without asking. "Shit deal," I said. "So what do we do?"

John shrugged. "Keep going," he said. "Things have to change sometime."

I looked at him. "You sound like a rev." That talk about things changing, how unjust it all was. Hell, I guess I sounded like one, too, in my head, but I knew I wasn't, and I don't think John was either. Just two guys in bad positions.

"Yeah, well. They're wrong about a lot, but they're not wrong about this." John shrugged, and stood up. "I've got patients. You're gonna be fine."

"Yeah," I said. "Good luck on your rounds."

He went, and I lay back and listened to the painkillers swirling in my veins. The door pulled open, and I didn't hear it shut. I looked.

"If I have any say in it, I'll get you that medal," John said.

The door swung closed behind him.

THE L7 GENE

◄ Jeanne Thornton ►

In her own teenage years, Sam, hyperconscious and pre-HRT, would have burned an hour getting ready, even if just for a late-night run to the gas station. But her brother Chris — she guessed Chris was technically sort of her brother; maybe science had no word yet for Chris — just threw on a terrible science-camp T-shirt, one Sam swore she remembered tossing out years before, and was ready to go. Sam's ex Roland was waiting for them in the car, the idle exhaust a dark swirl against the South Bay fog as Sam ushered Chris into the backseat. It was three in the morning; it was cold.

Chris laughed. You're not taking me out to murder me, are you?

Sam laughed too, and then she shut the car door over Chris' face. The satellite radio was broken, so they listened to nothing at all as they headed for the coast.

Chris's existence had been Sam's mother's Thanksgiving surprise. Sam had first seen him earlier that day as she climbed the iron-lattice steps of her family's house in Los Altos Hills: her former self, sitting on the living room couch. Seeing Chris's face was less of a shock, she figured, than it would've been two years earlier, before the estradiol. Chris didn't look like her current reflection, more like a cousin who'd hacked off Sam's stringy braids and replaced them with dire gel spikes. He wore a hoodie emblazoned with Sam's high school logo.

Oh, hey, he said. You're Sam, obviously! It's a pleasure to meet you. I'm Chris.

Sam flinched; he'd taken her deadname. Chris's eyes passed over her, much as she supposed hers had done to him.

You look very nice, he said, and she could tell he meant it, which surprised her — less the sentiment than the idea that someone who looked like a teenage Sam could say things and mean them.

She returned to the car to find Roland. I think my mom cloned me and made the clone cis somehow, Sam said. Can we go?

Roland's eyes grew wide. I wish my parents would make a cis clone of me, he said. I'd never have to let them down again.

But they couldn't go. Her dad, emerging like a crab from the shadows, scuttled her bags upstairs over her protests, and in short order the five of them were awkwardly assembled around the plastic-coated table. Chris initially took Sam's usual spot, his back to the living room with the old clock behind him, but sheepishly surrendered it to Sam on request. Her mother sat at the table's head, elated to begin explaining the situation. Sam could see how elated she was, could see it all over her face.

Sam's mother owned a genetic research company, and her research had led her into the areas of the brain responsible for the expression of sexuality, an interest she'd developed roughly around the time Sam had come out. She had finally isolated the L7 gene: the gene that, flipped on, caused a kid to become trans and, flipped off, left their internal anatomical map comfortably congruent with their body. And as she had already developed technology that would accelerate the growth of cell tissue, as well as technology to program memory engrams from online text and video samples, it would be impossible and uncouth, she felt, to decline to assemble the puzzle. She also had easy access to a supply of raw trans genetic material: Sam's shower drain and linens, following her last visit. The necessary proof of concept would begin at home.

So a viable clone had been produced, his growth accelerated to adolescence in a short twelve months. Chris would henceforth age in real time, just like a real child. The company was working on a way to develop consumer applications for the basic technology as well as on proofs of concept for variations involving other queer identities, as soon as the company's legal office could figure out good solutions to get around the stronger protections those identities enjoyed. Right now, Chris was the prototype in whom all their resources had been invested. After another series of tests and what would surely be an emotional personal testimony at the UN following the anniversary of the resolution next year, the company could secure international funding for additional human trials.

Are you Satan? Sam asked. Her mother laughed.

I thought that your, you know, your buddies would be the ones who'd be most excited about the news that we'd isolated the L7 gene, she said. It's final, scientific proof positive that you aren't deluded or lying to get attention. If you want to know, proving that you and your kind weren't lying is one of the major reasons I even did this, Sam. And to make the burden you're carrying a little lighter for you. We're working on a urine-based system, ideally effective from infancy so that parents can perform early interventions.

By interventions, Sam began, do you mean giving parents the high sign that it's cool to abandon their L7-positive newborn trans girls to die on the shelf while they brew up cis clone abomination boys to replace them?

Yes, that's exactly what I mean, Sam, her mother said. Brewing abominations and promoting infant death by exposure. Or, you know, maybe letting parents know early to purchase the right kinds of toys and clothes for their trans daughters. Getting paperwork and surgery schedules in order.

Her dad cleared his throat. You shouldn't call your brother an abomination, he said.

Sam pointed at Chris. Abomination, she pronounced.

Chris shook his head. I'm sorry, he said. I get that this is hard.

What are you doing with him? Sam demanded. Does he just live here, rent-free? Are you making him work at your company?

You don't have to talk about him as if he's not here, her mother said. Since the UN resolution last year, he's legally a person who gets to make his own decisions.

What decisions is she getting you to make? Sam asked, propping her face in her hands and blinking at Chris. He blinked back. Panicking, she suspected he was embarrassed for her.

I suppose for now, I'll work for the company? he said. I'm still sort of…figuring things out, I guess.

His face tensed into some configuration between awkward and polite, Chris looked into his plate of congealing rib sauce. It was late in the day, and the hair Sam had long ago scorched from her cheeks (yet another stupid thing she'd spent money on, she knew her mom thought, rather than saving for retirement) bloomed blondly from Chris's lip and jaw. Sam tried to remember what she'd felt like, prior to transition; if she'd ever held her head and jaw in the same way that he held his. It was a hard thought to fixate on, like trying to remember what her elementary school had looked like in the days she'd attended it. She'd since driven by, in adulthood, and the sight of the renovated playground had done something to her mind: She had pictured herself, a six-year-old trans girl dressed in boy drag, swinging from monkey bars that hadn't existed until long after her pubescence. The revision had replaced the original.

S he thought about this while they finished dinner and Roland talked about a project he was working on with Sam's mom. He'd freelanced for Sam's mom's technical support department for a while, both before and after the dissolution of his and Sam's relationship; Sam's mom paid their rent. Sam's mom was brilliant, Sam knew, and in the end she would pay everyone's rent. Everyone would all end up working for her.

She kept thinking about this as she failed to sleep later that night, downstairs in the rec room, with its giant TV and squeaking air mattress. (Chris had tried to offer Sam her old bedroom, which he had been sleeping in since coming home from the lab; Sam had demurred.) Roland was snoring on the futon across the rec room, and down the stairs, from the hallway to her mother's separate bedroom, she could hear the white noise her mother claimed helped her sleep. Over Sam's face loomed the regional sculptures her mother collected every time a new country honored her work; to her right sat the plastic Christmas tree, the box it came in unfestively stacked just behind it. It was a hideous tree, and Sam had picked it out. Why hadn't her mother replaced it? Apathy, Sam supposed, or else some impulse she found difficult to name.

She thought about the tree for a while, and then she got up, the air mattress sliding along the parquet beneath her.

Roland, she said, shoving him lightly three times, then punching him hard a fourth. Get dressed. Pull your truck around the block.

R oland drove; Sam sat in the passenger seat with the air vents angled toward her; Chris sat in the back, propped a little forward on his hands like a surveyor on a stagecoach board, yawning at the winding miles of moonlit asphalt.

So what'd you want to talk to me about? Chris finally asked.

Goosepimpling, Sam remembered that Chris had some of her memories. Just which ones did he have?

How's my old bedroom? she asked carefully. Comfy?

Chris bared his teeth. Look, I get why you wouldn't like me, he said. I came out here because, I don't know, I thought we should talk about it, not in the house.

He stressed the words *the house* the same way she did; she noticed that.

I mean, I didn't ask for this, he continued. I don't know how to deal with all these weird memories I just have. I'm nothing like you, I know that.

I'm glad you realize you're nothing like me, she said. I hope you think about that while you slowly take over every function of my emotional life. I mean, I'm glad I got one last Thanksgiving, anyway, before I stop getting invited.

Whoa, said Roland. That's maybe — unfair?

Oh, whatever, Roland, Sam said. Don't side with my mother! I know her. She's only two years into coping with the whole "having a trans daughter" project. That's hardly any sunk cost. Are you seriously telling me that any sane parents wouldn't do this, given the chance? She pointed at Chris, like a stab. That's his whole purpose. Poster child for the Cis Lebensborn Program. The final cure for gender identity disorder.

I'm sorry, Chris echoed, and then he got quiet. Roland drove, biting his lip.

The car crested the hills and was slowly descending to the shore. From the backseat, the sound of snot sucked into a familiar nose. Disgusting, Sam thought. She turned the fan up as high as she could, the better to drown it out, and then she turned it off.

What? she asked. What's wrong?

Nothing, Chris said. I don't want to bother you with it. You're right. I'm sorry.

She turned again, looked at him, their dark blue eyes meeting.

Do you and Mom — get along or anything? she asked.

He took a moment before answering.

She tries, he said. I mean, I try too. I'm not real, you know, so I have to try harder to make it normal for her. I hope this is okay to talk about with you?

It's cool, Sam said. Do you, like — I don't know anything about clones. Do you have other clones you can talk to about this?

Chris shook his head. None I relate to, he said. I mean, we were developed to be expendable, and that means we have like — problems? There's the ones missing limbs and kidneys and the ones with cosmetic-testing scars — you know, from before the UN resolution. And there's the wealthy ones whose immortality stasis crypts opened on the death of their originals. There are street crazies. How am I supposed to relate to people like that? I grew up in Los Altos Hills, in Mom's house.

TRANSCENDENT 2

Sam didn't reply.

I just think about having friends, he said. How nice it would be to have friends. Like that photo Mom has on the fridge, from that summer trip I took — I mean, you took — in high school. I keep staring at it whenever I see it. All those memories that aren't mine: me and Jared, ordering porn at the hotel, the guitar player in Washington Square while Jared lost all that money to that chess dude, racing back and forth across the Brooklyn Bridge to see if we could make the whole circuit before the trip schedule's two-hour time slot for doing laundry was up. You know? He frowned. The process can't fill in all the gaps. I mean, I have no idea what even happened to Jared. I couldn't call him up to go hang out even if I wanted to.

Again, Sam didn't reply.

Roland pulled the car into the lot just in sight of the visitor center. The noise of the engine stopped, and there were only the waves and the sound of other cars like breaths coming down the hills from the city on the other side. Sam's cheeks were growing warm.

Half Moon Bay, Roland announced. All ashore that's going ashore.

Sam and Roland had gone to Half Moon Bay once, toward the end of their thing. He'd recently started hormones, she hadn't, and she'd watched him cross the sand. Her hair was still short then, and her arms had shivered in a bare-armed Ian Curtis dishabille. Their relationship hadn't survived both of them transitioning, for the reason that Sam sucked. But they trusted each other — or Sam trusted Roland, anyway, enough to remember the section of natural seawall they'd staggered down together, the place where they'd sat on an overturned trash can and talked about how this fragment of beach would be an ideal place to murder someone.

The three of them split up as they descended to the strand, Pacific wind blowing around them under the starlight. Sam stomped in as straight a line as possible toward the breaking surf, and then, just at the moment of plunging in, she turned ninety degrees and walked parallel to the water, following the tightrope line of the surf.

The others' voices were faint. She thought she heard Roland asking Chris if he remembered the times they'd come here before.

Sam didn't think often about the photograph on the fridge; she tried to avoid it whenever she was home. She hated every person in it. Chris's description of her memories, Jesus — this grotesque major-key transposition of everything. She remembered that high school trip, hiding in the bathroom and running the shower water while Jared and his buddies hooted over the women's bodies that writhed and crashed into one another like F1 cars on the hotel big screen, loudly asking Sam how her masturbation was going, and then the teacher demanding an explanation for the hundreds of dollars of room charges in front of the assembled class, as she blushed and Jared beamed. And Washington Square: the quiet NYU student with bangs and serious Moleskine and books and peacoat who stood next to Sam, watching the guitar player while Sam watched her and thought about how badly she wished she could trade her own life for that student's and wondered why the woman would ever change her own life for one as bad as Sam's, all while Jared said racist shit to the elderly grand master who was taking his money.

Chris remembered none of this. He had the facts, not the interpretations. It was her L7 gene in operation: a gene that created its own interpretations, like dosing spiders with hallucinogens, then marveling at the faulty webs they start to spin. She marveled at her mother's ingenuity. Soon transsexuality would be over. Miserable people like Sam would be gone, and everyone could be happy.

Did one of your friends put you up to this? her mother had asked when Sam came out to her two years ago, as a deprogrammer might ask. Communication with other trans people was, clearly, brainwashing. Your new friends chased out your old friends; bad crowds stole your kids away. Against their lies, data was the only reality, the pretext you could believe in. Her mother had invested so much money and research into finding a pretext for believing what her daughter had told her. It was, in a way, love. And now her mother could give the pretext she'd found to the whole world, so that the rest of the world could love as well.

Up on the hill, she could see, Chris was standing close to the section of seawall she and Roland had long ago picked out. Chris was watching Sam; seeing her turn, he waved at her. She waved back. He had the facts about the seawall. Did he have the interpretation? What did he want her to do? What did she want to do?

She started back in his direction. And with each step, as she slowly climbed toward land and her brother — her abomination on the shore, who lined up with her in the old family force field, who kept his eyes on her now like fishing line — she thought very carefully about the sequence of actions she would take and which actions she would not take. It was very important, she knew, to be

RHIZOMATIC DIPLOMACY

◄ Vajra Chandrasekera ►

Talpo lived in the past tense now, unable to maintain the traditional human pretense of a pilot consciousness operating in simultaneity with events. Only a memory, that sense of control and purpose — and not even his own memory but Kvora's, from when he was still Kvora. It was the difference, Talpo thought, between drive and being driven. This loss wasn't an intended effect of his new phenotype — or if it was, Kvora had been unaware of it so Talpo didn't know either. So too the other unfortunate side effects: the tiny, weak jaw; the curved cleft in the roof of his mouth; the way his tongue seemed set too far back, making him feel like he was about to choke; (persistent, intrusive thoughts that he kept hearing in Kvora's voice, in what he used to think of as his own voice); chronic lymphocytopenia; the ominous promise of immunodeficiencies and the fluid already gathering in his lungs.

Breathing was never going to get any easier, Kvora had told him when he was born complaining.

She told him again, twenty-eight minutes later, when she pulled the oxygen mask off and let him down into the marsh. Paniskoi bombers were coming in for another run on the west quadrant so Kvora's helo lifted away fast, leaving Talpo with half an hour of life in the world and already alone.

Bog-poppers over the tree line puffed the rot of rotten eggs, but the marsh was out of the line of fire for now, temporary diplomatic/arable/adjudicatory ground. The marshwater was a sour curd slicked with oils that caught and pooled around his thighs.

"Bombers" being the wrong word, he knew that now. (Poor connotative fit, should be something like "soil rejuvenation initiatives.") The in-vitro language training, imperfect and still settling into the twisty nooks of his new brain — paniskoi languages were so frustratingly close to human languages, with even the same triune configuration of pheromones, somatics and speech, only ever *just* unspeakable, over the line that made misunderstandings likelier than in-comprehension. (In hindsight not even his Kvora-mind, his haphazard simula-crum of himself before his birth, would hazard a guess which of the two would have flowered finer casus belli. But what did it matter in all this fecundity? There was, in any case, no such thing as diplomacy uncomposted by the dead.)

Despite knowing the terms and conditions of his altered genotype and phe-notype, since his (fraught) first breath outside the egg Talpo's human memories still expected an easing, a longed-for regulation of the lungs, a breath that would finally catch and clear. He now saw (with the wisdom of forty-seven minutes of living) the wheezing horror of its lack, or the fragile efforts of his heart to pound, as like the waves he used to watch crash on the grim human pollution of Saliko City beach (memories not his own, but Kvora's, that black water quietly transmuted in memory's lazy eye into the dirty milk of the marshwater around him) as inevitable/historical events caused by forces that dwarfed in scale and scope the observer consciousness. Following along, never directing. Kvora had theorized this was how paniskoi saw the world, and made him in their image, or as close to their image as a human brain (and mind, or minds, if Talpo wanted to count himself a separate entity from Kvora, a distinction they had not had time to discuss in the haste of war) could achieve.

(This dissociation, she warned herself/him before he was even born, would be a brutal adjustment: the cessation of self-identifying as an agent. She had told herself this as firmly as she knew how, internalized it before they put her under for the procedure, prepared herself to wake up twice: once in terror and relief; once with purpose and in abandonment.)

It wasn't clear if paniskoi even *knew* they were at war. It was not known if they meant to commit acts of war or agricultural engineering. Ends had merely revealed intentions irrelevant. It wasn't clear if paniskoi understood intentions, either.

Kvora's plan (she said let's give it a go I won't make anybody volunteer I'll do it myself and meant it, because Talpo as Kvora remembered meaning it, and there was no way to tell at this range if that intent had included substrates of lies of second-order intent, or lies of fact, or lies of the unconscious variety for which blame could not be reasonably applied. There had been no ethics committee, no approval from Saliko City's Fourth Junta, nothing but expenditure of accumulated credibility and frontline assumptions about language) depended on Talpo's participation in his predestination, which he would have cared less about if only he could breathe easy. Blame came easier with the nearness of panic (and the risk of aborting himself in two feet of marshwater). The mission: find the paniskoi diplomat/farmer/soil-quality-assurance engineer/erosion control measure in this marsh and figure out how to say "we surrender" in paniskoi. Or "you surrender or else." Kvora didn't care what the message was, if this impossible communication could be initiated at all. There were other plans, contingencies, gambits, a choice of meanings to commit to that Talpo could no longer grasp, rapidly decaying into unintelligibility. Intentions have a short half-life and were instantly obsoleted in any case, by the undiscovered realities of what Talpo could or not articulate in paniskoi when the time came. (You're in the army now, my son.)

The damp air in every raw breath tasted like milk gone bad, which Talpo had never tasted but Kvora had once when she was young on her homeworld (hometown childhood home warm red tiles river-smoothed stones, bad milk sick and slick on the tongue), long before the colonial navy bought her and brought her to Saliko City under the Third Junta. Promotion, honours, lives and territories gained and lost.

Straight lines from A to B. Don't drink the bad milk because it will make you sick. Tiny unhappy cilia, an epithelium in revolt, formalised as the construct of disgust.

Overhead the bilious yellow overstory thick with alien xanthophylls and casting sunset at high noon. A jaundiced underworld with no void in it, all filled and entangled with leaf, branch and root. Talpo clambered under and through (not to worry about scrapes and scratches, about infections and immunodeficiencies, since in any case always already too late given his predestination), splashing whenever distant explosions (not so distant) rippled the water around him. He kept his lips closed tight. Don't drink the bad milk.

These foggy Kvora-memories from before his birth felt like a trick. Like Kvora had somehow betrayed him by not properly conceiving him as a separate person with his own history but only as a version of herself, a ragged continuation of her story, a brief subplot. Her genotype and her consciousness, her choices, her will: Talpo the product of *her* voluntarity, participant but not agent, behind the curve of will (of course this was quite sane from Kvora's theorised paniskoi point-of-view), and Kvora not his twin nor mother, but still a ghost-twin, a mother-dream. Call it his risk, his life, not hers but her voice in his head (don't drink the bad milk, but in the ghost of Talpo's memory, Kvora drank the bad milk anyway this time, tilted her head back and kept swallowing spilling and splashing down her chin) directing the choices made over an hour ago, in another life.

He smelled strange to himself, alkaline and dying.

The clearing in the marsh-tangle was formed in the interface between great mater roots from which much of the tangle radiated. Talpo had arrived here by simply following the pattern of the roots, with no consciousness of doing so. Talpo knew which way Kvora would have seen it (a straight and intended line from birth to this predestination, a clearing in which a planned meeting could be had) but not which way he saw it himself. Intention and simulation lay all before him like the tangled roots themselves, a structure grown mysteriously with its roots in alien milk.

The paniskoi smelled like nothing Talpo had an analogue for. When its emergences stellated, indicating awareness/airflow adjustment, he heard himself speak, and listened.

THE PIGEON SUMMER

◀ Brit Mandelo ▶

J. kicked the door shut and deposited hir armload of grocery bags on the floor. From the squat bedside table, one of the three pieces of actual furniture included in the price of rent, the rattling buzz of hir phone filled the room — a petite cacophony, but grating. And then it stopped. For a moment, one hand on the countertop and the other hanging limp, J. stood frozen in the silence. The shop below the apartment had closed in the afternoon. The building, though aged, did not obligingly ping and moan and settle. In the space of held breath the weight of quiet was suffocating, until the gentle burble of a bird's call broke the tableau. J. twitched like a horse shaking off flies and moved to the window, chewed fingertips on the warm glass, to peer out. On the ledge between gutter and wall there was a nest — tufts of fluff and prickly twigs. A pigeon rustled in it, one eye turned to the window, and cooed again.

"Some company, I guess," si murmured and turned to lean a hip against the frame, surveying hir domain: a trash bag full of clothes listing sideways in front of a shallow closet at the foot of the compact, hard bed, a laptop on the dining table, and a battered carryon case with handle still raised pushed up against the side of the kitchen counter. Si nudged open the drawer of the bedside table — inside, a slim black smartphone and a stack of twenty dollar bills not much bigger — and closed it again, then shut hir eyes and sagged against the thick old wall.

As the sun crept down, taking with it the bird's soft continual communication, J. paced across the creaking hollows of the uneven floorboards from fridge to bed and back, counting steps against the quiet. Si lost count at sixty-seven and collapsed onto the mattress, breathing careful and slow through hir nose. The sheets still smelled like long nights of sweat and restlessness. Si hadn't washed them before bundling them up and stuffing them in the trash bag. The streetlights below illuminated the cracks in the ceiling plaster; si rolled onto hir side and reached out, fingers resting on the drawer handle.

It slid open with a whispery squeak. Si picked up the phone and thumbed it on, swiping past the missed calls and texts, found the gallery and opened it. C.'s smile — C.'s arm around hir shoulders — C.'s shock of brunette hair wild and caught in a private wind. A wolfish sound ground its way from between hir teeth, breaking into a choke-breathed moan and the wrenching gasps that followed. J. cried ugly, cried alone, cried hot-skinned and lying on top of unwashed sheets in a shithole apartment downtown. The hard edges of the phone cut into hir palm.

Then came a crackle of plastic and a thud from across the room, followed by the sound of something rolling across the floorboards. J. lifted hir head, swallowing hard. A can of condensed soup bumped to a stop at a split board. The side of the plastic sack had been pulled down as if a curious hand had tugged it to peek at the contents. Skin tingling with a mixture of horror-movie curiosity and raw pain, J. staggered from the bed and circled the shopping bags, seeing no way for the culprit to have tipped itself open.

C. had used to watch marathons of *Haunted Hotels* in the fall. They'd done it together. It had become a joke, but the sort that maintained a sincere and childish hope: that it *could* happen. It would be almost too much for that mutual shred of belief to come to fruition, now, too late. Still si waited, lips pressed into a thin line, for the brush of a cold hand or the whisper of a voice — some sort of theatrical confirmation — and nothing. The air felt like air; the room, empty. Finally si unzipped the carryon and snagged a notebook from the assorted junk inside, opened it to write:

> *Dear ghost,*
> *I would know if you were C., and you're not. I guess you're my roommate now.*
> *I'm writing because I don't want to hear the sound of my own voice.*
> *Hope you don't mind.*
> *J.*

Si left the note on the table and stripped out of hir jeans and shirt, crawling beneath the covers and burying hir face in the pillow. Eighteen for two days — days like wrack-strewn islands — and already writing notes to imaginary ghosts. It made hir feel close to C., for a moment. Hir hand found the phone again, cradling it to hir chest: a fragile slip of circuits and plastic, a box of memories.

The vertiginous sensation of waking under an unfamiliar ceiling with the sun at the wrong angle to the eyes: J. swallowed it down with a dry mouth and cracking lips. The second morning was not precisely easier than the first, only less of a surprise. The body-hot phone dug into hir hipbone where it had slipped in the night. Si fumbled for it with loose hands and placed it on the bedside table, then sat up and swung bare feet down onto the sun-warmed boards. Before leaving behind hir bedroom and books and self, si often woke without remembering that *it had happened*, as if hir mind had shunted that knowledge off to the side in self-defense. But then as si would reach out drowsy to text C. good morning, synapses would fire quick and merciless — his fingers white and cold in the coffin molded around the striped hat he'd loved, the discreet agony of messages sent and not ever answered. Comparatively, waking already gutted and dizzy was preferable to being wounded fresh each time.

Going through the motions — clothes, bathroom while avoiding hir reflection in the mirror, a bowl of cereal — took barely twenty minutes. After, J. sat slouched at the table, hands in hir lap. The notebook sat open by hir empty bowl, its scrawled note stranger still in the daytime. There was no clock in the apartment. Time passed; the room grew warmer as the sun filled it more and more aggressively.

J. stood, walked back to the bed, and lay down. Si wrapped one arm around the pillow and hugged it to hir stomach. As if in an attempt to distract hir, the phone buzzed for attention on the nightstand. Si did not move.

Time passed.

"Fuck's sake," J. croaked as the phone went off for the sixth time in a row, buzzing incessantly. Si sat up, ignoring the twinge in hir lower back from so long spent lying on the unyielding mattress. The screen read, *Mom.* Si waited until the call stopped, picked up the phone, and toggled it to silent. These two days were probably the most hir mother had tried to talk to hir in years.

What am I doing, si thought.

TRANSCENDENT 2

Nerveless fingers scrolled through a handful of unread texts from people whose desperation could not touch hir. Si had nothing for them — no answers, no apologies — any more than si had for hirself. The thought of opening one, of facing the blinking cursor and a blank box into which si had to compress some sort of rational answer, was unfathomable.

But what am I doing —

On the table, the notebook wasn't open. Si dropped the phone onto the bed and crossed the room, thinking blankly of shut windows and still air, of a notebook that could close itself in a locked room.

The page with the note was the same. No spectral hand had scribed a response. All the same, J. sat down hard at the table and took up hir pen once more, flipping to the next blank page. The cheap, crisp paper wrinkled gently under the pressure of hir palm holding the notebook open. Si waited, poised to begin but unable to find the thread, the explanation, for what had put hir in the cramped studio downtown with a silenced phone and no one in the world to whom si felt accountable.

> *Dear ghost,*
>
> *I don't know what I'm doing here. I don't know who you are, or what you're sticking around for. I won't know your name. That's kind of a relief: I don't have to know you. I am unconnected to you, and you are unconnected to me. Just some disembodied something hanging around, maybe trying to figure me out. Good luck.*
>
> *There are some things I do know though:*
> *(1) I've paid two months' rent here*
> *(2) I don't have a job and I don't have much money left*
> *(3) My best friend is dead*
> *(4) I don't know how I'm supposed to* **be**
> *(5) Above all I am seriously fucked*
> *J.*

The aching in hir eyes recalled a three-day hangover, bruised and tingling. Si blinked, stared up at the ceiling until the dampness and burning passed, and took another look at the note. *I don't know how I'm supposed to* **be** — and next to that, si scribbled in addendum, *without C.* Below the signature, si continued: *it was us against the world right.* The aching spread in a shiver across hir skin from eye sockets to sinuses and out. Si shoved the chair back and stood, swallowing down bile and tears. The chasm inside hirself — a trench home to some devouring leviathan, waiting for the right moment to surface and consume — was like a physical wound, the kind it was best not to look at. A cut down to bone: the shock doesn't set in until you see the striations in your tissue and muscle and fat. So *don't look*.

The setting sun hollowed out the room, highlighted the bare lack of personalizing detail. Si wandered to the window while hir pulse pounded in ears and tongue. The pigeon wasn't in its nest; there were two eggs, pale and speckled as if with flecks of ash. Si watched, waiting, devoting hir energy to the complex task of breathing. Finally the pigeon returned and landed on the ledge with a few clumsy flaps, then hopped up into its nest. It settled in, fluffed up, blinked, all small bones and dynamic reality chugging along the tracks of its life. The pigeon didn't know how easy it had things. After standing until hir knees ached, J. dragged the chair to the window and sat instead, watching the pigeon watch the world. On the street below, the river-flow of people moved and moved, colorful and drab by turns, all alive and vital. J. rested hir head on the glass, gently, feelings its warmth.

D*ear ghost,* si wrote later in the dark, seeing by the yellow reflected glow of streetlights.

The question isn't necessarily if I want to live.
*It's whether or not I **can**.*

T he next morning, there were chicks.

Their naked miniature bodies had appeared suddenly — eggs during the night, birds come noon. J. wondered with a dull ache in hir gut if it was all right that the adult had left them so bare and alone, freshly extant in the world. Si took up hir post in the chair by the window to keep an eye on them. They didn't move much, huddled together, only a little twitch here and there. The stillness was agitating in and of itself, long moments of dread where those barely-birds seemed too motionless.

When the pigeon finally returned, si breathed out what felt like hours of tension. It cuddled into the nest with the chicks, hiding them from view. Released from vigil, J. paced to the fridge, bed and back. After seven circuits, si flipped open the notebook on the table and wrote:

Dear ghost,
There's a line about the terrible boredom of pain that seems really appropriate right now. I wonder how you deal with being dead. I guess I'm your pigeon — something to watch that's still moving.

Si paused, shifting on the creaking floorboards.

You're probably not real; this is a device, me giving myself therapy badly. But if you are, we're both in limbo. Not so unconnected after all, I guess.

— —

You know, we got into college together. Same program. We had a future. Seems like a different world. Not real.

J. spread hir hand over the words, pressing them down. Si had been so *ready*; they both had been, full of strategies and tactics. The world an oyster, a peach, a sun-hot raspberry from the bushes behind C.'s parents' house — and now husk, pit, bitter. No plans. Instead, the dedicated free fall of a life with the bottom torn out.

Goddamn I am so melodramatic

There was a thin-fingered handprint in the steam on the bathroom mirror. Towel in one hand and wiping water out of hir eyes with the other, J. attempted to correlate the odds that si was hallucinating against the odds that the ghost was real and — judging from the print — petite. Or, it had been left in body oils by some previous tenant and never wiped down. That seemed as improbable as the phantom; tiny and old or not, the apartment had been clean when si moved in.

"Are you going to communicate with me now?" si murmured, voice rough from disuse and echoing strangely in the closet-sized room.

The steam on the mirror didn't streak to life with words or finger-drawings.

Si wasn't, precisely, disappointed.

Dear Cordelia,
That seems like an appropriate name for a ghost. I feel like if I'm going to keep writing you it's too weird to do it in the generic.
It's not that I've never experienced loss. When I was a kid my dad left. Two years ago, my grandpa died. It hurt. But this is so far beyond hurt I can't ex-

*plain it to you. It's like being skinless, having your eyes put out, I don't know.
Something you should die from. To be honest with you maybe I'm a ghost too. I
am dead and this has killed me. God only fucking knows why I'm still walking
around staring at birds.*

*C. was a part of me. I came out because I had him to lean on, because there was
one person in the world I could bare myself to like that the first time: hey, this is
who I am, I know it's fucking weird, can you deal? And yeah, of course he could
deal.*

His whole business was dealing. **We dealt.**

And then he maybe killed himself, and I don't know what to do with that.

It's absurd: your **other half,** *your* **significant other***. I had one of those even
if it wasn't the kind most people think — C. didn't have to be my goddamn boyfriend to be the thing I most cared for. Binary system, self-supporting, closed loop.
Then it goes and ruptures, one day to the next, and you've got nothing and no one.
Because you're a weird motherfucker and — yeah teenage angst whatever, but really — nobody else gives a shit about you and nobody else understands you.*

I don't even know if I can feel betrayed.

The last half of the letter was jagged, words crawling over lines and sliding
sideways off the page.

There was a time limit in place, si reflected, slouched on the chair with one
bare foot propped on the windowsill. The rising and setting of the sun ticked
one more day off — one more day where the rent was paid, gone; one more day
with food to eat, gone. The time limit was some comfort, though, a guarantee
that this state of purgatory was not and could not be permanent, that si wouldn't
find hirself still mourning and half-alive in the tiny studio in three years. On the
ledge, the pigeon was preening. Si hadn't seen it feeding the chicks yet, but assumed it must be. Those birds had time limits, too, whether or not they knew
about them. So long to grow feathers, so long to learn to fly, so long to live,
then — nothing.

Si took up the notebook again, finding a fresh page.

Dear Cordelia,

Here are some clichés and some truths or both:

(1) I don't know how to live without him.

(2) I am lost and alone.

(3) I miss C. so much I could die.
(4) Life is too short.
(5) Life is meaningless.
(6) I am a coward.
(7) I just want some answers.
(8) Ghosts can't move on properly.
— J.

The notebook slapped to the floor, the pen clattering next to it. Si tipped hir chin up and wobbled the chair on its back legs, playing at risk. The chicks made the softest yelping chirps outside, barely audible, crying out at the wide blue sky.

No answers.

Dear Cordelia,

I'm starting to really identify with these birds. Probably a sign of my oncoming psychological collapse. I write letters to ghosts and I spend all day watching pigeons grow up. That's what I have left.

The question is: did he kill himself?

I don't know, maybe, maybe not on purpose. Keeps me up nights. **Haunts** *me even. I can't say that you're haunting me. I think I might be haunting you. Probably why you won't respond to these letters. There's a good enough mirror to write on if you wanted to.*

— J.

Dear Cordelia,

The pigeons are getting bigger — they've got fluff and feathers. They wobble around in their nest and headbutt each other seemingly by accident a lot. I've lost track of what day it is, or what else I'm doing but lying around in the bed or watching the birds. That should worry me, and it doesn't.

Maybe I don't need answers. Maybe I just need to man up and make a decision. It's a big world out there and it seems to chug along just fine without me.

One more thing: there's nobody left to tell me how much I have to live for.

Thanks, C. You're the best friend a person could have.

There was no more milk. J. stood in the chill wafting from the open fridge door, sweat prickling hir scalp, and stared at the empty shelves. The box of cereal on the table was the last of the actual food that remained from hir initial and only trip to the corner grocery. Si realized with a sick swooping sensation that si had not left the studio since that day. The grey wash of preceding mornings and afternoons and nights blurred, indistinct — countable only in terms of the dwindling supplies. Hir hair was a nest not unlike the pigeon's; toenails grown out; clothes unwashed. Si closed the fridge and took a calming breath before wandering to the spill of still-possibly-clean laundry from the tipped-over trash bag next to the empty closet. Si found a sweatshirt and a pair of jeans, despite the summer swelter, and tugged them on. A glance out the window revealed a bustling afternoon crowd passing on the street below.

Si walked to the door and put a hand on the knob. Hir fingers shook. Hir guts cramped — equal measures hunger and terror. There were, of course, people down that narrow staircase. There would be more at the grocery, and more at the checkout, and yet more on the walk back. Each would have their own manners of seeing and judging, their brief cruelties and petty aggressions. With C., there were certain possibilities: a reckless bravado, a bolstering effect — the crowd of two, ready to put backs together and fight. C. *knew* hir and *needed* hir, would be there to the end no matter bodies or pronouns or the harshness of strangers. Alone, J. was — si let go of the knob and banged hir head twice on the door — vulnerable. The shape and not-shape of hir had mattered less, before. Before, si had armor. Before, si hadn't felt raw as bone and dangerously visible.

But this was now.

Si picked up the box of cereal and poured a glass of water from the tap, then went to sit by the window. The pigeons, grown plump, cooed and wittered at each other and their parent. The three of them could no longer all fit in the nest together. J. ate fistfuls of the dry cereal, washing them down with lukewarm iron-tasting water. *Dear Cordelia,* si thought, *I am fucking terrified.*

J. paced, slept, ate the dwindling box of cereal to quiet an aching stomach. Life had come down to those simple but ineffably complicated behaviors, and the ticking of a phantom clock, the pressure of a phone that held more and more unanswered messages juxtaposed against the frightful silence of the void. In hir bones si felt it, the coming to a close.

The ghost had been neglectful, invisible; the pigeons were growing to look like their parent, no longer so devastatingly helpless and delicate. The rent would be due, soon. The food was nearly gone. C. was still as dead as he'd been weeks before, and would be for the rest of the weeks in the world.

TRANSCENDENT 2

Footsore and stiff from pacing tight cage-circles for hours, J. sat down to the red sun of evening in the chair by the window, notebook balanced open to a fresh page on hir knee. Si took in the stifling warm air of the apartment in one long inhale; let it out slowly. The city, their city, moved through life below.

Dear Cordelia,

If you were the real C.'s ghost, there would be some things I'd want to tell you. Some things that need to get said, I guess — I feel like doing it now.

So: Dear C.,

*I should have said it more, that I loved you. I should have said it into the stupid mess of your hair when we sobered up at dawn in the backseat of your car. I should have made you understand what I would have sworn to fucking god you **did** understand: without each other we've got nothing, because you're the whole world and all I wanted out of it.*

You left me.

You made some promises, to me, and you broke them.

I don't care. If I could have you back for five minutes, just five forever, so I could say goodbye — it wouldn't be enough but it would be something. It wouldn't be my stupid text "sup" and you not responding. It wouldn't be almost blacking out at your funeral and your fucking parents not caring, not understanding, that I had lost half of me.

I miss you. I miss you. I miss you. You heartless fuck.

I don't know how to go on, how to go do the shit we should be doing together — you should be in this apartment with me, crammed into that tiny bathroom in the morning and maybe having to get a second bed or just a bigger one we could share or whatever felt all right.

Nobody else had to get us, what we were for each other. I thought you thought it was funny, when kids couldn't decide to call us faggots or what. I got us. I thought you did.

You should have thought of me.

What would you tell me to do, without you? Couldn't even leave me a fucking note.

I loved you.

J. trailed off, silence overtaking the scritch of pen on paper, and heaved a chest-cracking breath. It felt as if the ink had crawled up from hir guts and ripped free onto the page, splattered there in a horrorshow of anger and need and pain.

This was what it was like, in words — insufficient, flat, a belly-shaking cry distilled into a page of symbols. This was what it was like to yank at the edges of the gash and look at the insides.

It, si thought, **hurts**.

Yours, J —.

The ticklish swipe of a hand brushing hair back from J.'s face woke hir to wide white cracks of lightning in the outside sky and the sound of thunder. Si froze, one hand clutching the pillow, as the nearly imperceptible touch skated across hir scalp, ruffling bed-wild hair and smoothing a hank of it away from hir face. Hir heart raced. The ghost — silent for days, more figment than phantom — had been stroking hir head.

This was not a hand-print on a mirror.

It was less eerie than si would have expected, more of a comfort. Si waited a moment for another touch, amidst the thunder's rumbling, then when none seemed forthcoming climbed out of bed and went to the window. Si looked out on the rain-washed street through the distortions of wet glass. The realization that the ever-present nest to the right on the ledge had only two occupants — and one was the adult — struck by the blaze of an arc of lightning from the sky. J.'s stomach dropped. The wind howled outside; the two birds huddled together close through the deluge. "Shit," si whispered.

The chick must have fallen out. Si wasn't sure how long it took pigeons to fledge; they looked big, but si didn't know enough to judge. What if it was lying on the ground below, trapped in the runoff water, cold and alone? The constriction in hir chest tightened inch by inch. Si threw on a pair of sneakers and a sweatshirt, shivering with adrenaline, and leapt to the door. There si balked, drawn up short. The knob was cold in the warm room, somehow, as if a chill hand had held it moments before — one equally incorporeal and helpless to open the thing as si felt in this moment. Outside was *outside*. Si ground hir teeth hard enough to ache. Hir metaphorical clock had stopped ticking, all hands pointing to midnight.

Si turned the knob and clattered down the dark staircase, opening the metal door at the bottom onto the courtyard. The rain hissed down in sheets. Si ducked into it, head down and hands up to shade hir eyes; the downpour was cold, soaking hir to the skin in an instant. Si traced the backside of the house along the garden row with the shop owner's flowers flattened and jerking under the assault of the wind and rain. Each step si took without finding the little bird was like a blow to the ribs.

It mattered. Si absorbed that knowledge while searching, water sloshing into hir shoes to freeze hir toes. It *mattered* whether or not si found the pigeon, whether or not it was all right. This was an individual act si had to perform to assure the continuation of some particular small world.

Then beneath a brambly bush that was doing nothing to protect it si found the palm-sized bird, scrunched miserably into itself as tiny as it could become. "Ssh," J. whispered, bending down and taking a knee to reach it. It did not respond to hir looming close, its eyes closed. When hir fingers gently closed around its warm thrumming body it struggled as if to flap away, but si held it tenderly. Hunching over and holding the bird close to hir chest, si struggled back to the stairs and inside the building.

The sudden cessation of rain was like surfacing from drowning. Si wanted to gasp for breath but held the urge so as not to frighten the bird quivering in hir hands. Si bumped the door shut with hir hip and walked up the stairs to the studio. Water trailed behind the pair, pooling under J. as si stopped inside the doorway. Si slopped across the room to the pile of clean laundry and, trembling with uncertainty, sat the pigeon there, opening hir hands slowly to release it. The bird flapped, agitated, and kicked at the old shirts for a moment. J. stepped back and it made a quiet noise that seemed thankful in the dark night, settling in.

J. stood in the center of the room, goosebump-spangled and soaking, and there: the soft weight of fingers resting on hir shoulder, the lightest grip of reassurance, silent and small and whisper-faint. Si closed hir eyes against tears, thought of the letters si'd written, and knew it didn't matter who had received them — just that, impossibly, someone had. The touch dissipated from one breath to the next, and si felt the wet and cold again, moved to strip off the sweatshirt, jeans, shoes, underclothes, each layer a weight and a symbol. Si lay down damp on the still-sleep-warm sheets then shifted, head to the foot of the bed, and pillowed hir chin on hir arms to watch the pigeon. It slept, bird-sized breaths making its body rise and fall.

One small world, one inexplicable life.

"Thank you," si whispered, not entirely alone.

In the morning, si opened the window onto the beginnings of a crisp, clean-breezy summer day. Stealthily si approached the pigeon and took it up, shirt and all, in loose hands; more than the night before, it rustled and fought. Hir heart fluttered like its trapped wings as si approached the window and leaned out, hip on the sill, to reach for the nest where the sibling bird rested. Si waited until the pigeon quieted slightly then opened hir grip a fraction at a time. It hopped onto the ledge, wobbled for a breath-stealing moment, and stepped into its nest again.

The fist-clenched tightness in J.'s chest eased, bit by bit, like hir own hands. Si closed the window and sat down in the chair to take up the notebook. Si wrote:

> *Dear Cordelia,*
> *The pigeons are okay.*
> *— J.*

After a long moment, si leaned over and picked up the phone from the bed-side table to scroll through the message box. C.'s name, there, and si knew what was in the thread: laughter, light, loneliness. Instead si flicked up to hir own unanswered texts and messages. Hir thumb tapped, deliberate and trembling, "return call."

THE ROAD, AND THE VALLEY, AND THE BEASTS

◄ Keffy R.M. Kehrli ►

The valley of my home is long and crooked and narrow, cut into the landscape like a knife wound. A river runs along the bottom, flooding often through the spring, drying to a barest trickle in late summer, and freezing in winter. Shadowing the river is the great old road, a broad expanse of weeds and cracked bricks that were laid by hands long since forgotten.

As a rule, we do not travel the road, as it is not ours to use.

Our town has no official name. It is merely a collection of houses rough-hewn from tree and stone for those of us who find ourselves here. There are never any visitors, and none of us ever leave, not by road, nor by river, and certainly never in the baskets of the dead. Perhaps the town had a name once, and the people who lived here before us decided that there was no need to keep a name if there was no one to speak with. Would we have names, ourselves, if there were never anyone to introduce ourselves to?

We are not born here, but here we die, and our bodies are buried in the cemetery tucked up against the eastern wall of the valley. There we rest with all those who lived here before, whether they gave the town a name or no, their own names obscured by lichens and mosses and worn away by the callused hands of time.

Why is there a road if it is not used? Ah, but it *is* used, frequently — only never by any of us.

There is a procession of giant Beasts that travels the great road past us twice a day, in the morning traveling upriver and in the evening traveling down. In the dim light of early dawn, the Beasts walk hunched and weary, their backs laden with baskets full of the newly dead, whose eyes stare and gleam in the dark, legs and arms limp or stiff depending on how long they've been dead. In the evenings, the Beasts pass us again, looking strong and refreshed, their baskets hanging limp and empty. Sometimes at dusk they whistle while they travel, the fluting sounds echoing down the valley for hours.

Somewhere, far away, there is a land where we are born. Somewhere, far away, there is a land where people are not buried when they die, but are taken upriver by the Beasts.

I dream of that land almost every day, whether I'm weeding the garden that my adoptive mothers have planted, or baking bread, or washing the clothes in a shallow section of the river. There are so many dead in the baskets of the Beasts each morning that this land they come from must be full of people, more people even than are buried in our cemetery, more than have ever existed in our small town. I wonder what things they have built, towers of marble, cathedrals of glass, bridges of gold that gleam red in the sunset...

My dearest love is a girl named Ria, who was given a boy's name when she first came here but let her adoptive father know that he was wrong as soon as she could speak. Although nearly adults, we two are the youngest living in the town, as it has been one of the longest stretches between new arrivals that anyone can remember.

In the evenings, Ria sits with me under the apple trees in my mothers' orchard, nibbling at my ears when she thinks that I have paid too much attention to the Beasts passing us by, holding my hands against her chest when I try to cup them behind my ears to hear the Beasts' strangely soft footfalls.

I prefer to watch them in the evening. They look happier, their burdens left behind them. Their springy coils of metallic hair bounce with each step. The lightened baskets swing down along their sides, empty and free. Their arms pump the air, all sinew and skin, and their long, long fingers snap quiet rhythms.

"Ria," I whisper into her ear, resting my forehead against her kinky black hair, "someday I will follow them home, back to where we came from, and I will find out why we were sent away, and how, and by whom, and then we will know who we really are."

She shakes her head, reaches behind us for a freshly wind-felled apple, and takes a bite before offering it to me. "Why should we care about who we used to be, or who we would have been, or those who never wanted us to begin with?"

The apple's flesh is crisp and cool and sweet between my teeth. "Aren't you curious?"

She rolls her eyes and runs her fingers through her hair. "Not about who I used to be, no."

"But what if…?"

"No."

"We could be princes, or kings, or queens, or long-lost siblings to an emperor, or…"

"Or babies too strange to ever be wanted, people with no past worth speaking of or remembering."

She takes the apple back, and I say, "I don't understand why you don't even want to know."

"You won't go, anyway," she says. "You've been telling me the same thing, making plans like wisps of clouds, since we were children."

"Someday," I insist. "When I'm ready."

Ria shakes her head, and she pulls me down beside her on the grass, staring up at the leaves and branches and softly reddening apples. Above our farms and the trees, the walls of the valley ascend far into the clouds on most days, so high that nothing can grow in the thinned air. We are ringed around by jagged black teeth, as though we rest in the back of a mouth tipped to the sky.

It is later, after we have made up, and kissed again, and reached gentle fingers under clothes and into all our favorite places, that I realize my mistake. It is not that Ria is not curious. It is that she prefers the morning Beasts, prefers waking before dawn, alone, and watching them walk.

In the mornings, their backs are stooped under the weight of all the dead. In the mornings, they walk like dead things themselves, their eyes tired and pained, their fingers not snapping, but instead dangling near to the cracked road beneath their feet. They do not whistle on their travels upriver, but instead they sometimes hum a dirge, a lullaby, for the dead they carry.

I do not always wake to watch the Beasts pass us in the morning, but I know that Ria does, so I crawl from the warmth of my sheets an hour before dawn, too early, too early, the exhaustion making my skin feel tight and achy. I wash my face in the basin of cold water, trying to bring myself to wakefulness, then grab two rolls left over from dinner the night before and slip out the door quietly enough that my mothers will not wake.

Ria is not by the trees in the orchard, nor is she on the hill beside the river, but when I climb that hill, I do see her sitting on a large stone next to the great road. I sprint to her, nearly dropping our breakfast.

"Ria!" I say, starting to feel the soft, shuffling footfalls of the Beasts upon the earth. They are so near, so near, just around the bend of the river and road. "Ria, what are you doing?"

"Shh," she says. "They don't mind if you sit so close to watch them, as long as you are quiet."

"But…"

"Come and sit with me," she says, "or go back to bed."

I climb up to sit next to her on the stone, and hand her one of the rolls. She sniffs it, smiles, and then puts it inside a small canvas bag she has slung over one shoulder.

"You spend so much time thinking about the land we've come from," she says. "Do you ever think about what might be further on down the road?"

I frown, my fingers tearing into the roll I have kept for myself. Crumbs fall to the road, and a quick and fearless crow grabs them before the Beasts round the corner.

They are as heavily laden this morning as they ever are. I have never sat so close to watch the dead. I recoil slightly, but Ria grabs my arm and steadies me. The dead are old and young and in between. Some look peaceful as they gaze out at the valley. Others are weeping tears of blood, or holding together grievous injuries with pale, bloodless fingers.

The Beasts ignore us, ignore the valley, pay no attention to anything around them, until suddenly Ria jumps down from the stone and dashes onto the road, dancing around the feet of the Beasts in the front until she is standing before the last of them.

I cannot breathe, and I cannot move, and I cannot save her.

The Beast stops, its feet slowing to a shuffle and I see that Ria is barely as tall as half its shin. It stares down at her, long fingers straying up to scratch the curly hairs on its chest.

"I wish to go with you," Ria says.

The Beast looks over her to the others in its procession, passing the orchard and the hill, and soon to be out of our town altogether.

Its voice rumbles in its chest, and I think that it is about to talk, but it does not. It hums to itself quietly, thoughtfully, and then reaches behind to the baskets on its shoulders. It palms something, and then holds out a hand the size of a small house to Ria. A child sits there, eyes wide and frightened, not looking nearly as dead as the others.

"Stay here," the Beast says, its voice like rolling thunder. "Safe, here."

Ria looks for a moment like she will argue. But the Beast is as tall and implacable as a mountain. Her shoulders slump as she accepts the refusal. She reaches out, and the child slides down off the Beast's great hand to stand with her on the road.

The Beast considers them for a moment, rubs Ria's hair gently with a single fingertip, and then steps over them, walking a touch faster than usual so that it can catch up to its fellows.

ABOUT A WOMAN AND A KID

◄ M. Téllez ►

An older woman came to town. By town I mean our little dark forest, which
is on the disconnected part of the city — the other side of the river where
the power's broken up anymore. She came in the morning when we were out
pulling weeds and foraging along the creek banks. She had a lot of useful things.
Machined tools and a collapsible no-puncture canoe — a really small kind I'd
never seen before. It fit into a pouch as big as a half loaf of bread. We were
all curious. She carried herself like a mountain cat, strong, gentle, moving easy
and deliberate onto the shore. A few of us exchanged intrigued glances. She ac-
knowledged herself. She knew about us, was happy she'd made it. Said she had
come cause she'd heard there were good mushrooms and many medicine plants
and deer. Also that we were all homos and witches. That made us laugh because
it's true.

Our forest is a damp kind that ate a city. Or part of a city, one that used to
cross the rivers back when they were smaller and the rain was less. We're the
people who stayed and gathered after everyone else left. The water changed the
land. If you knew it before the flooding years, you might be able to recognize
some of the old roads, the houses, the school buildings and stores. Most things
have long since left the hold of human design and order. And my little coven, we
live in one of the old stone churches that still has its convent and school buildings. Our neighbors live in a mosque and its buildings likewise. I suppose we live
a bit like nuns, all up in this church, but our reverence is for each other and the

stars and the land, not for that surveillance state, killer man-God they stole the profound crossways and put him on…

We asked the woman where she'd come from and how she'd heard about us. She looked right at me with a smile and said, "Your walker got me curious." The others all turned my way to see what my face said, and I stared back at her with my mouth in an *ohhh*. I'd been around a fire with her before.

We invited her to sit with us and snack and make some sense of everything. We grew a bit of corn, beans, squash, potatoes. There are a few fruiting trees we enjoy. We eat mushrooms. Meat sometimes. Eggs. We steal too. She asked if we ate fish. Said she loved eating fish when she could. We said no, the fish is unreliable still. There's plenty, but they get into something in the water that isn't good to us. We asked, did she cross the Schuylkill on her blow-up boat? She did. How far had she come. Quite a few days away, maybe sixteen, seventeen? She couldn't remember and didn't seem to care. Spent most of her transit on the canoe. Were the waterways dangerous? She said she tried to travel at night, wearing a sight mask, and besides, she was old and tough. She had cut her hair off short to travel. That's why I didn't ken her right away: here, she wasn't lit up with a bonfire glow, laughing with all that bountiful hair on her head. (I wonder if she saved any of it. Wow, what a commitment, cutting it off to come here.)

I keep my hair clipped down so you can't grab it.

Her name is Veo, but her lips purse together when she says it so it sounds more like "beh-oh." I remember then: my trip last spring to the healer's market hosted by the old gay farm in Tanasi land. I went with Kel, who is a good friend of mine, a flop-eared dog and a very good person to travel with. You go to these markets to trade in goods, skills, know-how, and enjoy sex with people if it's in the cards. (I was there officially to trade for herbs.) Sometimes the markets are called bazaars or meets, and they last some good days so everyone can get to them from where they're coming. Usually there's all kinds of other things planned around them, too, like roasts and fights and bonfires. I had seen Veo there, around a bonfire by the side of the creek. Her hair was long, piled up on the top of her head in a braid, lustrous and coiled dense like a snake. She had deep laugh lines in her face, and she opened up with a high, free giggle, mouth full open. I spent a long time watching her from across the fire, drinking and smoking herb for merrymaking with my own while she enjoyed herself among suitors. She'd catch me looking time and again and flash me a smile.

As it often does in gatherings, it came out that I'm a walker. That's just slang. They call em different things in different places, but walkers travel around usually between however many places they're welcome and can get to safely and swap info, tell stories, learn what's going on, for good or worse. They take all they get and weave it together, find patterns, make connections, and then tell their people. Anyway, I got to talking about our funny forgotten dark forest and all that, and Veo caught wind and came over to listen. Started getting to know Kel while I told about the land and how we live. What's good about it and what's hard. Then I shifted things, asking how it is everywhere else cause folks was getting a little too wrapped up in what I was saying. I just don't think it's right to take over the air with all your words, unless you're trying to war. You know, you have to fall back a bit sometimes, ask people about themselves, or just shut up. (That's how you stay safe as a walker, by the way. You read people. You listen to them. It's nice.)

The next day I got to do something I like best, and that's tell a story. I'm real good at those. The market was already full of speeches, feats of the body and mind, poets, musical acts. I did one from the old tales of Robin Hood. I change the details to be about our forest instead of Sherwood. It always goes over well. Veo was sitting in the audience listening to me.

I told myself I would ask her later, if she had come all this way because of that story or what?

Kel the dog remembered Veo from the fire too, and so the others welcomed her in with us pretty easy. She gets a lot of our ways. And the story of our encounter at Tanasi's market helped everyone to make sense of her quicker. She doesn't have any kind of untended psychic void. She's not up in here casting glamours on us. She's open about herself. My intuition says she's aight. Plus she's got those tools and knows a lot to do that we want to learn. It's all mutual. I like the way she spends time with Kel. I like the way she walks. I like the smell of her when she passes me by. And she likes to talk to me.

Veo knows she'll soon get the feel for the shape of our land and our neighbors' on this side of the river, but she comes to ask me about them when I'm sitting with Kel. I tell her we're a good few hundred spread four or six miles around the places and groups we like best. We live a little tough, try not to hurt ourselves, and get a hold of enough rare stuff from across the river and wherever else so we don't die real stupid. She seems suspicious of how easy I talk about it all. Is there no hardship? I say there's plenty, I just have to talk about it easy for my own good, and what's the rush. It's not even rainy season yet. Then I go on telling her how our different groups schedule congregations to share info and socialize. Me pregunta si puedo hablar español. Responda a ella, sí, si quiere que lo haga.

También en otros idiomas que el español. Pues, "Let me get this straight," she starts...

She takes to calling me kid like how she talks to the actual handful of children in our group. Sometimes people call me kid cause I guess I come off young and I don't like it at all, but she says it really nice to me. I don't know how old she actually is, but I know it's a little bit older than me. And I like her for that. For being older and still alive and always wanting to come talk to me. I spend a lot of time in silence, actually. Thinking too hard about what might happen next in the world, and will we live. Worrying will the power ever come back over here and what'll happen to us all then. I told Veo: actually, yeah, I am a kid. A stuck one that's been through too many adult things now to go back. She says to me, I known a few like you before, and I look at her like, have you? Then she nods real intently, looking right at me like she does. And I feel real hot and shy like I think she has. And I notice a little bit more what it is we keep coming to each other for. Then she smiles at me like, don't worry, kid. Says, "I like you," with her crow's feet dancing.

One day Veo comes find me crying on the hillside in the middle of the day. I turn around to see who approaches (sometimes it's a four-legged person when you expect two). She addresses me as La Llorona. Then she smiles and looks at me with her long gaze, and I lurch back into tears, panting, hoping I can get back to the world of words before she asks me what I'm doing. But she stays where she is, higher up on the hill behind me. Considerate.

"What did you come here for?" I manage to say without looking. I don't want to look. I don't trust the language of my eyes to protect me now.

"I came to find *you*, kid."

"What for?" I sob. The thought that she came looking for me, at this height of my despair, is terrifying. There is something I like too much about being looked for.

"You're in one of your moods again," she states plainly. I hear her step closer. The field of magnetism — electricity, energy, whatever — feels like it pressurizes around me. I crank my head over to peer at her from my shoulder. She is looking right at me, wearing a halo of kindness. I feel unworthy.

"What's my mood now?" I mewl out.

"I noticed you got a cycle." She pauses, then frowns. "It seems hard on you. You start to drink raspberry-leaf tea and disappear when you can. You stare at everything like the gravity's too high." I gape at her. "I could be wrong," she adds.

"No," I manage. She looks at me with heavy concerned eyes. Waits for me to continue. I don't say anything more.

"Well." She plods down the hill in front of me, rough hands on her hips. I zone out on the landscape of her sinewy forearms. "I came to offer you something, kid," she snaps me back. "If you're interested."

"What's that?" I sound miserable. Tiny. Pathetic. When she calls me kid like this, I feel myself get smaller. I wonder what she thinks of it. I wonder if she does it on purpose. I wonder if she...

"I wanted to come ask if you'd come spend some time with me."

"Right now?" She nods slowly. "What do you mean by 'spend some time'?" I'm confused by how simple it is. Her face bears a teacher's patient smile. The worn leather belt holding her pants up creaks as she shifts from one hip to the other.

"Sometimes, I find" — she touches a hand to her chest — "it can be nice helping someone to cry."

I'm breathing faster. I imagine sitting on her lap and feel flushed with heat.

"How does it sound to you?" she asks gently.

I look away, troubled. Then I open my mouth, stuttering. "It sounds...I'd really... You want to... How — what do you mean, helping me to cry?" I want her to tell me because I'm too scared to tell her what I think it means. I hear her chuckle like aren't you precious. I look up. She's saintly. Her serene gaze falling on me like warm sunlight. (God, we spend so much time in those church buildings, it rubs off on you.) Then a slow smirk spreads across her lips. Turns into a smile. She has crooked teeth and one missing in the front, which I always look at. She shrugs.

"I thought I would offer and have you tell me what would help, kid. How does that sound to you?"

"So...do you..." I'm struggling. I open and close my mouth several times. I'm tearing up again.

"You don't have to be shy with me." I suck in a breath, exhale loudly. Then she adds, "I know those are just words."

"I like the way you use your words," I say immediately. Then I look up at her face, my own twisted full of woe, clinging to my knees. "I...would really like to spend some time with you. Right now." I finish this agonized utterance and my whole body is flushed and warm, like something's gonna spill out of it any moment now.

TRANSCENDENT 2

"Why don't you walk with me then, and we'll end up at my place." Her place is a smart little shack with a medicinal garden she put together next to an old, still-standing automotive garage.

"Yes, ma'am," I say. Then she's close. She reaches forward and strokes my head, pushing it back in the same motion to make my gaze turn up to her. I like the force of it. I think I look scared. She only smiles, and then she raps me against the cheek with her fingertips.

"You're a good kid." She pats me on the cheek again, a little harder. "I can tell."

"Will you put me to work?" I ask, immediately tearful again.

"We can do what*ever* you like, kid. Whatever you need." The benevolent saint metaphors keep hitting me. She is luminous. She is warm. I am warmed before her.

I gulp on my swollen tongue and thick saliva. I stand up right in front of her, closer than we've ever stood before each other. I look for her eyes, then look down at her chest. Zoning out to another dimension through the patterns of grime on her sweat-sheened skin. I hang my head. Then I hear a laugh under her breath.

"*Mm'awww…* Come here."

I let her scoop me up. So close. My tears break, wetting her collarbone. I hold onto her dense body and feel like the weary bag of bones I am. She wanted to know where the hardship of the land really lay, and perhaps now she will find out. It is in me. It is in the knowing.

Destruction is coming. For us and this special land. It won't come right away. It could be a flood, or it could be any one of those private armies forming. We may have some many good years to forge memories on, or maybe just another full moon. I don't know why I worry about it so much when there's so little we can do, but I deal with so much information… A walker is a pattern maker. I don't know how to unmake.

But in her place, when she has me by the throat, dressed in lavender, telling me to look at her while I take all of what she gives me, I can surrender. I rest.

TRANSCENDENT 2

SKY AND DEW

◄ Holly Heisey ►

I brushed my fingertips over my lover's cheek, their skin growing cold and damp as the stone beneath me. Above us, swirls of color — dancing reds and shades of blue — ebbed back into the world from which they'd come. The incursion of voices in the corridor faded to whispered snatches of conversations, never fully heard. From stories below, the deep murmurs thrummed. The Hallows was safe again.

My lover's eyes were open and unseeing. To save us, to save the magic that fed the city above, they had broken their vow of silence and spoken one word with their lips and voice. Now those lips were still.

I carried my lover to the Chamber of Broken Vows. Blue cold-lights shone in sconces along the polished stone walls, and shadows sat heavy on the rows of still forms laid on slabs. These were all who had broken their vows of silence.

I hesitated on the threshold. I could already feel the deep chill of the stasis reaction in my lover's body, aching the bones of my arms and cramping my muscles. I had to lay them on an empty slab soon or frost would overtake them, and they would be truly lost.

Another acolyte came in, white cold-lantern humming in her hand. She brushed pale hair back from her face under her light blue hood. I did not know her name before she had come to the Hallows, but I called her Daisy in my mind. She reminded me of sunshine, and brighter times.

She reached a trembling hand to touch my lover's lips. She looked around us at the other vow-breakers, lying in stasis. Her eyes were wide and glassed with unshed tears.

Daisy gestured toward my lover, in the simple hand-talk we used. *Did they save the city?*

I closed my eyes. It was the question always asked. Did the acolyte break their vow of silence out of carelessness, or to protect the Hallows and the city above?

I called my lover Dew, because they smelled like morning dew on the grass after sunrise.

Dew and I had been deep in the Hallows, deep enough to feel in our bones the bass murmurs from the Lost Emperor's own chambers below. We passed a corridor mouth and heard an incursion of whispers from another world. The whispers were common enough, but when we entered the corridor, we saw the colors had come as well.

We must protect the Emperor, and the city above, Dew gestured to me. Their face was set and solemn. This would not be an easy canceling.

We listened to the intruding sounds, and began to hum a frequency to cancel them out. But the colors spilled into our world too quickly. I could not find the right frequency, and Dew's voice alone was not enough to send the colors back. Reds and blues swirled and tried to close in on us, forming into shapes like men.

I tried to hold my fear in check. We could not let them through. The Emperor's murmurs would be disrupted and stop the flow of magic to the city above. The crops would stop growing, the city would lose power, the river would dry up. Maybe not right away, but if we did not stop the incursion now it would spread. It might be days before we could control it, days edging toward blight and desolation above.

Dew opened their mouth. I knew what they were about to do, and our eyes met.

I shook my head, no. My breath caught, and my focus threatened to tatter, but I brought all my concentration to bear on finding the right frequency.

Dew turned to the colors and spoke, "Dissipate."

It was not the word itself that held power, but the cadence and frequency of syllables that could not be expressed in a hum. The colors began to fade. The intruding voices calmed.

Dew collapsed.

In the Chamber of Broken Vows, Daisy caught my attention with a flick of her hand, and then asked a second question.

Do we leave them here, or do we take them below?

I had been dreading this. Other acolytes had gone below when friends and lovers broke their vows, but no one returned from a visit to the Lost Emperor. The priests told us they were affected by the murmurs, and now served the Lost Emperor in his own chambers. It would be a trip with no chance of return.

I could lay Dew on a slab in the Chamber of Broken Vows. I could visit them, and touch their hands, but never be touched back. I could always look into their vacant eyes, and wonder if they saw me but could not move enough to say.

Or I could go below and see if the Lost Emperor could save them.

Daisy saw my resolve. *I will go with you,* she signed.

No, I said, a sharp gesture. She and Dew had never been lovers, but she had been Dew's friend before I came to the Hallows. She among us had known them the longest. But we didn't both have to stay trapped down there.

Daisy caught my arm. *I want to go. Do not deny me this.*

If I was being honest, I did not want to make the trek down to the Emperor's chambers alone.

And so we took turns carrying Dew down the circular stairs, around and around the open center of the Hallows. The deep murmurs were quiet for now, as they often were at this time of day, leaving only an echo behind them to fill the space with charged air. As we passed corridor mouths, drafts cut the cold of Dew's body deeper into mine. Sometimes, there was the ghost of whispers from other worlds, but never enough for us to stop and cancel them out. The voices always came, and often faded on their own.

On the eleventh story down, the deep murmurs started again. They came like a sigh at first, then a gust, then an almost-formed word. On the nineteenth story down, my body began to shudder with the murmurs. Dew had made their sacrifice on the twenty-first story.

On the thirtieth, I set my teeth against the buzz of sound in my skull. I had never been this deep before. Only the most experienced acolytes and priests had come this far, and if I went much farther, only the priests.

We passed two brown-robed priests on our way down. One glared at us. The other flashed a look of pity. They knew they would not see us again. Not in the upper regions of the Hallows, at least.

I pulled Dew tighter to me.

TRANSCENDENT 2

We reached the last of the stairs and stepped onto flat, rough stone. My heart thrummed a counter beat to the droning that filled my ears and my mind and my soul.

Daisy had Dew now and was puffing under their weight, so I raised her lantern and we stared at the double doors ahead. Cold-light sconces on either side of the doors traced out elaborate carvings on the pale wood; shells and waves and plants of the sea.

Our hair floated, then fell, floated, then fell in the wind of the murmurs coming from the other side of those doors. My teeth chattered with the vibration. The cells in my body began to feel less solid.

Daisy and I shared a look. We had come this far. If we stood here much longer, we would be dispersed by the vibration of the murmurs.

I took a chattering step forward, touched the door handle, and pushed inward. The murmurs broadened into a great crescendo. Then, mid-word, they whispered into a sigh and there was silence.

My skin pricked as we entered the chamber. The air felt different inside, not damp like the rest of the Hallows, but warm and stale. Had we passed through a stasis field?

Daisy still held Dew, but I reached for them now. I needed to be their shield against whatever was inside.

Cold-lights lined the walls, the most light I had seen in one place in five years. Red and purple curtains hung in a wall across the room, swaying in an unknown breeze. A shadow moved behind the curtains. I pulled Dew closer to me.

I had never seen the Lost Emperor. I had heard his story, of course. He had come to our world many years ago, bringing with him the power of his words. None could listen to his speech without it first being funneled through the Hallows corridors, or their ears and souls would burn. I believed that now, having felt the raw power of the murmurs just outside his doors. As the story went, when first he came, he'd been dressed richer than the king, and his tanned face carried the visage of a god. He'd made the crops grow again, when they had been withering with blight. He'd made the river flow, when it had been dwindling to a stream. He flared the city's magics to life, fueling lights and machines and industry, when the magics had been dying.

I stepped forward and Daisy made a whimpering noise, quickly staunched. I ignored her and passed with Dew through the curtain wall.

A man sat on cushions on the floor, a checkered board of polished wood on a table in front of him. He was moving stones around it, but looked up when I entered. His black hair was grayed at the edges, and small creases enhanced his handsome, tanned face. He couldn't be the centuries-old Lost Emperor.

He flowed to his feet, and he spoke.

I flinched and drew back, my stomach knotting. No one could speak anywhere in the Hallows but in the initiation chamber, and then only a few words could be risked at a time, and only by the priests who gave the acolytes their vows.

The man looked at me expectantly, and then sighed. He set the checkered board down on the floor and motioned for me to lay Dew on the table.

Dew's body was hard enough now that I could not make them lay flat.

The man spoke again, and this time I registered that I did not understand the language. But it was an itch to my ears, something that might have made sense if I tried to puzzle it out, like conversations from childhood memories.

Then he was the Lost Emperor. How was I even still alive? Did the stasis field of these chambers protect me from his words?

I met his dark eyes. I motioned to him, and then to Dew, and to Dew's mouth. I indicated that Dew had spoken.

The Lost Emperor nodded impatiently, and said more words. They grated up my arms and down my spine, causing disharmony. But they did not harm me more than that.

I heard a sound behind me. Daisy had come through the curtains and now watched with wide eyes, though her mouth was set in a line of courage. She held her lantern as if it would ward off some darkness, though it was not needed in the near daylight of the room.

I looked around. Plates with half-eaten food were strewn on gold-leafed tables; cushions in velvet reds and purples were spread across the floor; a pile of richly engraved books sat on a table, dusty and unused.

The Lost Emperor leaned over Dew and I snapped my attention back to them. My body hummed with danger and I stood ready, though what I could do here, or what I would guard against, I did not know.

The Emperor tilted his head as if to listen for Dew's breath. I tried to motion that Dew was in a stasis field of their own, but the Emperor waved me away. He spoke words into Dew's mouth.

I waited. I watched Dew's graying lips for any sign they would come back together, that their dark eyelashes would flutter.

The Emperor rocked back and growled an oath that didn't need translation.

TRANSCENDENT 2

He stood and began to pace about the room, now and then kicking at the cushions. He stopped once, and looked past the curtains to the open door beyond them. There was a sadness in his face, and a hunger. A madness.

I stood where I was, unsure of what to do. The Emperor could bring magic to the world above, but he could not help one who had pledged their life to his service. Who protected the Hallows from the incursions of other worlds and the breaking of the Emperor's magics.

He was not a god. He was not all-capable or all-knowing. He looked then like a beggar addled by the sun, only dressed in finer clothes.

I swallowed.

The curtains rustled. Daisy was gone.

I shifted toward Dew until I touched the coldness of their body. I had known I would not be leaving here. I did not see any other acolytes around, those who had come before. I did not know what had happened to them. But I could not leave Dew.

I waved to the Emperor to catch his attention.

He shot me an annoyed look. "San sa-henne ha?"

He'd spoken here, and his words had not caused him to go into stasis, or caused me more than minor discomfort. Would my words work the same? What choice did I have left but to try?

I cleared my throat. "Do...you...understand me?" The words came out soft and thready, and my throat constricted with the speaking of them. But nothing more happened.

"Shen shani henne at?" he asked. No, he did not know our language. How could he, if no one ever spoke it to him?

I listened to the sounds of his words, felt their slight warping of the air. I let them permeate who I was.

And then I spoke them.

Days passed, or maybe weeks. When the priests opened and closed the outer doors, the Emperor passed through the curtains and came back with a plate of food. He always shared it with me. He smiled, an expression that smoothed his lined face.

Dew lay on the table between us, an eternal statue, as the Emperor taught me his language. I taught him mine, until the priests who brought the food left a note: *Do not speak the language of the city in this sacred chamber.*

When I read it to him, the Emperor snorted and made a rude gesture toward the doors. But then he smiled. "It is good to speak, even if in only my language. Good to speak not just to make the magic work, but to talk with another."

And it was. I had not realized how much I'd yearned in the Hallows not to be silent. I only wished Dew could share my relief.

For every span of time we spent learning, the Emperor spent twice as long speaking solemnly to the wall in his own language, to feed the murmurs to the city above. His voice was rich and rough, and as the time passed, the effect of his words on me became less of pain and more of music.

"How long have you been here?" I asked him.

He ran hands through his long hair. "Too long. Years, surely. They *grentanakan* me." I didn't understand the word. We gestured for a short while, then I nodded. They had captured him.

I was beginning to suspect that the story the priests had told us was not the truth.

"I came through into here," he said, and motioned around him. "Not this room — a large cave. There were men dressed like you, blue robes. I asked where I was, and they went stiff and collapsed, and the lights that they held flared bright. One who was still far off witnessed this and ran away, and so I also ran. Of course I ran." He passed a shaking hand over his eyes. "I got lost in the caves. When they found me, and brought me here, and poked at me until I spoke again. This time, they did not collapse." He paused. "I have seen some of the priests age — go from young-faced men and women like you to old and worn and gray. Is it true? Are they grow old while I do not?"

I nodded. It must be the stasis field. The Emperor spoke the murmurs clearly in here, but out in the corridors of the Hallows, they were long and bone-rattling deep. The stasis field kept the Emperor from aging more than a few years in a few centuries. He would supply the city's magic for centuries to come.

"They think I'm a god," he said. He eyed me in my blue robes. "Do you?"

"No," I said. "No, I know you're not a god." I looked down at Dew on the table. Frost had formed on their lips and open eyes. Maybe, when I'd first decided to stay here, I had thought I might learn something to save them. But I did not fool myself now that they would come out of a stasis that deep. I did not fool myself that there had ever been a chance.

"The others like you," the Emperor said, "the ones who brought me people to heal, did they return to you?"

TRANSCENDENT 2

"No," I whispered. Fear raised the hair on my arms. What was this place? This Emperor was not a god, and the priests whom I'd trusted — who we'd all trusted as faithful servants of the Emperor — were lying to us.

"Did I do this?" he asked, waving at Dew. "I try, I always try to bring them back. I think maybe I will find the right words one day. Or maybe I only make it worse."

I shook my head and stood. I didn't know.

The Emperor looked from me to the doors and back to me. Panic flashed across his handsome face, glinting the madness in his eyes. Maybe I should have been afraid of him, but I was more inclined to pity. More inclined to anger. No, the Emperor had not been able to cure Dew. But the priests kept him here a prisoner, to speak their murmurs. Whatever harm the Emperor's words had caused Dew was at their hands.

"Thank you for staying," the Emperor said. And I knew then that even if the priests let me leave, I couldn't leave him alone again.

The Emperor helped me carry Dew through the curtains into the outer part of the chamber. As much as I did not want to relinquish Dew to the priests, having them still and unmoving in the chamber had begun to fray my edges. And so I said my goodbyes. I spoke them aloud, in the Emperor's language. And then I spoke them, more quietly, in mine, and damn the priests who would forbid me that right.

"I have two children," the Emperor told me the next day. "They are likely grown by now. Or maybe, if you say time moves more slowly in here, they are already dead. Perhaps I can see their children, if I return."

I moved another stone across his checkered board, and captured two of his pieces. I suspected he let me. Or maybe he just did not care. Time moved differently in this room, but he was no less old because of it. Years weren't always measured in time.

"Why do you stay?" I asked. "If you can put anyone outside this chamber into stasis with your words, why don't you just put them all into stasis and leave?"

He looked up at me with steady eyes. "I have tried. More times than I wish to count, I escaped into the tunnels, but the priests know when I leave. They know when anyone leaves. They know the tunnels better than I do, and they catch me quickly. When I speak to defend myself, they hum and aren't affected by it. Their humming addled my brains for days after, though they made sure I did my duty to speak."

The priests could hum to counteract the Emperor's words? Could I hum to counteract their humming?

I didn't know the tunnels this deep in the Hallows. But if there were two of us, and one of us a trained acolyte with a sense for the sounds and winds of cross-corridors, maybe we would have a chance.

If I could hum to stop an incursion from another world, maybe I could hum to make an incursion of my own.

"What if I could get you home?" I asked.

For a moment his face shone with naked hope. But he shook his head.

"I know my speaking keeps others alive. I have resigned myself to that task."

"But what if the priests have only taken the easiest way to fuel the magic of the city above, because they could?"

He glared at me. Then he rose and retreated to a cushion in the corner, picking up a book he couldn't read.

We spent the next days as we had before, with one alteration. When it was nearing time for one of his speaking cycles, I sat and faced the wall and started speaking instead. I spoke a story-rhyme I had learned as a child, about the wisp-men who came out of the sea. The rhythm wasn't quite right in his language, but it worked well enough. He sat and watched me the whole hour, his mouth a straight line.

When the priests came that night, they said nothing. And so we began to alternate the duty.

"I can teach others your language," I said. "If I do that, you won't have to stay."

"What others?" he asked bitterly. "The only ones who come here are the priests, and those who want me to fix the ones I put into stasis."

"We'll ask the priests —"

"No," he said. "They are not on our side."

"If we leave, they will have to learn." They could not have kept watch over the Lost Emperor for so many years and not have learned something of his language. They had to have a plan for if he finally escaped, or if he died. "They'll take over the murmurs."

Hope flickered in his eyes and did not burn out so quickly.

In the times between speaking the murmurs, we began to talk through his memories of when he'd first arrived. We reconstructed the route the priests had used to bring him here from the caves. It was all hypothetical, we told ourselves.

TRANSCENDENT 2

Then, without any spoken agreement, we began to eat less as we stored up food. The priests brought two plates now, one for the Emperor and one for me.

One day, just before our sleep cycle, we left.

We carried cold-lights plundered from the chamber, bobbing blue-white ellipses on the walls of the deep tunnels. We did not speak. Though I had grown acclimated to his language, I didn't know what our words would do to each other outside the stasis chamber, or even if I could hum them away.

We moved quickly and did not sleep, and when we paused to rest or eat, it was with quick efficiency. My sense of direction was honed from years of silence in this living tomb. I followed it with reference to the Emperor's memories, and we only once heard the rustle of the priests' footsteps from a cross-corridor. We slipped into a crevice and covered our cold-lights until they passed.

After hours or maybe a day, our cold-lights began to dim. I had never seen a cold-light dim before. Was it because we had stopped the murmurs? We hadn't been away that long. Was even the Emperor's absence from his chamber enough to dim the lights in the city above? How long until the rot seeped into the crops again, and the river ran low? How long until the seas became thick with the algae that made the fish too poisonous to eat? I tried not to think about it. I wouldn't be away that long, I hoped.

But once the tunnels had turned from cool cut stone to damp natural cave walls, the Emperor touched my arm. Yes, that formation was as he had described it. We picked up our paces.

And then, finally, the Emperor made a wordless exclamation and rushed us through a narrow passage. We broke out into a cavernous space, lit with streaks of light from above. Sunlight. The cavern was dank, but with a promise of sea air.

The Emperor shouted, "Here!" and it echoed around us.

I tensed, waiting for his word to fell him, or me, but he flashed a grin so wide he hardly looked like the same man.

"Yes," I said, in his language. Again, nothing happened. Maybe a month ago I would have fallen stiff at the sound of my own words, but the Emperor's language was starting to feel more natural to me than my own.

The Emperor dashed to one side of the cave, skidding to a stop near a stone slab. "It was here." He turned to me, then looked past me and stiffened.

A group of priests stepped out from behind a large rock formation. They had wraps over their ears, and carried spears and knives and rope.

They'd known we'd come. Of course they'd known we'd come here. How could we not have considered that, or that there was another way into the cave than the way we'd come? We'd been too eager, too willing to try, and the trip through the tunnels had been too easy.

I darted to the Emperor, and he gripped my arm as if to steady himself. He was too pale in the raw rays of sunlight.

"Whatever you're going to do," he said in a low pant, "do it now."

I clasped my hands together, and shut out what might happen if this did not work. I let go of my focus on the cavern around me, and the priests, and the Emperor. I formed the scene he'd described to me in my mind: a man in a carriage, dressed in fine but ordinary business wear, traveling a stretch of road that held nothing in particular. The horses' hooves struck packed dirt, the carriage springs creaked. Outside, grass continued for a ways until it stopped, and the cliff dropped down to the sea. The driver clicked his tongue at the horses, and began an off-tune whistle.

I listened to the whistle, and began to hum along.

Outside of myself, I watched a different scene entirely. The priests advanced on where I stood with the Emperor, spears outstretched.

"Stop!" the Emperor shouted to the priests. Some of them cringed, the word affecting them even through the wraps on their ears. But it only slowed them down.

Still, the Emperor saw his power over them and pressed his advantage. He poured out a torrent of words. He was good at this. Nonsense words mostly, or sentences strung together in a loose, manic storyline. Something about a hunt chased to the sea, and the whitecaps rolling in to steal the catch, and a fishmonger's wife...

The priests braced themselves as if against a crippling gale and continued to advance.

My hum gained rhythm. I found harmony to the music of the Emperor's words, and spoke words of my own. I wove in the poems and rhymes that I had learned as a child. The second rhythm shuddered the priests. Our words together quivered the air, and the air between the Emperor and myself began to ripple. The Emperor saw it and stopped speaking to stare.

"No, keep going, keep going," I said, not breaking the rhythm of my sing-song hum. And then, "Can you repeat the rhymes with me?" I said one quickly, then again, and he nodded and said it with me. We chanted, the words falling into a strange and echoing dance. The air between us formed rings like a stone dropped into a pond, rolling outward until we could hardly see one another.

Colors began to bleed through, and my muscles clenched in the long-learned reflex. I wanted to hum them away, to protect against them. Instead, I tuned to them. The sound of these colors was not so different from the rhythm of the words I was speaking, and I adjusted my pitch and rhythm to match.

The Emperor stopped speaking. He was only a blur of a shape through the translucent ripples, but I knew he was looking within them.

I raised my hands and spoke to push the sounds toward the Emperor. My breath almost caught as I realized in that one moment what I was doing, letting go of my only ally, someone I would call a friend.

"Oh…" I heard him gasp. It was a word of wonder. I had found the right frequencies. I pushed them over him until the ripples enfolded him. And then I slowed my rhythm, pausing between words, and gradually letting them fade away.

The colors ebbed, the ripples grew more shallow, and then dissipated. The Emperor was gone.

Tears stung my eyes, and I stared at the place where he'd just been, the sounds of my sing-song still echoing in my heart.

Rough hands seized me. Fire exploded in my head, and then there was nothing.

It was long days in the Emperor's chamber, despite the priests' frantic gestures and threats, despite the danger to the city above, before I could bring myself to speak the Emperor's words again. Before I could not hurt as much at the lack of his presence here. Before I could remember that my duty was to the city, and not to the priests.

Then I sat in the Emperor's chamber and spoke. I read aloud from the books on the table, translating as I wove the words. This had been my plan since I'd first pressed the Emperor to leave. He had a family to go back to, even if generations late. I had no one, so I would protect the city above. But I hadn't understood how hard it would be. I was alone, where once I had not been alone.

After a time, it was no longer the Emperor's chamber. It was my own.

One day, days or weeks later, the curtains rustled and a figure stepped through. I stopped speaking and stared. Dew.

Their black hair was tied up in a knot, green eyes sparking with life.

My face crumpled as I tried to understand this.

Dew looked around them, their eyes widening at the opulence of the chamber. I had grown used to it, and only now noticed it again.

Dew gestured. *You are...the Lost Emperor?*

I gave a startled laugh. "You can speak here, Dew. It is safe."

Dew's brows knit, and they picked their way across the strewn cushions to sit across the table from me. The checkered board and stones were arrayed on the surface, and Dew inspected them, briefly touching one stone before pulling their hand away.

They looked up at me. Swallowed. And I saw the courage it took for them to say, "Safe?"

Dew flinched, but when nothing happened, they sank back, putting their face in their hands.

I dropped the book I'd been reading from and scrambled around the table to sit beside them.

"What happened?" I asked. "How are you awake — " How were they alive?

They swiped at tears. Their voice came thin and hesitant, because it had not been used in years. "When the murmurs stopped, the magic faded. I...thawed." They shuddered, and I wrapped my arm around them. Dew was warm, and smelled like the dew of morning grass.

"A few others thawed, too," they went on. "But not the ones who've been in the Chamber of Broken Vows for years."

I pulled back. "But it's been weeks." Weeks in my time — months outside this chamber?

"I had to recover," Dew said. "The priests only now told me that you were here." They looked around again, frowning at the chamber. "That is you, making the murmurs?"

I nodded.

"And...where is the Lost Emperor?"

I looked down. I didn't want to think about him. I had been successfully not thinking about him while I spoke the murmurs. But the checkered board sat on the table in front of me, the stones arrayed across it, waiting. "He went home."

Dew nodded, accepting this. Trusting me. "That was when the murmurs stopped. Thank you."

That was when I'd stopped the murmurs. No one had told me what damage I'd caused in the city above with my days of silence, though I knew from the priests' desperation there had been damage.

TRANSCENDENT 2

I closed my eyes. But I hadn't known this would happen. If Dew had somehow come back to me, maybe my choices had not been a mistake. Not as big of a mistake, at least.

I curled my hand around theirs.

"But you can't go back," I said. "The priests won't let you leave now. And I can't leave."

Dew closed their hand around mine. "I know." They looked into my eyes. "I know, Sky. Teach me these words, as the Lost Emperor taught you. I will stay with you. We will keep the murmurs and the city alive together."

My breath caught. The Emperor hadn't had a choice in staying here, but this was the path I had chosen. I had given up any thought of a life above first to save Dew, and then to keep the city thriving. Then, I'd thought I'd always be alone.

But I did not want Dew to be trapped here, too.

Dew kissed me, a sweetness I'd never thought I'd feel again. "My choice, Sky," they said. "This is my choice to stay."

They pulled back, a wry smile tugging at their lips. "You scared the priests. They don't want the murmurs to stop again. They will send down more to learn; I'm a new sort of acolyte. We will be the ones who keep the murmurs alive."

My throat was tight but I nodded. I had lost the Lost Emperor, but here was Dew, returned to me again. I traced my fingers over their face in growing wonder at this miracle.

I was still confined here, but the air was different in a place where you were not alone. Where you were with someone you loved.

I kissed Dew back, murmuring the word for love into their mouth. Dew shuddered at the sound of my new language, as I once had, and then kissed it back to me.

THE NOTHING SPOTS
WHERE NOBODY WANTS TO STAY

◄ Julian K. Jarboe ►

The veil is thin immediately outside the Salmon P. Chase Municipal Junior High School. A dense perimeter of flowering thorns grows two feet out from the exterior walls, and between the plants and the bricks is a zone dense with magical energy. Especially suggestible students and teachers can sense it, the stunted or abused into rupture, the intuitive, those in a state of spiritual drift. Like all liminal spaces, this one can be elusive, and sometimes it's hungry, draws you near and lures you in. It gives, and it takes away.

The school building is newly renovated and the grounds heavily trimmed. It's the drippy-snot-nose part of March in 2002, and the students file outside in assigned pairs because Mike Johnson — obviously — left a bomb threat on a stall in the yellow-wing boy's bathroom, but the teachers are officially telling the students there's a fire drill. They have to be sensitive to the handful of earnestines who take every Sharpie pentagram and locker room firecracker stash at face value. The other four-hundred or so children know that this, like the "rabid dog" lock-downs, is entirely about someone and something else.

Jamie is the only student who has ever experienced the aftermath of public violence, and he wanders away from the crowd with AJ, leaving their assigned buddies to buoy in place with one another. AJ is sure a teacher can see them sneaking off into the bushes, in their ski coats and L.L. Bean super-sized mono-grammed reflector-tape backpacks, the clacking multitude of novelty keychains on the zip pull, but nobody stops them. AJ is used to anticipating trouble, even though he's with Jamie, and adults let Jamie do anything he wants now.

Out of view, the boys crouch over the buried treasures of their hiding place, Tupperware and pencil boxes stuffed full of contraband from the strip mall on the edge of town. The underpass and the mall parking garage are both reachable directly through a portal from the junior high school bushes. The portals present themselves when beckoned, but seem to possess a will of their own and something like a sense of humor — once they tried to get to the train station and it deposited them on the tracks with just enough time to dodge the approaching train.

Jamie believes this will is a reflection of his and AJ's subconscious. AJ is not so sure anything that powerful could come from them.

Jamie pops open one of their boxes and pulls out a king-size candy bar they shoplifted last weekend. He twists it in half and they lean against the wall, gnashing at the toffee and the nougat. When they finish, Jamie takes a deep breath, adjusts the crotch of his jeans, and turns to lean onto AJ, pressing his erection against AJ's hips.

"Do you feel that?" he says, and smirks.

"Yeah," AJ responds, and licks the milk chocolate off his hand.

Jamie kisses AJ with tongue, smears of candy still on his lips and stuck in his braces, and rocks his hips on AJ's in a performed and disembodied way, going through the motions with no regard for what might feel good. AJ coughs into the kiss, and Jamie takes it for a moan of pleasure and fishes his hands up under AJ's shirt to fondle his breasts.

AJ's had sizable tits since fifth grade, the only thing about him, he's certain, which earns him some kind of use value for others, an idea so loudly and consistently reinforced by the lust, envy, and scorn of others that his dysphoria around having them at all won't surface consciously for another decade. In 2016, when AJ wakes up from his top surgery, his first thought will be, "Well, now I'll have to rely on charm alone."

For now, AJ thinks, they keep Jamie interested, and it mostly feels good. They're achingly heavy, and Jamie grabs them like he's catching a ball, squeezes, pushes them up toward AJ's chin. This is the way every boy will ever touch them, like he can't believe his good luck but needs to relocate them skyward like a button-mash code to unlock some next-level fondling. It's sloppy, but a welcome relief from gravity, and it's so easy to just stand there and allow it to happen.

AJ wants to touch Jamie in return, kiss Jamie's whole body with his clothes off. For some reason, the thought of acting on these things then and there, in the same semi-public way that Jamie acts on all of his desires, does not occur to AJ.

What does cross his mind is an urge to steal tapes. He passively suggests they head over to the mall for some release.

Jamie's made a wet spot on the crotch of his jeans but tucks himself away and repeats AJ's thought as though he's just thought of it.

"Good idea," AJ tells him.

The rest of the school is filing back into the building for the last two and a half class periods of the day, and Jamie wipes his mouth and focuses on opening a portal. He holds AJ's hand because he believes this makes the magic stronger. If a teacher does see them, they're not going to do anything now that Jamie's got that serious look on his face. Jamie doesn't have to take any tests, or even really keep coming to school, and the guidance counselors have recommended private therapists and grief groups but he won't let anybody try to help him, not even his mother, Eileen. Everybody wants Jamie to talk, so they keep telling him yes, and he hates all of them.

AJ doesn't ask Jamie to talk, which is how they've gotten so close, but AJ wants it just as much as everyone else. He thinks that the trick is to be so reliable that any day now, all this time together is going to add up to something meaningful and Jamie will open up, finally, to AJ and nobody else. The saddest boy in the whole school will tell AJ things about his dad, and say "You're the only one who understands," and it will be the single most flattering and fulfilling burden of AJ's whole life. He lies in bed at night and imagines the whole scenario. Sometimes he rehearses the hushed, intimate tone he's going to respond in.

They figured out the veil and the portals in the first place because Jamie was looking for a spot to set his diary on fire last Halloween, and AJ had been the one to bring him a lighter and show him how to use it. They burned the barely-filled notebook — what could possibly be in there, AJ wondered, as it burned — behind the bushes and buried the ashes under the mulch, and that's when they saw other transient places in the town, the nothing spots, where nobody lived or worked and nobody wanted to stay for very long, and they could reach out and touch them and step into them and find themselves there.

Jamie tried to use it to go back in time, but it never worked. AJ knew Jamie had tried to go back to September 10th alone, was never going to ask AJ to go there with him, but he had tried and failed and AJ knew this because one day Jamie got really philosophical about what the portals were and how they worked. People always get deep after they don't get what they really want, AJ thought.

They rip a wound in the world and walk through it together, still holding hands. They exit in the food court behind the photo booths, and separate inside Suncoast Video. AJ peels the shrinkwrap off an anime boxset and slips the individual tapes into his cargo pockets while Jamie dumps a handful of coins onto the counter and asks the clerk how much candy he can get for five dollars in loose change. This takes enough time for AJ to inconspicuously slip back out of the store and appear to be idly browsing bachelor-party gags in Spencer's Gifts by the time Jamie joins him again. They have it down to routine, but this time Jamie takes more than an hour to rejoin. When he does, AJ is running out of excuses to browse the joke book section without buying anything.

"Sup," Jamie says with forced coolness.

"I don't get what the thing is about mother-in-laws," AJ says, closing a book and returning it to the shelves. "What took so long? Are we in the clear?"

"Yeah, yeah, just had to make a side trip."

They head to the basement level of the mall parking garage and climb through a portal back to school, in time for the procession of SUVs at the front circle. AJ rushes to change out of what he's wearing and into the clothes he left home in that morning. When he's done, he and Jamie meet out front and climb into the back of Eileen's car for a ride home.

Eileen greets the kids wearing a leather blazer and her hair styled for volume, cinnamon shoulder-length curls. She looks resilient, tired, and handsome. Jamie eyes the luxury jacket with suspicion. He wonders where her cat-hair covered fleece is, her usual abundance of bobby pins coming loose.

"Happy Friday," she sing-songs, and Jamie crosses his arms over his chest. She turns to AJ and asks him if he's attending Crystal Sazerac's sweet thirteen with Jamie that evening.

"Oh yeah," AJ responds, a soft fog of dread setting into his mood. "I'd forgotten about it."

Eileen hums along with the radio as she drives AJ home. The two boys wallow silently in their respective conjecture, slumped down, AJ with his knees pressed against the seat in front of him and Jamie twisted onto his hip, face and shoulders leaning onto the window.

AJ's mother had not forgotten that the next door neighbor's daughter was turning thirteen, though she is still at work when he gets home. Set out on his bed is a hideous too-large jumper dress and an already-wrapped present.

Even if AJ wanted to wear girl's clothing, the things his mom picks out and mandates are humiliating. She still buys him little kid stuff in incrementally larger sizes, with no sense of context, telling him he looks "cute." The word "cute" feels like an insult for the rest of his life. He puts on the dress, practically swims around in the garish materials.

It's no use arguing. His mother thinks his discomfort is an attempt to hurt her. He doesn't yet know most other children's parents do not physically restrain and slap them for wanting to dress themselves. This is how he started shoplifting in the first place. He wanted a denim jacket, unisex, well-fitting, so he nicked one from Kmart. The desire was so practical, but it gave him something he never had before — a secret, a part of his life he could control.

The party invitations went to Crystal's actual friends, plus a pity list of neighbors and losers like AJ and Jamie. They were almost too old for this sort of forced mingling. In high school, AJ sensed, there'd be no pity list, which was almost a relief. But Jamie didn't seem to know that yet. He got an invitation to everybody's birthday, bar mitzvah, and pool party since the fall. Eileen made sure he went to all of them.

AJ arrives early, mystery gift in hand, in the ugly dress, and fusses with his hair by the chip and dip table, then fusses with the food, fills his discomfort with Tostitos.

The trade-off Crystal had clearly negotiated with her parents was that if randos had to come, then her chosen few got to be co-ed, too. Her boyfriend Derek is there with the rest of his lacrosse team. The atmosphere is relaxed — the "fire drill" had made the Friday especially casual and Crystal herself isn't a status-conscious girl, just eager to please people like Derek, who most certainly is.

AJ inks into the shadows of the evening, melts into the wallpaper and the carpet, lurks by the French doors leading out to the patio of the Sazerac's back yard which abuts his own. Mrs. Sazerac's daffodil buds spear out of the garden on the edge of the property line. He watches the deep dark of the suburban night saturate the lawns, the daffodils, the patio.

Jamie arrives just as the conversation turns into a game of truth or dare. He's gel-spiked his hair, has too much cologne on, carries a distinct turquoise gift box. AJ recognizes it from the window displays of the Tiffany shop at the mall. By the size, it has to be the silver heart pendant, easily the most popular piece of jewelry among the rich girls at school since the end of Christmas and Hanukkah break, when they conspicuously appeared around the delicate necks and wrists of blossoming princettes. Getting one from a boyfriend, much less a boy at your birthday party, was unheard of.

"Hey, you look pretty," Jamie says to AJ as he approaches AJ's spot by the patio doors. AJ squirms.

"Jamie, that's..." AJ says, pointing an accusatory finger at the gift box. "She's gonna know you stole it, and Derek is going to beat the shit out of you."

"How do you know what it is?"

"Jaim, you can't give her that. It's like a step below a promise ring."

Jamie defensively pockets the box.

"Yeah, Jaim," Derek snorts. He slithers over to the boys, but seemingly hasn't overheard their argument. "You smell like a hooker."

Derek punches Jamie in the arm. Crystal is engrossed in truth or dare across the room, and doesn't notice either Jamie's entrance or Derek's comment.

"Leave him alone, Derek," AJ says. Derek stares down AJ with sparks of that unhinged loathing unique to bigotry.

"I don't need you to fight for me," Jamie snaps at AJ. Derek is a bully but at least that script is safer than letting a mouthy tomboy stick up for him in the middle of their own argument.

"Look, fag," Derek digs in. "You're only here because everyone feels bad for your stupid dad dying in Nine Eleven, but everybody fucking hates you and wishes you'd stop coming to shit our moms make us invite you. The two of you should stay home and pee in each other, see if it makes an ugly baby to keep you busy."

Jamie is silent and still. AJ's eyes well with tears, and he imagines himself gouging out Derek's eyes, twisting off his balls, anything, but he can barely stop his lip from quivering. He might like to kick Jamie in the shins, too.

"Oh my god, are you going to cry? Freaks." Derek rolls his eyes and rejoins the main group of the party. Crystal looks up and greets him with a smile, oblivious.

When they were very small, AJ and Crystal used to play Barbies together. They used to have fun. For some reason, this pops into AJ's mind as he chokes back sobs. With hands shaking, he grapples for the handle of the French doors and lets himself out onto the patio. After a stunned pause, Jamie follows.

AJ stares up at the light in the kitchen window of his own house. The light falls in long green stripes from the windows to the lawn, where it dissolves as the world between the houses tears itself apart and a portal offers itself to the boys. In the dark, dark night outside, only they can see that the veil has come undone, is dissolving completely.

Jamie steps up beside AJ.

"My mom is on a date tonight," he says.

"What?" AJ asks, barely able to fathom language in his fury.

"I said my mom has a date tonight. She's out with a guy." Jamie takes the Tiffany box back out of his coat pocket and fidgets with it.

"Oh," AJ responds, watching the world crumble around them. The portal swallows the daffodil garden and envelops them both, taking them somewhere indiscernible in the dark.

"You can't — " AJ thinks aloud to the sound of the pedant rattling inside the box. "You can't just give people really nice things like that. It's too much."

AJ waits for a response but there's only the knock of the silver against the cardboard and the howl of the veil, closing again like curtains around their unknowable destination.

LISA'S STORY: ZOMBIE APOCALYPSE

◄ Gillian Ybabez ►

People die every day but when they don't stay dead it becomes a real problem. Especially when they attack the living. Sometime during the fifth day the internet gave up all pretense and just started calling them zombies.

Several of my neighbors packed their kids and some stuff into their cars and took off. If I had a car, I might have tried to leave as well. The nearest National Guard-established safe zone was a couple hundred miles away. God bless Texas and its open country. Not.

A couple of days later, the power went out. It was getting worse. Power outages across the country. A safe zone in Kansas had dissolved when someone died inside. Fifty more people died before they were killed for the second time.

The last of my neighbors left the apartment complex. A zombie wandered by the next day and broke into a nearby apartment. One of my neighbors had left their dog behind. The dog got away. I barricaded my front door with sofas and the two big front windows with mattresses and bookshelves after that.

I waited for a sign that it was all over. Surely we were pushing them back, right? There was no way mindless zombies could really take over, right? The power might be shut down but that couldn't last for much longer. We couldn't really lose, could we?

A few days later I realized, this is it. This is how the world ends. I looked out at the quiet apartment complex. I was alone and no one was coming for me.

I counted how many days of food I had left. Seven days. If the stove wasn't electric I could cook rice or pasta — there would be enough for several more days.

I counted my hormone and anti-androgen pills. Enough for a few weeks. I could do without them if I had to but I'd rather not. Would it be hard to break into a pharmacy?

The water was still flowing but how long would that last? I needed to find more water before that happened. I had to go out or die in my apartment. There was a convenience store a few blocks away that would be a good first stop. Beyond that there was a superstore that had to be overflowing with supplies.

But first I had to deal with a problem closer to home.

When I moved into the apartment, my roommate and I had split the cabinet and refrigerator space. Since the power went out, I had eaten all of my perishable food but hadn't touched hers. Out of obligation to the roommate code I had respected her food rights, even as I piled her mattress against a window. I had believed she would be coming back after finding her father but now I doubted that I would ever hear from her again. I wished I had eaten her food. It was starting to smell.

Sorting through the leftover food I realized none of it was salvageable. I briefly argued with myself over a block of mold-spotted cheese but decided against taking the risk. I repeated the process with the freezer. All the spoiled food went in a trash bag that I tied shut.

I moved the sofas and I armed myself with a baseball bat, left over from that time I tried joining a local amateur team. I looked out the peephole, watching for a few minutes before opening the deadbolts. They scraped and squeaked as I twisted the knobs to open them. Had they always been that loud? I made a note to get oil for them. With the trash bag in one hand and the bat in the other I slipped out of the apartment.

Fresh air blew across my face for the first time in over a week. I took a deep breath and looked around. Most of my neighbor's cars were gone. A few cars remained, not that they were any good to me without keys. The neighbor's door was busted in.

The door was dented but still on its hinges. The frame, however, was cracked and split around the deadbolt and knob. I turned away, glad that I had remained undetected. I closed the door but didn't lock it behind me, I wouldn't be going far or for very long.

The garbage cans were in the alley between my building and the next. I kept watch on the deserted complex during the walk. Once around back I quickly dropped the bag in a garbage can. Four cans sat in a row, one for each apartment in my building. The one for our — my apartment was almost empty. Two women just don't make a lot of garbage, especially if they recycle like we did. The other three were covered so I couldn't tell how full they were. It would only take a second to peek but I didn't have that much interest. I didn't want to spend more time out here than I needed to.

I turned around and started to walk back to my apartment.

As I rounded the corner, I saw a person walk through the entrance to the complex. I recognized the dark blue of the city's police uniform. I should have ducked back and watched. Instead, I walked further into the open. Gut instinct said "Don't hide, suspicious people hide from police" and when you're not white suspicious usually means guilty to the police. After hearing numerous horror stories, I had no desire to find out firsthand what happens to trans women in jail, so I had always tried to not be suspicious.

He saw me and began walking in my direction. He seemed to be trying to run but his left leg seemed too short and hobbled him. Then I noticed his leg wasn't too short; he was missing his foot. It wasn't a man. It was a zombie. In only a few seconds, it had nearly closed the distance between us. With no more time to think, I gripped the bat in both hands and as he — it got close, I swung at its head.

Its head flew to the side and it stumbled from the impact. I froze for a second, watching it regain its balance until it turned and lunged at me. I raised my bat high and brought the bat down on its head. It cracked and crunched but the zombie didn't fall. It staggered back for a second but renewed its single-minded attack. I swung to knock it off balance one more time before running away.

I ran between the apartment buildings and turned the corner behind my own. Behind me, I heard the shuffle-thump of it following. Looking back I saw it stumbling along faster than a person missing a foot should be able. It will follow me until I can't run anymore, I realized. It won't get out of breath or tired or hungry. I could make it back to the apartment but then what? I have to kill it. I can do this, I told myself. It's hobbled and off balance.

I turned, grabbed the bat in both hands again, and swung as it reached me. It stumbled but this time I didn't give it time to recover and smashed my bat down

TRANSCENDENT 2

on its head again. It doubled over from the impact so I hit it across the back, sending it to the ground. I circled around to its head and began smashing its skull before it could get up. After a few minutes my bat began to ring out as it hit concrete more often than flesh. The zombie wasn't moving any more, it hadn't been moving for a couple of minutes now that I thought about it.

I snapped out of my killing frenzy. My heart was pounding and I was breathing hard. Looking down at the now mostly headless corpse made me feel ill. I swallowed back my nausea, then I noticed the black gore coating my bat, my arms, splattered on my clothes, and presumably on my face as well. I took a few steps away and retched.

Taking deep breaths, I forced myself to concentrate on what had just happened. I had smashed in a zombie's head. Should I move the body? Obviously I didn't need to hide it from the police but just leaving it to rot didn't seem like the best idea.

Would it rot? These things didn't seem to be really alive. Besides the grayish pallor to the skin it didn't look like it had been rotting and it didn't smell like rotting meat either. It obvious didn't need or have much blood judging by the missing foot.

What did people in movies do with dead zombies? Leave them lying around? If I wasn't behind my apartment building that might have been an option. But I didn't want dead bodies lying all around.

So I needed to move it, but where? I needed to at least move it away from my apartment building. The complex was four buildings, two buildings on a side facing inward. Parking spaces in front of the building with extra against the back fence. The zombie had chased me between two of the buildings until we reached the back of the buildings, where I had stood my ground. The wooden fence around the complex meant I was mostly hidden from prying eyes. Ideally I should remove it from the complex but I had no way to move it other than dragging the body. I decided to haul it to the back corner of the complex near the fence. It would be out of sight and hopefully far enough away that if it did start to rot I wouldn't have to smell it.

I walked back to the body and stood over it. I avoided looking too hard at the ruined mess that was left of the head. Its arms were bare, meaning I had to touch its flesh. Grabbing one of its wrists, I grimaced at the cold flesh. No, not cold, just not warm like a person. It was firm and dry, not squishy and wet like the rotting meat I thought the zombies were made of. With a wrist in each hand I began pulling against the body's weight.

It didn't move, at first. I threw my weight back and managed to jerk the body forward a few inches. Again I put my weight into pulling the body and dragged it a few feet before its foot snagged on a crack in the concrete. Slowly, I jerkily dragged it past the apartment buildings to the fence.

My first zombie kill. It had been a lot messier than movies made it out to be. I was covered in stuff that I really didn't want to think too hard about. If I didn't know these zombies weren't infectious, that you had to actually die to become one, I might have been worried instead of just disgusted. I walked back to the scene of the crime and picked up my bat from where I had left it while dragging the body. What if another one of those things had come along? Trying to fight one without a weapon was not something I wanted to think about. I needed to keep my weapons close at all times.

Wait, I thought, it was a cop. I walked back to the body and checked its belt. Empty holster, a couple magazines? clips? of bullets for the missing gun, pepper spray, a small flashlight, and handcuffs. Would pepper spray work on zombies? Probably not but it would work on other humans. I took it and the flashlight.

Once back in the apartment, I locked the door, refortified it, and walked straight to the bathroom.

Half an hour later I was physically and mentally clean of zombie head gore. I dropped my shirt and pants in a trash bag. Before everything went to hell, I would have tried to salvage them. The pants especially, since before I didn't have many pairs and wasn't exactly rolling in cash. If things went well on my trip, I wouldn't have to worry about clothes. If they didn't, I still wouldn't need to worry either.

I re-dressed for my first trip out into the new world. T-shirt and jeans for ease of movement. A sports bra in case I had to run. My hair was pulled back into a sporty ponytail. I dug a duffel bag out of the closet and adjusted the strap until it was tight against my back. Baseball bat and pepper spray for protection.

I moved the sofas from in front of the door and peered through the peephole. I didn't see anyone. Was I being too cautious? The deadbolts scraped and squeaked as I twisted the knobs to open them. I reminded myself to get oil. From the main entrance to the apartment complex I headed north, staying close to the complex's fence while looking around. At the corner I looked down the cross street. No one in sight. I dashed across the open ground of the first intersection to the relative cover of the nearest house. The smaller residential street I had been following met a larger four-lane street bordered by a few small businesses. I stopped by the dry cleaner on the corner and looked around. On the other side of the street was the convenience store. Around it was lots of open ground. Good for me to see zombies, bad for me to have to cross.

The area between me and the store looked clear. Farther away I saw motion in my periphery. At least I thought I had.

There was nothing there when I focused on the area. Maybe it had gone behind something. I looked around again, seemed clear. It was now or never. I separated from the dry cleaner's wall and began walking to the convenience store. Across the dry cleaner's parking lot, the four-lane street, and across the store's parking lot. I kept a steady pace while looking around, especially behind me, until I reached the front doors.

As I pulled open one of the doors I realized I wasn't the first person to come by. The store was almost stripped clean. I began searching anyway. A package of Snoballs on a rack and a couple cans of beans on the floor. Bags of chips torn open, their contents spilled all over the floor. They crunched under my shoes as I walked between the aisles looking for anything else that had been left behind. I heard chips crunch behind me. Spinning around, I raised my baseball bat and found myself face to face with a skinny white guy also holding a baseball bat. He flinched and jumped back. I stopped, heart beating fast, teeth gritted, panic flooding my mind.

"Whoa, whoa I'm not gonna hurt you," he said releasing one hand from the bat and holding it palm out. "I wasn't sure if you were a zombie or not."

My panic faded as I breathed slow and deep. I grabbed a shelf to steady myself as the post-panic dizziness set in.

"Hey, are you okay?" He looked at me, concerned, as I tried not to collapse.

"Yeah, just give me a minute," I wheezed.

"Okay, um…I'm Andy," he said.

"Lisa," I replied. Andy's brow furrowed slightly. I cleared my throat, smiled, and said in my most feminine voice, "Hi, I'm Lisa." He smiled, mollified by my femme voice.

"What are you doing here?" he said.

"I was looking for water and food." I stood up straighter.

"Why?" he asked, "The water is still running here. Did it stop where you were staying?"

"Not yet but when it does I want to have some water around."

"Good point," he said.

TRANSCENDENT 2

"Looks like you got cleaned out," I said gesturing around the store.

"Yeah, when the power went out I tried to close the store but the customers didn't want to leave and started taking stuff. Some of them started fighting, so I locked myself in the back room until they left."

"You were here alone?"

"No one else would work. I was the only one not to bail on my manager. I kind of wish I had now."

"How long have you been here?"

"Since the power went out. A week, maybe a little more."

"Why didn't you just leave?"

"I don't have a car and no one was answering the phone at home. I didn't want to try walking with everything that was going down. What about you, why are you still here?"

"No car either and I couldn't get in touch with anyone." I pointed at the chip-covered floor, "Did you do this?"

"Part of it. When they started grabbing stuff, some chip bags got busted open and dropped. I just spread them out. I thought it would help to alert me to someone coming into the store." He grinned at his cleverness.

"You could have just locked the door," I said, "I guess I'm going to have to look somewhere else for water."

"There's a pallet of bottled water in the back," he said. "And I packed everything they didn't take back there too." I looked toward the open door he had come from. "I probably shouldn't have said that. I would share…" he halfheartedly offered.

"No," I said turning back to face him, "You have to protect what you have. I'd do the same."

"Oh yeah," he said, "Hey are you staying some place nearby?"

"Uh…I don't think…" I trailed off, not sure how to say, "I don't trust you."

"Hey, don't worry about it. Sorry I asked."

"No, it's not like that. I don't know you. You don't know me either, remember. You have your storeroom with water and who knows what else that you need to protect. You don't know if I'm going to kill you for your water and food."

"I don't think you would — " he protested.

"But I might. You should start thinking like that." I already had, apparently.

"I should start thinking everyone is out to get me?" he asked.

"Look at this place. They took everything they could and that was before it got really bad. When I spun around, I could have killed you. I almost did out of instinct. I could have taken everything you have." He paled as I talked. I might not be as strong as I used to be but I was still taller and a little bigger than him. "I'm going to go now. Lock the door after me."

"Wait, you can't just leave me here alone," he pleaded.

"I…I can't trust you either. You could leave. Try to find a house nearby to hole up in," I said.

"Is that where you're staying?"

I locked eyes with him, "If you follow me I will kill you."

"What?"

"I don't know you. I can't trust you," I stated. Guess I was over being shy with my emotions.

"Come on, this isn't some post-apocalyptic wasteland. Everything was normal a couple weeks ago. Why wouldn't you trust me?"

I turned and walked a few steps away from him, putting a shelf unit between us, before turning back, "I'm transgender."

"What does that mean?" he asked confused.

"It means when I was born the doctor looked between my legs and said, 'It's a boy,' and everyone believed him but I'm not."

"You're a guy?" his brow furrowed.

"No, I'm a woman, just — a different kind of woman." I watched him thinking through it. Watching for him for signs of violence.

"You have a dick?" he finally asked.

"Yes," I watched his eyes flick back and forth, his face scrunched up in confusion, "And that is why I can't trust you. Right now you're trying to decide how to treat me now that you know I'm a woman with a penis. You're trying to decide if I've tricked you. You're trying to decide if you should be angry. You are trying to decide if you should attack me."

"I…I…"

"It's okay, I'll see myself out." I walked down the aisle away from him and made my way to the door. I turned back to him and said, "Don't forget to lock the door after me."

He said nothing, just watched me leave.

I walked away from the store, past the dead pumps, the package of Snoballs still in my hand. I thought for a second about taking it back as some sort of peace offering for rejecting him. No, I thought, I have the right to be defensive. They've always killed us but now there really was nothing to stop them.

A few hundred feet ahead, a superstore loomed over a mostly deserted parking lot.

HAPPY REGARDS

◄ RoAnna Sylver ►

ONE MONTH BEFORE CHAMELEON MOON…

It was Evelyn Calliope's birthday, and for one day everything was almost perfect. It almost seemed like Parole stopped being Parole. Her small house was full even on ordinary days. Full of plants, machines, people, and laughter. And today it was filled with balloons, brightly wrapped presents, and the smell of delicious treats slowly baked to perfection.

The first surprise came a day early, and it wasn't for Evelyn. Not exactly.

"That's a pretty drawing, honey," Rose said as she sat down beside Jack and his collection of papers and crayons, all in varying shades of red and green. "Is that a cake?"

"Mm-hmm." He nodded, adding another slightly more magenta, pointed shape to the top, completing the circle. He had a faraway look in his eyes that Rose knew well; she'd seen it often enough when Danae started work on an especially intricate project, or Evelyn was writing a new song. She supposed if she looked in the mirror when she was deep in thought, she'd see it in her own eyes. But this might have been the first time she'd seen it in her son. Maybe he'd discovered his calling, she thought with a little thrill. They hadn't had a visual artist in the family yet that she knew about. Or maybe he just got really excited about baked goods. "Tomorrow."

TRANSCENDENT 2

"That's right!" Rose resisted her delighted urge to pick him up and hug him; that might break him out of his newly discovered creative groove. "It is Mama Ev's birthday tomorrow!"

"Mm-hmm." He nodded again, still not looking up. He added a rectangular shape around the cake, like a frame, or as if it were floating in a doorway, held by unseen hands, or suspended by invisible strings. "Strawberries."

"Her favorite." She grinned. The warm love and pride that swelled in her chest was one of her favorite feelings, and Rose tried to savor like she did every time. The memory would make the next hard Parole day go a little easier. "What a wonderful idea. We'll bake her a strawberry cake — a bunch just came in the other day too! Perfect timing!"

Now he looked up, shaking his head a little bit as if just now coming out of a daydream. "Is it a good present?"

"The cake? It's the best. She'll be so glad you remembered!"

"No, this! It's not done yet." He held up the drawing, eyes entirely clear and focused on Rose now. When he smiled, it was filled with pride in his work, though he still watched carefully as his mother took in the art, then the artist. Now it was her turn to look dreamy for just a moment, imagining all the art and birthdays to come. "Will she be happy?"

"I can't think of anything she'd love more. It'll be a perfect day." Even in Parole, they still happened from time to time.

So when the next day came, Jack stood on a chair to reach the kitchen table, working with two of his mothers to create that elusive perfect day for the third. The house was decorated, bright, and cheerful, but the cake wasn't quite done, and Evelyn was taking the night off to come home early. She'd be home soon, and every minute counted. In front of him was the masterpiece he'd designed — or soon, it would be. The kitchen was warm and filled with the mouthwatering smell of oven-fresh cake, and the fact that so much frosting had gone onto its hubcap-sized surface and not into their mouths was a testament to their dedication. Nobody was beyond temptation, but at least the cake was getting done.

And the top did read "Happy Birthday Evelyn" now, in bright red letters.

Strawberries, big as both his small hands put together, pointed up around the top of the red-frosted cake in a ring like the points on a crown, and Jack and Danae were halfway around when they ran out. Rose went to politely request some more of her homegrown ingredients (it was very important to be clear with your intentions and say please and thank you, she reminded Jack before heading into the adjacent, skylight-bright and vine-thick room, petting the head of a giant

Venus flytrap as she went), leaving Jack and Danae to continue painting more red icing and food coloring onto any missed spots and sneaking licks off the spoons.

This kind of normal was the strangest thing in Parole.

And it never lasted.

Danae and Jack both jumped as a shrill cat's screech cut through the air, followed by thunderous barking. Then, the rapid, harsh scraping of metal claws against wood and tile.

"Dandy?" Danae called, voice instantly tight with anxiety at the guard dog's alarmed bark, putting down the large bowl of red icing and turning around quickly, just in time to see a metallic animal zip into the kitchen from her open workshop door.

It wasn't Toto-Dandy. It was much smaller, and even though it didn't look quite finished — more like a metal skeletal frame with a more-completed head than a fully formed animal — it moved much more like a cat, crouching low, almost flat, and scooting along the ground. It zigzagged wildly around the kitchen, briefly scrabbling at the kitchen door, before it ricocheted out into the hallway, ears flattened against its shining head. A moment later, Dandy himself followed, bursting into the room with a much louder, wilder, entirely doglike bluster.

"Oh no." Danae paled, face filling with rapidly growing horror. "Dandy, no. Stay!"

The huge, black-fur and shining-steel wolf paused for a moment, staring at his two surprised humans as if weighing his options. Then he chose one. Toto-Dandy dove after the cat toward the living room in a fresh explosion of barks and answering furious yowls.

Crash.

Toto-Dandy was not always one of her more graceful creations. On his way out, the huge metal wolf slammed into the kitchen table, and everything on it jolted to the side and a good three inches into the air, including the lovingly crafted cake.

"No..."

Breathless, paralyzed, Danae watched it happen from across the kitchen, but it might as well have been from a mile away. Horrified, she couldn't move a muscle — then she moved all at once. Her legs were propelling her forward before she knew to jump, arms outstretched, but she was too late and too far; she would never make it in time. The cake and its plate slipped off the table, fell —

TRANSCENDENT 2

And landed safely in Jack's waiting arms. The huge cake was almost too heavy, too unwieldy, too much, but he planted his small feet and stood firm.

"Good!" Danae almost collapsed with relief before she reached him, but managed to steady herself, and then Jack, keeping herself between him and the noisy animals still yowling and barking up a storm in the living room behind her. "Oh, good job, Jack, you're my hero. You are my absolute hero."

"I was just in the right place at the right time," he said, and she had to laugh. One of Evelyn's favorite saving-the-day phrases. Kids really did pick things up fast. Looked like he'd picked up the truth-and-justice part too.

"Yes, you were." She sighed, hands on his shoulders for a moment before slowly, gently taking the cake (almost bigger than the boy who'd saved it) and placing it on the kitchen counter, out of reach of any flailing animal appendages. "Now. *Dandy!*" She let out a sharp whistle.

A huge, black canine head appeared around the doorway to the living room, bright blue eyes wide. They didn't need to be human, or even organic, to look guilty as hell.

"Over here." She patted one thigh and pointed at the floor. "Leave the kitty alone, it's a work-in-progress." She could still hear somewhat grating hostile feline noises and caught a flash as it ran past at the end of the hall; it must still be in a panic and trying to escape.

Dandy didn't move, but his head drooped a little lower.

"I know, boy, you're just doing what you know best. But you know you're not supposed to play with — "

"These should be enough," Rose said from behind her with a bowl full of fresh, huge strawberries. Surprised, Danae turned to see her wife entering through the kitchen door that led outside, not the open doorway she'd left through before. "Serena didn't feel like letting me borrow any more berries, so I thought I'd — "

"Rose, look out!"

"What?" Rose looked up sharply at the alarm in Danae's voice — so she didn't see the cat shoot between her steel ankles and disappear outside.

"No — *no!*" Danae's face fell, then her eyes widened as a huge black shape careened past her and directly toward Rose. Danae launched herself into the air, landing on Toto-Dandy's back and tackling him to the floor. "Dandy, *stay!*"

"Was that your new project?" Rose had fallen back against the counter, still clinging to the bowl of strawberries like they were precious gems. Or perhaps a flotation device, in case of an emergency landing. Jack had climbed down from his chair and seemed unsure whether to laugh at the strange sight, be nervous because his parents were, or both.

"Yeah! It *was!*" Danae struggled to keep her biggest and, right now, most infuriating creation pinned to the floor. The second he threw her off his back, he'd chase directly after the cat — she had to admit, Dandy's instincts there were flawless. Though right now he seemed more like a mechanical bull than a wolf. "Took me six months! Almost done! Special stealth alloy! If it's lost, gonna turn this one into a weedwhacker!"

"Okay." Rose set down the bowl and chewed her lower lip, looking up at the kitchen wall clock. "Half an hour until Evelyn's show closes. You stay here, finish the cake! I'll find the cat!" Rose called over her shoulder as she dashed through the door, leaving it open behind her. A second later her head poked back through. "Everything's going to be okay!" *Slam.*

"Yeah, that'd be great," Danae muttered, still holding onto the thrashing metal wolf at least twice her size, wrestling him across the kitchen floor and back toward her workshop to cool down. "Come on, boy! Work with me! Jack, can you — "

"Dandy!" Jack was already at the workshop door, holding it open and waving. "In here, please!"

Toto-Dandy's triangular ears perked up immediately at the sound of his voice. He moved across the kitchen and down the short hallway so fast that he dragged Danae a few steps before she let go, flopping onto the floor. She lay there for a few seconds, seizing the opportunity to rest and take a quick breather. Then she sat up to see Jack reach up to pet Dandy's thick neck fur and get a face-lick in return; the giant synthetic wolf allowed the little boy to gently steer him through the door and shut it behind him, and Jack turned around with a triumphant grin.

"He listens to me."

"Maybe next time I'll just ask you to pass on a message," Danae said, wondering if her guard dog's priority subroutines were enough out of alignment to tinker with, or cute enough to leave. Maybe she'd just practice giving off a more confident Alpha vibe. Danae never felt right about messing with any of her creations' heads, not if she could meet them halfway. Especially with something as easy as saying "please." That was what Jack had done, she realized. It was the magic word, after all. "Anyway, got that under control. Now it's time for the fun part," she said with a conspiratorial grin. "Just gotta stick the berries on…"

"And then what?" His eyes grew round with anticipation.

"And then you get to lick the bowl!" She giggled when he did, relieved that they'd managed to get the day back on track. "Then we wait for Mama Ev to get home — and ahhhh, the look on her face! It's gonna be sw — "

As they came back into the kitchen, something flew directly at Danae's face. It hit before she even had time to scream.

Outside and a few blocks away, two men headed down the narrow, smoky residential back street. Unlike most people in Parole who found themselves walking outside this close to sundown, they didn't hug the inner edge of the sidewalk or peer around corners, glance over their shoulders as they walked, or even seem in all that much of a hurry, despite their destination. Or the sheer number of Eyes in the Sky who would love to see the both of them dead.

Nobody knew how many members made up the infamous CyborJ Syndicate. Nobody knew what the elusive leader of the cyber-revolutionary group looked like, or if the virtuosic hacking force in question was one person at all. Rumor and speculation abounded as to his — or her — or their — identity, ranging from single allegations to long lists of names.

The only known facts came from observation. Ten years of devastatingly effective virtual blows against Eye in the Sky, and meticulously rebuilt electronic infrastructure. Parole had a working internet free of policing and surveillance thanks to their tireless efforts. And nothing, not even super-powered resistance, had saved more lives than their organization's flawlessly synchronized operations. They moved with surgical precision, leading city-wide simultaneous strikes coordinated in perfect unison. CyborJ was everywhere at once, appearing like a ghost out of thin air, leaving a wake of technological devastation and/ or wonders — and vanishing without a trace.

The most popular theory was that "CyborJ" was actually an elite group within the Syndicate, comprised of at least ten and as many as fifty individuals.

But sometimes the truth was stranger than fiction. Sometimes it was more mundane. Sometimes it was both at the same time.

"Listen, Stef, babe, towering teddy-bear cyber-pirate sentinel who guards my slumber and my heart and my nerd-cave — which is pretty much my heart, and also my brain — much as I love Evelyn, and I do, I really do, she's a freakin' delight…they know I can't stay away from the command center for more than a couple hours, right? Wait, they know who I am, right? I don't know if I've actually told Rose directly who I am. And they didn't *tell* anybody who I am? Right?"

TRANSCENDENT 2

The mysterious — but definitely singular — entity known as CyborJ pushed his black mirrored sunglasses further up the bridge of his nose and pulled the strings on his gray hoodie a little bit tighter, stuffing his long black hair more firmly down into the neck. He cracked his black-gloved knuckles a few times, a nervous habit, then tugged at the straps of his backpack, adjusting them to better center the long, irregularly shaped gift-wrapped box that stuck out and far above his head. He walked quickly down the street with long-legged, slightly off-kilter strides, pulled off-balance by the unwieldy package.

"Oh man, I can't even remember how much they know about me. Stefanos, how much do they know about me? My brain's so fried right now. It's been a weird month...year. Maybe it'd be easier if I really was like fifty people or whatever everybody thinks now. I mean, I made 'em think that, but..."

He was definitely only one person: a tall but slightly hunched at the shoulders (terrible posture even without the backpack and long gift-wrapped box), thin (even without regularly forgetting to eat) young Tsalagi Native American man in dark shades and a baggy, faded sweatshirt and torn jeans, moving in a vaguely forward direction, but also constantly zigzagging and trying to look in every direction at once, all while obviously trying to appear as casual and normal as possible. It didn't work. In Parole, like everywhere else, nothing tended to attract attention like such obvious attempts to avoid it. And right now he was looking more than a little on-edge and hyper-vigilant. Beneath that, exhausted, and like he wasn't quite used to being out on the physical street, like he'd just stumbled out into a brave new century after cryogenic stasis, unfamiliar with the world in general. Or maintaining balance while walking.

Sometimes it was amazing how somebody so brilliant and powerful in one arena could be so vulnerable and make such an easy target in another. Fortunately, he wasn't alone.

"Take a breath, Jay. You're fine, they know, I'm not walking you into any place we can't walk right back out of." The second, much larger man beside him also walked just a hair's breadth behind, ready to extend one arm in case he tipped right over backwards thanks to the backpack and its top-heavy center of gravity...and the simple fact that stranger things had been known to happen when CyborJ abandoned his nerve center and started to walk down physical corridors instead of virtual ones. Things occasionally got...unexpected. "This is why you need to relax a little more, especially while I'm gone. Talk to people. Breathe some relatively fresh air."

TRANSCENDENT 2

"I should know this," Jay continued, only half-listening. "I mean, Danae has to know who I am, right? So that means Evelyn knows. So Rose — no, mistake to assume anything, we know that. Standard story? I'm in the top ten Syndicate members? That might be safer..."

"It's all right, they know who you are," Stefanos said, deep voice level and calming. "And no, they haven't told a soul. They know the score, believe me. I made sure of it. They're safe. But if you get there and something feels off, we can bail."

"Okay, good." Jay spun on his heel three-sixty degrees to look around the entire street. Stefanos kept his catching arm ready, just in case. "Just making sure."

"We're not being followed. You can relax." He wasn't dramatically taller but he was much more substantially built, broad shoulders and thick muscles dwarfing Jay's thin frame. Long, thick, curly black hair fell down his back, and his equally thick beard fell almost as far down to his chest. Like Jay, he wore loose, dark-gray and neutral clothes that were easy to move and easier to hide in — but he would have had trouble blending in no matter where he went. It wasn't because he had scales or wings or anything one might expect in Parole; his difference was both more subtle, and more significant. It had been ten years since UV light had filtered through the barrier, and most people who lived in Parole tended to be unhealthily pale and develop vitamin-D deficiencies without the use of personal sun lamps. His visible skin was a healthy tanned bronze, as if he'd been out in full, unobscured sunlight recently.

"Oh, you relax, you're the one looking at me like I'm about to fall over! I'm not about to — okay, thank you for that. I think it's these shoes. They're outside shoes. I'm outside. Anyway, I know, I've got like thir... sixteen checks and fail-safes in place right now, but I just wanna make sure. Nothing beats my plain old eyeballs. I mean, maybe except for yours."

"I doubt it," Stefanos chuckled. "I might have spectral scans and infrared, but you see the strings that control the system. And those are tougher to pick out."

When Stefanos smiled, his eyes glittered in a quite literal sense. They were golden, metallic, obviously synthetic, with several rotating rings around the pupils' exteriors that spun as he focused near and far like telescopic camera lenses. Occasionally, other rings or metallic shutters would flicker in front of his gleaming metal eyes, switching the lenses into a new mode or rotating them in a different direction. The gyroscopic optical implants were wonders of engineering, and even if he didn't quite seem to belong in Parole, they certainly did.

"Feel better?"

"Mm." Jay still looked nervous despite the empty street, but he nodded. "Parole will just have to get by without my watchful eyes and guiding hands for a few hours."

"It'll be fine. Everyone knows you're very busy and in high demand," Stefanos assured him. "They're honored you emerged just for one day."

"Hey, they should be." Jay stopped walking and flicked his sunglasses down to look over their lenses for a moment, raising his eyebrows. "That sounded snarky but I mean it, I don't leave my darkness and keyboards for just anybody. Only for emergencies, and family occasions."

"And which one is this?" Stefanos' tone wasn't as quick or energetic, but just as dry.

"Well, if it was anyone else throwing the party, I'd say emergency." Jay shrugged with a slightly embarrassed smile. "Actually, I wouldn't say anything at all, I'd already be running. But...your family is mine."

"Yes, they are." Stefanos reached out to pull Jay close, wrapping one arm around his shoulder and giving him a squeeze. As he did, his sleeve slipped up and his hand caught the light of a pale streetlamp. It gleamed dully metallic, artificial but in effortless motion, made of as many intricately articulated working parts as his optical implants' myriad gyroscopic rings. "Danae's been looking forward to seeing you again as much as me."

"See, that's not even fair, we both got genius sisters, but yours actually likes you." Jay dropped his head and pulled his hood a little bit tighter to hide his rising blush. "And me. Dunno how I got that lucky. And, okay, Maureen would definitely like you, so there's that. And not just in a 'wow, look at your cool eyes and arm and leg' way — I mean, she would, the nerd — but like, as a person and junk. Ha, after ten years, we might even get along a little better."

"We'll all find out one day. Soon." Stefanos shut his golden eyes for a moment to the sound of a clearly audible whir. "But for tonight, don't worry, we won't stay the whole time. And if you start to need some air, let me know. They'll understand too."

"Oh, I know they will, they're all good ladies. But maybe..." His confident tone faltered for the first time. "I mean, I'm *who-I-am*, that's a handy excuse right there. The city always needs saving from the clutches of evil. I'd just — I don't want 'em to think I don't want to be there. I do. But if I start to feel zidgy, I'll — I don't know, tug my ear or something, so you'll know..."

"Urgent cyber-revolutionary business. I'll excuse us, politely."

TRANSCENDENT 2

"Awesome. I'll definitely say some awkward, anxious nerd bullshit the second I open my mouth — so thanks for doing the talking."

"Any time. I do appreciate you coming with me, Jay." Stefanos' tone dropped slightly, and Jay looked up, attention caught by the change. "Evelyn Calliope deserves one good day. More. Not just because of all the good days she's given Parole. And not just because she's my sister-in-law. But just living her life, right in the spotlight? On the stage, off it? Being herself, *here* of all places?"

"Yeah, I gotcha." Jay said in an uncommonly serious voice, though one now free of nervousness. "It's…important, isn't it?"

"Very." Stefanos smiled, metallic eyes flashing like the sun nobody in Parole had seen clearly in ten years. "Seeing somebody like yourself not only walk through fire and keep walking — and come out the other side a superhero, bulletproof, the person they were always meant to be? Not just transition, and not just survive, but live and conquer? Makes you think maybe you can too. I wouldn't be the man I am today without that woman."

"Best domino effect ever." Jay was smiling. "Guess I owe her a lot too."

"And one happy birthday doesn't begin to cover it, but we can at least make an appearance. I'll give her my present and you can give her your…" Stefanos shot a glance at Jay's oddly shaped gift. "Whatever it is you have there."

"Excuse me. It's called a key-tar." Jay reached back to tap the end of the oblong package sticking out of his backpack. "An iconic instrument. Seminal. This one can do a cool holographic light show effect — well, it *couldn't*, but I messed with it, now it can."

"Uh-huh."

"She'll understand its musical importance, unlike *other people*."

"I certainly hope so."

"Well, it's more creative than a new microphone! You realize she probably has like six million microphones, right? And if she doesn't, the Emerald Bar does. I'm not trying to criticize your gift, I'm just saying it's not too late to put both of our names on — "

"Grappling hook."

"What?"

"When you twist the base, it fires off a grappling hook." Stefanos didn't look down, but gave a slow, satisfied nod and kept walking. "Took me a while to find one. Took longer to find one that didn't curve off to the left."

"I… Of course." Jay nodded after a second. "Because every girl needs a good grappling hook, why didn't I think of that?"

"Might come in handy at her second job. Being a superheroine." Now he shot Jay a look. "No, you're not putting your name on it."

"Mine's still more fun."

They walked in a comfortable silence for a few steps. Jay's brief flare of anxiety from a moment before had faded, but after a moment, so did his smile.

"So when do you ship back out?" he asked, voice light, but the kind of studied lightness that covered something else. "Out to the great big outside world?"

"Next week. This run'll be upwards of a month. Turret's up to something big out there, and it's going to take a little longer than usual to scope out exactly what."

"You got any kind of hint? Or a plan? At all?"

"The world's almost as big a mess outside Parole as it is inside. Turret's to blame. The plan is damage control, that hasn't changed."

"So you're just walking out there into who-knows-what like usual?"

Stefanos smiled at the combination of curiosity and frustration Jay made no effort to hide anymore. "I'm lucky the FireRunner still has clearance to leave freely at all. I'm almost starting to get the feeling that man doesn't trust the Captain and me anymore."

"A month." Jay made a face, sticking out his tongue so his disgust was clearly visible even with his sunglasses and raised hood. "A whole freaking...great. I *love* waiting around not knowing if you're dead or alive. Or anything else. That's my *favorite* thing to do."

"You could come with me." The simple offer wasn't a casual one, or empty, or easily withdrawn. Stefanos never made them.

"What, just sneak me out? I'm a little bit high-profile. Kinda a big deal."

"It's been done a few times before."

"Okay, yeah, understatement. Ha, they think this thing's so impenetrable." Jay nodded up at the barrier arcing far over their heads. "But every firewall has a back door. Especially if your name's...me." Jay was entirely still and quiet for a moment, a rarity that indicated some seriously deep thought. "You really don't think your friends would mind me hanging around? Could you even do it?"

"Like I said, we've done it before. Many times. You'd just be on a more temporary basis than most, that's all." His shining eyes swiveled down; Jay found it hard to look away, and for a moment, harder to make up his mind. Neither one was something he experienced often. "And no. They wouldn't mind you being there. If they did, they wouldn't be my friends for long."

Jay didn't answer right away. But after an even longer few seconds of consideration, he shook his head. His answer sounded casual, but that was all. "Nah. How would Parole survive without me? The man, the legend, the one they call… eh, you know what they call me."

"You've got a point there. Wouldn't last five minutes. I'd bring you back and the place would be a smoking crater."

"A bigger one, you mean. It's already pretty much a smoking crater."

"Mm. I couldn't be responsible for that." It wasn't always easy to tell when the big man was smiling or not; his heavy, curly facial hair hid some of his more subtle expressions, and his synthetic eyes made a hell of a poker face. But his voice was another story; it softened and warmed, and Jay's wide grin melted into something softer as well at the sound. "My heart valves haven't been upgraded enough to handle that kind of guilt."

Suddenly, something zipped between them and kept going; something small and very low to the ground, with four legs and a tail. It zigzagged across the street, then slipped into a seemingly impossibly tiny hole in the rubble of a fallen building, disappearing from view.

"Was that a cat?" Stefanos' golden optical lenses whirred as they rotated, focusing on the wreckage where he thought the animal had disappeared.

"What? Where?" Jay whipped off his sunglasses and snapped instantly into the moment, as if the mere presence of a cat was much more exciting than their actual destination.

"I don't know. Probably nothing." Stefanos shook his head, abandoning the search and silently hoping Jay would too. He'd only caught a glimpse, but it had really looked more like a cat skeleton — which told him it was either something they didn't want to mess with, or his optical implants were malfunctioning.

"Nothing? There's a cat around here somewhere!" Jay, however, seemed much more optimistic about the idea. Stefanos couldn't have been less surprised if he'd made a direct and concerted effort. "Somehow, one brave little stray managed to survive this hell city! Oh, that's a good sign, maybe we're not all doomed! You sure you didn't see where it went?"

"Sorry. But I'll keep an eye out." He couldn't help it; Jay's infectious enthusiasm won over common sense any day of the week, and today was no exception. He gave one gyroscope eye a whirl in a mechanical wink. "You know you can always play with the dogs at the library."

"I'll pretend I didn't hear that." Jay closed his eyes for a moment, as if gravely disappointed. "I mean yeah, yes…Ash does good work, dogs are great, they all need good homes…but I'm a cat person, Stef. I mean, living in Parole for ten years, you get to miss a lot of things, right? Family. Home. Um, obviously. Mostly." His eyes dropped to the sidewalk. "Anyway, growing up we had a ton of cats. Always like five at once. So…"

"It's okay." Stefanos' deep voice was gentle and his large flesh-and-blood hand on Jay's back was warm. "You don't have to explain."

He did anyway, and Stefanos wasn't surprised. "Dogs just don't — you can't compare them! Apples and oranges, HTML and CSS, *Wars* and *Trek*…you have no idea what I'm talking about right now, do you?"

"I did about the family part."

"Thanks. Figured you would."

Stefanos opened his mouth but stopped before he got any words out, holding up his synthetic hand and giving Jay's shoulder a slight squeeze. It was second nature by now, but he didn't have to: they could both hear the strange and ominous noise coming from behind them. It was regular, fast, like someone running in heavy steel boots — and getting closer. He and Jay both immediately edged away from the middle of the sidewalk and into the shadow of the nearest building, listening closely as the footsteps got closer, but not turning around or otherwise drawing attention to themselves.

They rounded the next corner. Then they held very still, pressed their backs against the wall, and held their breath. Jay shot Stefanos a quick glance and received a nod in return, confirming their next move. As soon as their pursuer passed them, they'd bolt the opposite direction, and if necessary, Stefanos would fire a disabling shot with his arm cannon — which he began to power up with a growing electrical hum. Together they held their breath, counting silently down from three, two, one…

Someone sped past them in a flurry of clanking metal legs, loose natural black curls, flowers, and vines.

"Was that Rose?" Stefanos held Jay gently back as he began to immediately rush off, one large hand across his chest. He looked slightly confused as he peered around the corner — though he was already powering down his arm.

Jay's sunglasses had come loose in his attempted dash, and now he flicked them back on. "Looks like the party's starting early."

They did burst out of hiding together, but it wasn't to fight back or run away.

"Rose!" Stefanos called, trying to keep his voice level to avoid frightening her, but she'd be too far away in a second. "Hey there, Rose!"

TRANSCENDENT 2

"What?" She whirled around, flowers flying and hands coming up defensively in a stance everyone who lived here picked up quickly — so they both stopped immediately, raising their own hands in a similar but much less aggressive one. As soon as she saw who stood several respectful feet behind her, she let her breath out and gave them a relieved smile, but kept her arms raised, letting them see the small forest of wickedly sharp thorns protruding through her skin. "Oh! Perfect!"

"Sorry about that." Jay gave her a sheepish grin and a wave as she stepped closer to them, arms still held at shoulder height so they could see the thorns recede. When they were fully withdrawn back into her skin, she gave her hands a shake and let her arms drop, sighing as she relaxed from her dash and startle. "Didn't mean to scare you. We were just on our way, wh — hey," he stopped, noticing the way she kept looking around, brow furrowed with worry and confusion. "You okay? Something going down, city in peril?"

"Not so far." Rose looked back at him and laughed, a little breathless. "Just a minor birthday complication."

"Oh, no, what happened? Maybe we can help."

"Missing cat."

"I told you!" Jay pounded Stefanos' metal arm with his fist, to which the much bigger man barely reacted at all, except to hide a smile in his beard. "Wait. You have a cat? You never told me!"

"It's one of Danae's works in progress," Rose explained, frustration coming back into her eyes as she recalled that morning's chaos. "Somebody left her workshop door open — "

"Somebody." Stefanos snorted.

"Mm-hmm. Anyway, the cat's not done, still being built and programmed and everything, but it can walk around — and run — and it still doesn't have fur or all its working parts, but I guess it looks and smells enough like a cat that when it got out..."

"Dandy."

"In about three seconds." Rose shook her head, looking like she was caught between laughing and letting out an annoyed sigh. "We managed to catch him, but that thing was gone. Danae and Jack are home finishing Ev's cake. I'm hoping there's a chance I can find this cat at all, you know how things disappear in this place..." She chewed her lower lip for a moment. "This is Danae's star project right now. And it's Evelyn's birthday, I just...it'd just be great if we could get everything back to normal and start over. It was going fine until now."

"Say no more," Stefanos said in a soft, low voice. "We'll help however we can. Right?"

"Absolutely." Jay nodded. "No job too small for Parole's elite resistance. Battling the forces of evil by night, rescuing stray cats and delivering perfect birthdays by day, that's what we're here for."

"He sounds sarcastic but that's just because he doesn't actually know how to stop," Stefanos said, giving up his attempt to hide his smile. "Anyway, shouldn't even be too hard to pick up on personal sensors. Danae's fancy alloys are even easier to trace than body heat." His eyes clicked and hummed softly, then began to glow a bright green. The light beamed out in a vertical line, sweeping smoothly over the nearest brick wall. "Which I keep telling her to do something about."

"She knows," Rose assured him. "That's actually what this prototype is for. One of its purposes, testing a new experimental alloy. Much harder to trace. You might actually have trouble finding it, I certainly have been."

"Well, good, if we can't, then SkEye won't be able to either. If one of her little friends ever fell into the wrong hands..." He frowned, beam emanating from his eyes growing both brighter and greener as he intensified the scan. "What was the final mix, if you know that?"

"You'd have to ask her about the exact percentages." Rose shrugged. She was just glad when nothing exploded, as happy as Danae was when she didn't wake up to find that their house had become a thick forest overnight. "This morning she was talking about tungsten, but just in a 'wish we had it' way."

"Tungsten? Here? She's dreaming."

"That's what I said! Actually, I said, 'Okay, put it on the idea list, honey,' because you know how she gets if you just shoot down one of her plans, no matter how wild, she'll go on a never-ending quest for every bit of tungsten in Parole just to prove she can...'"

Jay didn't even attempt to appear engaged in the conversation. Instead, he stretched out his arms in front of himself, opening his hands wide and wiggling his fingers like a stage magician about to levitate a string. The other two didn't even pause or look over when he cracked his knuckles — extremely loudly — or when he clapped his hands a couple times, activating the holographic interface in his gloves.

A couple small blue-white screens hovered above his palms, staying where they were when he turned both hands over, then used one to flick through the various notifications and messages. Nothing pressing, though he did tap one square to remotely activate a hidden shock mine, reveling in the knowledge that five very surprised Eye in the Sky troops were currently — ha, he had to chuckle at that, pun not intended, but enjoyed — smoking in their body armor. They wouldn't try breaching the library roof for a very long time.

Message break completed, he waved "goodbye" to make the hovering screens wink out, and instead pointed decisively at the ground. A small red dot appeared where he pointed, and he made a few quick practice circles. Like Stefanos' eyes, his glove was now emitting its own light. The beam was just much smaller, more focused, and not for scanning; a LASER pointer.

Not even a full second later, the tiny red light was attacked by a pair of shiny metal paws.

"Ahem." he grinned as Stefanos and Rose turned to look, nodding down to the small metal cat-skeleton-with-a-head that rolled around on the ground and wildly batted at the LASER-pointer light. "Would that be the cat in question?"

"Sure is." The relief in Rose's sigh surprised even her. All day, she'd been the one reassuring Danae that it would be all right if everything wasn't absolutely perfect. But clearly her own hopes had been higher than she'd thought. "Thank you so much."

"It's nothing! Cats are cats. No matter what they're made of." Jay kept smoothly conducting his finger and LASER-dot in a figure-8. The cat-in-progress showed no signs of getting bored, still batting at the light whenever it came within reach, long, whip-thin tail waving behind it like a startled snake. "Next time try a box. Wouldn't even have to put anything in it, probably, just a box."

"*AF-FIR-MA-TIVE.*"

Everyone jumped. The harsh electronic voice that had so vehemently confirmed the statement didn't belong to Rose or Stefanos — or anyone human. The cat abandoned its pursuit and looked up, green eyes unblinking and fixed on Jay as if suddenly finding him much more interesting than even the most fascinating wiggling light.

"Was that…" Jay stared back, finally falling still. He let his hand drop, a programmed glove motion which extinguished the red light. The cat's eyes flicked briefly down to follow, then right back up to his face. "Did that cat just say — "

"It's not done yet," Rose explained with some secondhand embarrassment. Danae hated it when people saw her projects before they were finished; she said it was like people seeing her half-dressed. Rose thought there was something fascinating about seeing the animals especially without their fur; it was like seeing the levels of scaffolding and detailed blueprints that went into the construction of towering buildings. You could more easily see the intricate moving parts and appreciate the works of beautiful genius, rather than go an entire day forgetting you weren't petting a real cat. But Danae insisted — no seeing a new model until it was done. Otherwise, people saw and heard things like —

"*AF-FIR-MA-TIVE.*"

"It won't do that when it's done," Rose said hurriedly. "It'll meow just like a normal cat. And have fur and everything, you'll barely be able to tell. Really, it's — "

"*Amazing!*" Jay practically squealed, crouching down and reaching one hand out, knuckles toward the cat's metal nose — which it immediately sniffed, then nudged with its forehead. "It's already amazing! Why would you change it? I mean, what if someone wants a cat that talks in a cool robot voice?"

"That...hasn't come up yet," Rose said. "Though I suppose it's always possible. We get all kinds of custom orders."

"I'd be fine with plain old fur and meowing." Stefanos folded his arms and gave the small animal a baleful stare. "Anything else gets a little weird."

"Oh, come on, be nice! It's just a kitty!" Jay and the cat both looked up at him, and somehow Rose was sure its bright green eyes wore a matching look of reproach. "Perfectly good, normal cat, just with metal bones instead of bone-bones, right? We like people with metal bones."

"Right," Rose said, nodding, then shaking her head, then nodding again. "Everything she crafts is alive. In a w — I mean, yes, they're very much alive." She'd never been exactly clear on how. A different kind of life than her plants, a different kind of life than humans, even, or other animals. Maybe even different from what (little) she knew of artificial intelligence. All Rose knew was what Danae insisted: that her creations, from the objects that only appeared inanimate, to the ones that clearly looked you in the eye and protected and loved you, like the giant wolf who'd caused all this trouble, and the cat currently rubbing against Jay's shins, were just as alive as the human woman who had created them. "We tell everyone to just think of them as very advanced therapy animals. They can actually recognize when you're having a panic attack or flashback. Or perform complex tasks and understand what you say a lot better than flesh-and-blood animals."

"Well, that'd be pretty nice to have around," Jay mumbled, scratching behind the cat's ears and admiring their delicate movements. Rose remembered the hours Danae spent on each individual ear, citing the Sydney Opera House for their multi-layered shutter design. "Instead of a hundred anxiety attacks a day, maybe I'd only have ninety. Cute and useful."

"*AF-FIR-MA-TIVE!*"

"So did Danae build her custom for someone, or can you like, adopt them, or — how does this even work?"

"How about we walk and talk?" Stefanos suggested mildly, both metallic eyes swiveling over to Rose, who gave him a grateful nod. "Didn't we have to be getting somewhere?"

"That's right, we'd better head home. Evelyn's coming home right after the show, and Danae might need some help finishing the cake. But no, nobody's claimed this one yet. She'll go wherever she's needed most."

"Mm-kay." Jay nodded and stood up — and as he did, the cat immediately jumped up onto his back, curling around his neck to drape around his shoulders like a scarf. Jay gasped and held very still, but looked unable to keep from trembling with wonder and joy. "Guys…look! It's…I'm…"

"I'm looking," Stefanos sighed, looking resigned as a soldier on a long and lonely night before a battle he knew would be his last. "Rose?"

"Imprint protocols." Rose kept the laugh out of her voice, and hid a smile behind the sway of her hair; a thick curtain of vines and blossoms came in handy sometimes. "This is why Danae keeps all her projects inside and away from people until they find their homes. They tend to imprint on the first people they see who aren't us. It helps them bond with their new family… No promises, but let's talk to Danae."

"Imprinting… Do you know what this means?" Jay whispered, overjoyed. "She likes me! *I've been chosen.*"

"*AF-FIR-MA-TIVE!*"

"No promises, I said," Rose insisted, though the thought of separating this man and this cat was quickly becoming more and more impossible. Especially considering the fact that after this strong an imprint bond had formed, the only way to reset it was just that — a hard reset, wiping the project's memory entirely and starting from scratch. And (maybe in some cases unfortunately) such a memory wipe was impossible for humans. Even considering that seemed cruel, unusual, and as far as Rose was concerned, out of the question. But just in case… "Ask Danae. She might have plans for this one that I don't know about, and I don't want you to get your hopes up, all right, Jay?"

"Okay, okay, yeah, sure, yes." Jay nodded quickly, clearly making an effort to keep his face very serious, grounded, realistic, and like he wasn't already picking out cat toys for his small, dark, computer-filled apartment. "No promises, got it."

"Walk and talk," Stefanos said again and kept moving on as the other two followed, but it wasn't hard to see the smile hidden behind his bushy black beard, and glinting in his golden eyes. "So...your new friend got a name yet?"

"Seven. Like the brilliant, efficient, complex, and yes, beautiful, Seven-of-Nine...Lives. Because this 'borg's a cat." His grin only widened as Stefanos slowly turned to stare at the both of them. As before, the synthetic feline face seemed to smile too. If Rose hadn't known better, she might have checked for yellow feathers; that cat had to have just eaten a canary. "No — 'Tails.' Seven-of-Nine-Tails. Like cat-o-nine-tails, and like Ninetales, and — see? Layers. Layers upon layers of wordplay and self-referential naming brilliance. Just like her human."

Rose decided right then and there that if Jay couldn't convince Danae to let him keep this cat — Seven — she would. It probably wouldn't come to that, though. Danae had a heart. A particularly big, passionate, and generous one. It was one of several reasons Rose married her. She didn't see much to worry about.

"Amazing," Stefanos marveled. Instead of sounding sarcastic, he was smiling. Rose realized that in the (increasingly remote) event she'd had to argue to keep Jay and Seven together, she wouldn't have been alone. She didn't expect the warmth that rose in her chest, but she hadn't expected much of anything that happened today either. "Absolutely amazing."

"I know! I can't wait to show Re...runtime partner!"

"You could have brought him, you know." Rose couldn't quite hide all of her disappointment. "How many years has it been, and we've never met him?"

"Yeah, he doesn't really do parties. Or names." Jay reached up to pet his new friend, actually giggling when she started to very gently nibble at his fingertips. "Cats, though? I can't wait. He'll love her. So will Rowan — and Annie, and Ash, everybody! Everybody's gonna love her!"

"I...hope you're right," Stefanos said, not looking at all convinced. "But you *really* might want to wait until she has fur. And actually meows, instead of...talks. Like that."

"Why would I wait? She's perfect the way she is. Isn't that right? Yes it is right, that's a great big *af-fir-ma-tive* right th — " Jay almost missed a step and tripped when Seven showed off a new, previously hidden feature. "This is the best day of my life..."

They walked the rest of the way home to the way of slightly metallic cat's purrs.

Rose's sincere wish was that by the time she returned home with the missing cat, and two guests, everything would have returned to normal. But like so many things in Parole, "normal" was once again too much to hope for.

The kitchen was spattered with bright red. It covered the floor, the countertops, even the walls, spray had made it all the way up to the ceiling. The only thing more stained than white ceiling or yellow linoleum was Danae, standing very still in the middle of the devastation, looking like she'd survived a massacre — but not without scars.

"Oh." Rose's mouth fell open. She couldn't form a question, no more words at all. A chill didn't just run down her spine; she felt the cold adrenaline shoot through her veins as she automatically prepared for a life-or-death fight. But she couldn't make herself move, she could barely think. Jack. Where? Danae, hurt, how?

Slowly, Danae looked up, raising her eyes to meet Rose's. Her thousand-yard stare spoke of horrors, of dark deeds and brutal desperation. "Need more strawberries."

"What?" Rose's words came out in a dry, choked whisper. "What happened? Where's Jack?"

"Clean shirt. Sticky. Juice everywhere. Cake...ruined."

"Ca...oh." Rose let her breath out in a rush. "It's just strawberries. Danae," she hurried the last couple steps between them and pulled her into a hug, not minding the mess. "You scared me! I thought — "

"I know what you thought." Danae wrapped her arms around Rose and let her head drop down onto her shoulder. "But no, everything's f...no it's not, look at this mess! I'm so sorry! Everything happened so fast, as soon as you left — "

"*James Tiberius!*" came Jay's shocked voice from behind them, and they both turned to see him and Stefanos in the doorway, Jay staring at the ominous stains and Stefanos' arm already powering up. "What happened here? Is it over? Are there any hostiles — "

"No, it's fine — it's strawberry and red food coloring, it's fine!" Rose rushed to reassure them.

"It's not fine!" Danae flopped her head forward and rubbed at her raw eyes, sending a small chunk of cake and icing flying from where it had been stuck in her hair. "Party's cancelled! Call everything off! Hi, Stef." She sniffed, mellow-ing somewhat and looking up at him. "Thanks for coming."

"Wouldn't miss it for the world." He shut off his arm-mounted cannon, shak-ing his head and letting out his breath in a rush. "What happened here?"

"I — cat! Dog! Plants — everything's ruined!"

"Well, then we'll fix it. Now why don't you take a few deep breaths and tell us what happened?"

"It's still ruined! Look at this," she rubbed at a particularly nasty stain with one finger, to absolutely no effect.

"Well, it could have been ruined a lot worse! It looked like — just a lot of bad!" Jay's voice pitch still hadn't come down. Seven, still riding on her new favorite human's shoulder, sat up a little to nudge his chin with her forehead and re-sumed purring, but softer this time and on a different frequency than before; the rhythm was slower and much more soothing. "Oh. That's nice. That's re-ally…nice."

"Anti-anxiety frequency purrs…hey!" Danae looked up as if noticing the metal cat's presence for the first time, face lighting up in a relieved smile. It seemed that Jay wasn't the only one getting some good out of the calming purrs. "You guys! You found it!"

"Aw, it was nothing." Jay shrugged with his free shoulder, smiling and breath-ing much more easily than he had just a few seconds before. "Pretty sure Seven wanted to be found anyway."

"Seven…?"

"Of-Nine-Tails," Jay finished, suddenly looking both very nervous and tenta-tively hopeful. "And…I guess she's technically yours. We just found her. For you. Um, it. We found it — your missing model. Work-in-progress. Unit."

Danae gave the pair the briefest of scrutinizing glances before shaking her head, but her smile didn't waver. "Well, those are some hardcore imprint proto-cols right there. I dunno if — Seven?"

"*AF-FIR-MA-TIVE.*"

"Yeah, she's not so mine anymore."

"Really?" Jay asked with wide eyes, as if hardly daring to believe it.

"Congratulations." She nodded, not seeming at all annoyed that her creation had apparently made up its own mind. "You got a fully functional mechanized therapy and companion animal. I tweaked my usual alloy mix to something a lot more stealth-friendly. She won't stand out like a sore thumb on SkEye's scan-ners — so you in particular should be able to get up to all kinds of fun together.

Nice human choice, Seven." She gave the cat a nod. "Twelve different therapeutic purr frequencies for anxiety, panic, flashbacks — and a full health-scan mode, she can monitor heart rate, blood pressure, body temperature, all that good stuff. And you can probably figure out how to soup her up even more. What else? Oh!" She snapped her fingers. "Wi-Fi hotspot, directly configured to boost your signals and block SkEye's, actually. Enjoy that."

"I will," Jay said in a reverent tone. "This just keeps getting better. And it's not even *my* birthday."

"It does seem like it was kinda meant to be. Oh, but I can totally get rid of the voice-box weirdness if you want, she'll meow just like a bio-kitty."

"Uh, lemme think about that one. I kinda like it the way it is."

"Okay, your call." She shrugged. "I always liked their original voices too, but people always seem to find them creepy. How about fur?"

"Fur is good. Can you do Himalayan?"

"Anything you want. And it won't make you sneeze."

"Thank you, Danae." While Jay petted his new friend with barely contained glee, Stefanos reached out with his non-metal hand and picked one of the bigger chunks of pink icing out of his sister's hair. "We were hoping you'd say that."

"*We* were?"

"I can handle robot cats." He smiled down at Jay, and when he spoke his tone was warm, steady, and free from any of his previous misgivings. "Even cats that talk in…that voice. As long as they make you happy."

"I can't believe we're related when you say stuff like that," she said, but she was smiling. "I could never say that kind of mush with a straight face."

"You can't say anything with a straight face."

"Oh! Damn! Never mind, I see the resemblance."

"All right, focus." Rose sighed, and surveyed the wrecked kitchen. "That's one crisis resolved, onto the next. Next time just remember…dogs chase cats."

"It wasn't Dandy's fault!" Danae protested. "He was just doing what dogs do. But he'd never cause a mess like this, he's a good boy. He would never, ever, not in a million — "

"Take a breath," Stefanos advised as her face began to redden again. "If Toto-Dandy didn't make the mess, what happened?"

Danae opened her mouth — then stopped, an entirely joyless smile spreading across her face. "I'll show you." She bent down and picked up a fist-sized strawberry that had rolled under the kitchen table, then crossed the room, stopping before she reached the doorway that led into a much sunnier and more open space. The next room seemed to contain an indoor forest, thick with hanging vines and explosions of flowers soaking up the pale sunlight filtering through the skylight windows. This was Rose's indoor conservatory, home to around half of the flora that spread throughout their house's in- and exterior, filled to bursting with green life.

She held up a finger for everyone to wait and pay attention, and slowly extended her arm with the strawberry toward the door, standing well away from the threshold. After a few seconds, an enormous leafy head snaked through the doorway at head level with surprising speed, and unhinged a gaping pair of jaws with long, needle-sharp teeth.

"That!" Danae pointed a trembling finger at the snapping, straining giant Venus flytrap as she jumped backwards out of its reach, narrowly avoiding its fangs. "That's what happened. That thing has always hated me, and today it — it *struck!*"

"Oh, Serena," Rose said in a soothing tone, hurrying over to pet the giant head that swayed back and forth on its thick vine-neck, its needle-point teeth dripping a clear liquid onto the linoleum. "Did you get scared too? It's okay now, it's all over."

"She wasn't scared," Danae said in a much more level but no less vehement tone. "She was the one turning everything into her own little kitchen of horrors!"

"Really?" Rose turned back to face her, still petting the giant carnivorous plant and now eyeing Danae with the barest hint of doubt. "Serena made all this mess?"

"She took advantage of the chaos! She waited until you were gone! No, she *lay* in wait, until when everything was quiet, and when you left to find the cat, and I put Dandy in my shop, she — she *struck!*"

"Struck you?" Rose's eyebrows shot up.

"No, the cake! When Jack and I were shutting Dandy in my shop, the monster plant ate it! First she ate the 'Happy' part." Danae tilted her head to stare at the plant's suspiciously smile-shaped mouth. "By the time we got back, she was going after 'Evelyn.'"

"Thank goodness she didn't get her," Jay snickered. "Parole needs its superheroine. Eaten by a giant flower, wh — "

"I'm not done." Danae turned her sharp gaze on him and he shut his mouth immediately. She reached out and grabbed something from the counter that none of them had noticed before amid all the rest of the devastation. It was a small, crumpled white T-shirt, which she shook out to reveal the word 'BIRTH' in bright red. The distorted, dripping letters and spatter all around looked like something right out of a campy horror movie.

"Jack tried," Danae said, starting to look a little dazed again. "I put the cake down on the table while I fought off Serena and he climbed up and tried to protect it. Just like his moms, I guess… instead he fell."

"Poor kid. How's he doing?"

"You know, better than I would. Better than I did, maybe. He's four years old and already cool in a crisis. I dunno if that's good or bad."

"And what a crisis. Gets attacked by a giant plant, falls into his mom's birthday cake — there's something weird and symbolic about that, isn't there? — looks down, his shirt says 'Birth' in creepy bloody murder letters. I dare you to psychoanalyze this, Rose."

"My analysis is," Rose said faintly, gently shooing Serena back into the conservatory, "thank you for not showing that to us until *after* you told us it was strawberry and food coloring, Danae. And I'm so sorry about Serena, I don't know what got into her!"

"Ugh, it's not your fault." Danae dropped the shirt to the countertop again, then sighed and flopped back against it herself, finally exhausted. "Any more than Dandy's mine. At least I could always program him not to chase cats. Not that I'd ever impede on his…never mind. It just happened so fast."

"I know, honey, but hopefully we can get it cleaned up just as…almost as fast!" Rose gave both her shoulders a squeeze. "Evelyn won't be home for a little bit. We can still salvage the evening, you'll — "

"Hello!" Evelyn's voice reached them moments before the sound of the opening door. "If there's any surprises waiting, my eyes are closed!"

"Oh no," Danae whispered as she and Rose stared into one another's eyes and matching expressions of quickly dawning horror.

"Evelyn?" Rose called in an only slightly tight voice, turning around quickly and hurrying down the hallway toward the entrance. "Baby, keep your eyes closed for a second longer!"

"Don't worry, it's not blood!" Danae tried to sound as cheery as possible, but some things would never come out any other way but disturbing. She grimaced as she turned to the potentially terrifying room, frantically pointing at the fallen chairs, strawberries, and the worst smears and stains on the walls and floor. "Help me clean this up!"

"With what?" Jay whispered back as Stefanos shook his head and followed after Rose. After a moment's hesitation, Danae shoved a crumpled white-and-red cloth at him—Jack's stained shirt. But before either of them could continue, Rose returned, and she wasn't alone.

"I promise, we'll have everything cleaned up before you know it, don't worry about a thing," Rose reassured Evelyn as she led her by the hand. "We want you to enjoy tonight, really, we just ran into some…road bumps."

After ten wild, harrowing years in Parole, there wasn't much that could make Evelyn Calliope stare. The magenta-haired superheroine was still in her stage clothes, punk-rock spikes and ruffles making her instantly stand out wherever she went, but especially at home. She had the familiar air of exhaustion and exhilaration that followed a show, and looked like she wanted nothing more than to change into something much more comfortable (with lower heels) and enjoy a quiet evening with family and friends before bed. Or that had been the plan at least. Coming home to find the house looking like a juice-bomb had gone off inside had not been on the night's schedule. She was staring now.

"This…this isn't your surprise," Danae said weakly.

"Well," Evelyn found her voice at last, but still seemed lost for words. "It's still a pretty good one."

"I'm just so sorry," Rose sighed. "This did not go as planned."

"That's an understatement." Danae snorted. "Ev, we suck. If you want to call this whole thing off and go out for pizza or something, we'd understand. This has to be pretty much the most disappointing birthday ever."

"Now that's where you'd be surprised," Evelyn said in a flat, almost deadpan tone, and nothing more.

"I wouldn't," Rose shook her head. "Not with how you grew up."

"I know!" Danae shot an accusatory glare at the remaining "Day" cake. "That's why we wanted so bad to give you something really nice, Ev."

"It's really fine." Evelyn smiled, and after a fraction of a second it looked convincing. She was clearly still processing the shock of this and all other associated birthdays, but like always, she recovered by moving forward. "Let's just get this cleaned up. And—are we waiting on anyone else?"

"No, just us," Stefanos said after the briefest of hesitations, as Rose started picking up the overturned kitchen chairs and Danae went to get a broom from her workshop. Hopefully by now the worst of the icing would be dry enough to just sweep up, though the actual juice and dye stains would be trickier. Unfortunately, her mechanical animals weren't as good at cleaning up food-messes as they were at creating them. "Ash went out on a run, and Rowan doesn't—"

"Doesn't do parties, that's right," Evelyn finished, then turned to Jay before he could add the customary, perfectly-reasonable-in-Parole, but still-somehow-disappointing excuse. "And neither does your runtime partner."

"Hey, you'll meet him! Eventually," Jay said with only the briefest of hesitations. "He can't hide forever. I swear I'll drag him into society one of these days. And I'll even tell you his name! Or better yet, he will."

"I really would like that." Evelyn smiled again, and although it was tired, it looked like it took less effort than her last one. She was starting to regain some equilibrium, and talking about something else, something not quite so close to home, seemed to help. "You've been running together for — what, eight years now?"

"Coming up on it!" Jay never made a habit of hiding his happiness or pride, but he wouldn't have been able to now, even if he tried.

"And in a weird way, he feels like family already. Never seen his face, don't know his name but…" There was a little mischief in her smile now, a glitter in her eye. "I hope I know it before we meet at your wedding."

Stefanos chuckled and went to throw his arm around Jay's shoulders — but he found his usual spot newly occupied by Seven, so he pulled Jay close by the waist instead. "Now is it me, or do you get the feeling she just dropped several hints at once?"

The noise Jay let out wasn't quite words, but wasn't entirely a giggle either. His cheeks flushed a brilliantly deep red, joining the warm palette that seemed to make up this day. "We, um. Haven't picked a date yet."

"We'll let you know as soon as we do," Stefanos said much more serenely as Jay grinned down at the ground, busily adjusting his ponytail. "Wouldn't be right without you there. Or your music, if you were so inclined."

"As if you have to ask," Evelyn said, though there was no mistaking the way her eyes lit up when he did. "I'd be honored. Oh, speaking of — have you asked her yet?"

Evelyn shot a glance across the room at Danae, who looked up, despite not being able to quite hear the exchange. Seeing Evelyn deep in conversation with her brother and his fiancé, she waved and gave a smile that was only mildly laced with suspicion. These misgivings might not have been so quickly confirmed if the three of them hadn't all smiled and waved back exactly at the same time.

"I'm gonna go get Jack," she called, rolling her eyes and heading down the hall-way toward the bedrooms. "He should be done with his present now. Try look-ing more suspicious, guys."

"Not yet." Stefanos shook his head as he watched her go. "Figured you and Rose would want to be there."

"Oh, we will. She's gonna lose it. In the best way, I mean, she'll be thrilled. We all are, but really, she'll just love being a part of this."

"Aw, that's sweet." Jay chuckled, then a look of vague concern slowly crossed his face. "She does know they're just rings, right? Like, they're not supposed to explode or shoot LASER beams or…wait." The concern faded, replaced by curiosity. "Actually, I take it back, could — "

"That'll all come later," Stefanos rumbled, arm still around Jay, but favoring Evelyn with a gaze that was easily read as warm and fond even with metallic eyes. "Tonight is about you, Evelyn. I'm sorry your party turned out to be such a bust."

"I keep telling you guys, it's fine," she repeated, a little more firmly. "If I just get to stand around and talk with my family and friends and not have anything collapse or catch fire, that's still better than around ninety percent of birthdays I've ever had."

"There's looking on the bright side. And hey!" Jay nodded to the single remaining piece of cake, battered but not broken. "No 'Birth,' no 'Happy,' but we still got a 'Day' left."

Knock-knock-knock.

The room immediately fell silent. Everybody stared at the door. Even on party nights, unexpected visitors were rarely a good thing in Parole.

"I thought it was just you two who were coming," Rose said quietly, hurrying over to stand beside Evelyn.

"It was." Stefanos' golden eyes narrowed their targeting focus at the door and he raised his weaponized arm. "Want me to get that?"

"No!" Evelyn shook her head and crossed the room with confident strides, pushing Stefanos' arm down as she went. "Whoever it is, I'm sure they're a friend. And if they're not…they came to the wrong house."

She took a deep, steadying breath, and opened the door.

"I haven't come to the wrong house, have I?"

Garrett Cole stood in the doorway. He wore his customary sequins-and-glitter ringleader's top hat and tails, and a wide smile. In one white-gloved, red-cuffed hand he held a silver platter, and on that rested an ornately frosted, multi-layered red velvet cake, delicate strawberries anchoring each long icing curve.

"Garrett." Evelyn stared at her old friend, as if out of all the bizarre and fantastic things she saw in Parole on a daily basis, this was the most impossible. He was hardly long-lost; they'd seen each other at the Emerald Bar not a full hour ago, and now he was here. "You made it after all."

"I had an opening in my schedule." He gave a disarming little shrug, as if he was every bit surprised to find himself here as she was. He turned to give the cake in his hand a good, evaluating stare, then looked back up at her for approval. "I do hope I'm not too late to save the evening from disaster?"

"It's perfect," she whispered, aware of Rose's gentle touch on her shoulder as she came up to stand beside her, but still feeling caught in a half-dream state. This had to be some kind of birthday miracle. "My favorite."

"I know."

"How?" she marveled.

"If it's happening in Parole, I either caused it or I know about it," he said simply, as if the alternative was a remote afterthought. "Big or small, important or incon-sequential. And this is most definitely…" He extended his arm, and the cake, to-ward Evelyn, who carefully took it, her smile bright and eyes moist. "Important."

"You didn't have to do this. I didn't expect it. Ever."

"I know that too."

It was true. Evelyn hadn't expected it in a million years. But after ten years of Garrett Cole's uncanny and consistent habit of seeing, hearing, and knowing things no ordinary man could, being places he couldn't possibly be, and turn-ing up time and again like a bad penny (or a good friend), maybe by now she should.

"Thank you so much. More than I can say."

"Then don't say anything. Just have a perfect night, and may the best be yet to come." Garrett Cole had many smiles; most of them flashy, showy, and meant to be clearly seen from the back row of a packed house. This slow, gentle one was for her eyes only. "I told you before that if you ever needed anything, I'd be there — and I meant it. I keep my promises."

"Yes, you do. Always have." Evelyn cleared her throat and set the cake down on the kitchen table, taking a moment to collect herself, and a deep breath. When she looked up, her eyes were clear and her smile was bright. "Well, let's get this party started! I couldn't ask for better company — oh! Danae, Jack, look who it is!"

Garrett turned to give the both of them a slight, elegant bow from the waist, which Danae did not return.

"Hey," she said very slowly and carefully, while Jack stared up at the newcomer, eyes wide as he took in the circus-style top hat and tails, and the red and gold shimmering sequins that cast hundreds of tiny lights around the room.

"It's the guy!" Jack said in a hushed whisper, small hands clutching at the not-quite-finished drawing he'd brought with him, just before he remembered to be gentle with it.

"That's right, sweetie." Evelyn nodded. "You've met Mr. Garrett Cole a couple times. He runs the Emerald Bar where I sing, and sometimes he sings with me — and tonight he brought me a cake! What do we say?"

"I knew it!" Jack gave a decisive nod, a grin spreading across his face. As he ran over to the sofa and coffee table in the small living area in front of the kitchen to put the finishing touches on his drawing, he yelled an afterthought over his shoulder. "Thank you!"

Evelyn looked up at Danae, as if repeating the same question she'd asked Jack a moment earlier. Danae stared at the cake with an expression most strangers would have called a poker face. Rose recognized it as a "barely controlled glaring daggers" face, and took a few subtle steps to the side, so she was standing roughly between her and Garrett. "Good cake. Nice present."

"Well, thank you very much," Garrett said in his deep, resonant voice that could move mountains and bring tyrants to their knees when properly applied. "I sincerely hope you all enjoy it. Happy birthday, my darling Strawberry."

"Thank you, Garrett." Evelyn beamed at him. "Now, the first slice is mine, but after that, you're joining us, right?"

"Oh, I do apologize, but I can't stay." Garret shook his head and took a step toward the door. He gave the room at large a nod, but when he tipped his hat, he kept his eyes on Evelyn. "No rest for those who hunt the wicked. Busy night in the city tonight. But I had to at least drop by and wish you all my many happy returns."

"Well, thank you from us too," Rose said, giving Danae a look that went entirely ignored. "You really didn't have to do this."

"Wouldn't dream of missing the occasion," Garrett said smoothly, opening the door and stepping through in a motion just as fluid as his voice. "Now you ladies have a wonderful rest of the evening. Evelyn, I will see you tomorrow night. Gentlemen," He nodded to Stefanos and Jay (and Seven, whose eyes remained fixated on his every shiny, fascinating movement). "Keep up the good work."

"Can't do any other kind," Jay affirmed, raising his cat-free hand to shoot him some metalhead horns. "Uh, sir. Thank you, sir."

TRANSCENDENT 2

"CyborJ, you are more than welcome. Congratulations on your upcoming bliss, to the both of you." Garrett favored them with a bright smile before turning his attention where it always returned: back to Evelyn. "Oh, and one last thing. This arrived at the Bar shortly after you left. I thought I'd better pass it along."

He held up a small black envelope between his third and index finger like a playing card. The thick black wax seal — pressed with an ornate "T" — in the center was surrounded by fine black lace. Evelyn gingerly took the envelope, careful not to tear the delicate paper.

With that, Garrett Cole exited, quietly shutting the door behind him and extinguishing his sequins' glittering lights.

Danae stared at the closed door, face gone very pale under her freckles and lingering streaks of dried strawberry icing. "Ev, your boss is a scary, scary man."

"Oh, I wouldn't say that." Evelyn was still looking after Garrett too, but with a much less suspicious and slightly mistier gaze. "He knows…enough."

"I can't believe he's coming to our wedding." Jay grinned, looking almost dreamy at the prospect. "It was already gonna be the event of the season, because come on, I mean, us getting married, Evelyn Calliope headlining the reception, but yeah, that just put us into Parole annual holiday territory. Good job inviting him!" He leaned fully back against Stefanos, crossing one ankle over the other.

"I didn't invite him," Stefanos frowned, eyes flickering rapidly like an old-fashioned camera's shutter as he thought, then focusing in on Evelyn. "And he didn't say he was coming, he just gave us his best wishes. Ev, did you happen to mention something to him?"

"Hm? No, I was waiting for the okay to start shouting it from the rooftops," Evelyn said absently, still admiring the cake's masterful craftsmanship. "That's just Garrett. He hears things. I wouldn't read too much into it."

"I hate it when he does that. Brrr…" Danae shivered, then nodded at the black envelope, as if glad for any change in subject, even a slightly ominous-looking one. "Wanna open your…weirdly depressing birthday card?"

"Oh!" Evelyn picked it up, careful not to disturb the fine black lace that surrounded the wax seal, or the delicate paper, just barely more substantial than tissue paper. "I almost missed that. Let's see…"

Inside was a single piece of folded parchment much thicker than the envelope itself. The heavy paper itself was almost reminiscent of an ancient scroll, or a historical document one might see on display in a museum behind thick glass. It was blank, except for a single word of elegantly scrawled calligraphy in the center, surrounded by a proliferation of elaborate swirls and loops in gleaming black ink: *REGARDS*.

"Ah." Evelyn nodded with a smile that looked almost fond, but not at all surprised.

"What?" Danae stood up on her tiptoes to look closer over her shoulder, as if there was something about the single word and ostentatious swirls she was missing. "What 'ah'? Who sent that?"

"Who else?"

"Liam." Rose's unusually dry tone made them both look up, hold her gaze for a moment, then stare back down at the elaborate penmanship.

"Jeez, this must've taken an hour." Danae shook her head. "Not even 'happy regards' or anything."

"Happy?" Evelyn laughed. "No. That's not…no."

"You sure it's from him?"

She ran a finger down the thin black lace bordering the wax seal. "Yeah."

"Are you sure your family's last name isn't Addams?" Stefanos' eyes whirred as he focused on the card, briefly flashing green as if scanning it for potential threats. Behind him, Danae shook her head and wandered away, looking as if she'd finally run out of steam.

"Bite your tongue!" Jay scolded through a mouthful of cake; Seven's eyes followed as he waved his fork for emphasis. "The Addams Family are loving, and supportive, and would never…" He glanced up at Evelyn and swallowed, the easier to backpedal apologetically. "I mean, Evelyn, I'm sure your cousin's a fine excuse for… I mean, example of a…"

"More cake?"

"Please, before I make any more brilliant observations."

"You guys just make yourselves at home," Evelyn said, smiling as Jay offered a forkful of cake to the mechanical cat on his shoulder. To her knowledge, none of Danae's creations ate actual food, instead absorbing the toxic vapors and carbon monoxide smoke from Parole's ever-burning fires — but the newly named Seven gave Jay's fork a curious sniff anyway. She'd seen many worse human and therapy animal pairs in the time Danae had been setting them up. "I'll be back in a little bit, just gonna check on someone."

With that, she moved over to where Danae leaned against the wall, head hanging low and pinching the bridge of her nose between her finger and thumb. For a moment neither of them spoke. When Danae looked up and opened her eyes, her smile had the same combination of love and embarrassment she'd worn more today than she could remember. The warm blush in her cheeks joined the other shades of red icing and juice smeared across her cheeks. "Hey, birthday girl."

"Hey." Evelyn joined her in wall-leaning, entertaining a brief memory of high school dances.

"I'll be awake in a second," Danae mumbled, shutting her eyes again. "Just re-charging my batteries real quick."

"I don't blame you. Birthday chaos always takes it out of me too. Especially mine."

"Sorry about…" She slowly tipped her head back against the wall, gesturing to their house and its more-than-passing resemblance to one of Parole's war zone streets. "Everything."

"Like I said…wouldn't be my birthday without a little chaos, would it?"

"Just kinda hoping this year would be different." Danae didn't open her eyes or move. She might have been equal parts exhausted and relieved, but exhaustion weighed a lot more heavily. "You deserve it. You deserve perfect."

"Corny as it sounds, just having family and friends who tried so hard to make it perfect is perfection in itself." Evelyn gently reached out to nudge Danae's arm with one elbow, then took her hand. "Even after ten years, you don't really for-get what it feels like to go from not having that to…"

"I know." Danae opened her eyes halfway, giving Evelyn's hand a squeeze. "With your…everything you grew up with? That's why I want every year with us to be different. I just — God, everything you do for Parole, and for us, every day? For one day, that's what we want to do for you, or at least try to come close. Just give you everything you never got, and should have."

"That right there?" The sigh Evelyn let out wasn't exhausted, but maybe more contented than she'd felt all year. "You wanting me to have a perfect day and fighting to make it happen? That's why it already is."

"You're right. It does sound corny." Danae shook her head, laughing. "But you're so freaking sweet I don't even care, and I already sounded way cornier — God! You and Rose both turn me into the biggest sap. Guess that's how you know I'm in love. Anyway!" She pushed herself away from the wall. "Less mush, more party. Want some cake?"

"Sure do. Bet it's great even without strawberries."

"The hell you talking about, Garrett brought a crap ton of strawberries, be-cause of course he did…" Danae looked up fully to see Evelyn smiling back at her. "Oh my gosh. Really? You actually want my smushed, ruined, flytrap-eaten disaster?"

"I want your everything. Besides, you heard Jay. Even without 'Happy' or 'Birth,' we still got a 'Day' left." She hesitated. "It didn't actually fall on the floor or anything, did — "

"No!" Danae insisted, as if swearing on her last remaining honor and everything she held dear. "I protected that thing with my life. That's your birthday present, Ev, one of 'em. I'd take a bullet for it, I'd battle an army — Serena's wily, she got the jump on me, that's all. Never again." She blew out a breath through loose lips like a horse, messy crumb-filled hair flying. "Outsmarted by a plant. Amazing."

"Hey, like you said, she's mean, green, and crafty…" Evelyn reached out and plucked an entire intact berry out of Danae's hair. "And maybe out for revenge for her little friends."

"No way." Danae shook her head, dislodging a couple more leaves. "Now you're just making stuff up."

"Seriously, did you ask first? Rose always talks to her plants — not just 'hi, pretty flowers' way, but 'excuse me, I need exactly twelve berries, I apologize for the discomfort, I'll give you some of the extra good fertilizer later, thank you.' I dunno if it's just a Rose thing, making deals with the shrubbery, but…it couldn't hurt."

Danae remained silent for a few seconds, staring at the strawberry in Evelyn's hand. "I will apologize to Serena," she said, sounding half-dazed, half-enlightened. "And when I am done making amends to a giant plant that hates me, I am going to take a very long nap."

"Sounds good, you earned it." Evelyn chuckled. "Oh! But first… Did you say that the cake was only *one* of my birthday presents? If I wasn't supposed to hear that, don't worry. I have a very convincing 'joyful surprise' face."

"I know," Danae said as a slow, devilish smile spread across her face. "I've seen it. And don't worry. Part two comes later. When the three of us are alone."

"My favorite kind of surprise. Mmm, you, me, and Rose…" Evelyn grinned to match now. "I don't care how the rest of the day goes if it ends with the three of us in each others' arms."

"You mean the four of us. I've been thinking, and I bet I can come up with a way to make it up to Serena *and* give you a sexy present all at once." Danae held her gaze, all decisive planning and steady resolve — for around a second. Then the snort was too much to hold in, much less keep a straight face. "Surprise!"

"You're ridiculous."

"You love me."

"I do." Evelyn pulled her close, first kissing the top of her head, smearing crumbs and icing all over her own face, then her lips. Danae tasted exactly as sweet as she expected. "I really do."

A small distance away, Rose sank down into the overstuffed couch cushions and watched and listened to her wives relax and celebrate in their own, quietly doing the same in her own. From here she could see Jack putting the finishing touches on his drawing from this morning. Nearby, Jay smiled when Stefanos held out his synthetic hand for Seven to sniff, then laughed when she started licking his fingers, rough metal tongue giving off tiny sparks. He pulled the big man down into a deep kiss, then started speaking words she couldn't hear. Or begin to guess at. She couldn't imagine what it would take to make Stefanos blush like that. But then, CyborJ was supposed to know every secret in Parole…

Steel feet up and the rest of her surrounded by soft pillows, Rose finally let herself breathe easy. No cake (she didn't care if she never saw it ever again after today, quite frankly), no stress, and for a little while, no problems. She'd be awake again in time for that surprise later, after their guests had gone and Jack was in bed, but right now she was content to bask in the glow of a job extremely well done.

And a house that would need a serious day of cleaning tomorrow. But that could wait. It could all wait.

"Hey, sweetie," she whispered to Jack as he set down his crayon and began to study his drawing, four-year-old face serious and focused in intense scrutiny. "Is your present ready?"

"Mm-hmm!" Jack quickly pushed it into her hands, folding his small arms and looking up at her expectantly.

Rose smiled and looked down at the drawing — then her smile froze.

There was the strawberry cake in the middle of the paper, right where it had been this morning. But now someone was holding it.

A man. Wearing a top hat with a wide brim. Red sparkles drawn all over the wide, pointed collar. Gold. White gloves. Red cuffs. His smile stretched almost to the edges of his face. The lines were elaborate, not just in detail but with crosshatch shading, hundreds of red and gold stars and circles to represent sequins and glitter. No four-year-old Rose had ever seen drew at this level, but that in itself wasn't what made Rose shiver.

"This is so beautiful," she said when she could keep the tremble out of her voice. "Mama Ev's gonna love it. When did you find the time to draw this, baby? With the cake and Toto-Dandy and everything?"

"Right after you left," he said proudly, smiling. "I was quick. I almost got done!"

"You're getting so good," Rose said, staring at the man whose sharp smile she recognized, no matter how distorted. The truth was staring her right in the face. It could only be Garrett Cole. "Why don't you go grab your moms — we can show her together."

"Okay!" He hurried off, and Rose hurried to find her center before she had to think very fast and explain yet another potentially ominous wrinkle in their lives.

But she did find it. After just a few deep breaths, Rose could smile again, and mean it. That was the nice thing about feeling safe and surrounded by unconditional love; it was always easier than expected to leave the gnawing fear behind.

Rose looked up as Jack hurried back, pulling his other two mothers by their hands, and resolved not to let gnawing fear or ominous possibilities ruin this night. Danae and Evelyn welcomed her with open arms and berry-sweet kisses, and Rose forgot her worries in moments. Everything else seemed so small. Vague feelings of foreboding, chaotic days of hungry giant plants and runaway cats — it could wait. Just like the house cleaning, everything else could wait.

Tonight belonged to Evelyn, and the people she chose to share her life with. They could take a moment for themselves to simply be together and celebrate their lives together, the ones they loved, and the fact that they were all still here for one more year. Like the stains on the floor and the crumbs in the carpet, all the complications would be there when they got back.

Parole never stopped being Parole. Not even for a day.

TRANSCENDENT 2

THE WAY YOU SAY GOOD-NIGHT

◄ Toby MacNutt ►

I moved in with the goddess in spring, after a month and a half of cautious emailing and coffee shop conversations. She had placed an ad in the classifieds: "Seeking housemate: 2br bungalow, countryside, owner occupied. Artists, writers, LGBTQ, introverts welcome. Quiet hours & amiable presence a must; mutual support preferred." The rent was reasonable, utilities were included, and the explicit mention of queers and introversion intrigued me. Mutual support sounded nice, but I had my reservations.

We emailed, and emailed, and finally in April met. I didn't notice straightaway. She hadn't said, in her ad or in her emails, and she wore her strangeness subtly — I'm not sure how I would have responded, either, which I guess is why she didn't mention. Everything odd about *me*, on the other hand, is right there on the surface. Even the most sheltered of country-mice could probably recognize my queerness, marked as it is in my name and hair and clothing, even inked into my skin. I don't hide it and I never have. You can read my disability in my body now, too, without much effort. It was hidden once, camouflaged, but it has accumulated visible accessories: the splints, the sticks, the wheels. And most of the time now, I don't try to hide the pain. I'm up-front about it. Her bungalow was single-story, step-free; that had been the first question I asked.

Her name was Arielle — "call me Ari" — and she was a slight, unassuming woman. Dark hair framed her pale face; a tousled sort of look, just beginning to grow out from a short crop, maybe. She cradled her mocha to her chest, and kept her hands around the mug even after it was empty. In her emails her tone had been formal, reserved; in the coffee shop, she looked nervous — her narrow shoulders tensed tight, her eyes not quite finding mine, she'd picked a shadowed corner — but her voice was even, low and velvety. We talked about the vacancy. It sounded perfect.

She asked to meet again. Spring was burgeoning; the sun was out at last, and the pale blue of winter skies had just begun to deepen into one a little more succulent. The sunlight was still watery, but warm enough that the breezes couldn't steal its heat. Ari was inside, despite the fine weather, and tucked into a corner once again. The sunlight didn't quite seem to reach her. As she leaned from her niche to hail me, her hair swung forward and I did a double-take. It was past shoulder-length, curling over itself. It had been short, last time, I was sure — or maybe just pulled back, I supposed, some kind of messy and unobtrusive up-do.

"Thanks for meeting me. Sorry for all the runaround, but, I just need to be careful, you know?"

"It's all right, better safe than sorry, I know." I settled in.

She drew a deep heavy breath. "I feel pretty good about you. I think we'd do okay living together. But," and she hesitated, hands tight around a mug she'd emptied before I arrived, "I haven't been entirely honest with you, there's something I still need to tell you."

I felt myself guarding — my belly tensed, my shoulders pulled forward. "Okay…"

"And I guess part of why I think we'd be okay is, I think you might understand. I hope. So — all right. The thing is, what I need you to know is — I'm not quite normal. You know I'm a night person? There's a reason, I was born with an aspect. Night-aspect, particularly."

I relaxed. "Is that all?"

She startled, clearly surprised. "…yes?"

"Not so different, I don't think." I shrugged. "I'm a mutant of sorts, and queer, and I haven't found a gender that fits. We aren't the same shapes, you and I, but we both got made with odd molds, and we're living with what that means." I could see her evaluating this statement, suspiciously, slowly coming to terms with the fact that someone might say that and mean it. I guess acceptance had been rare for her; that's people for you. But this wasn't the first coming-out I'd been privy to, and goodness knows I'm strange enough in my own way. Aspects aren't that different from mutations, just less well-understood, and carrying baggage of prophecy more so than medicine, though our histories twine some there, too — in visionaries, the possessed, those who spoke in tongues; those who were seen as crazy, malingering, fraudulent. And they're still so rare, even now. I'd never met one, not knowingly.

"You're sure? That doesn't bother you?"

"Does it bother you that some days I can walk and some days I can't? Or that strangers on any given day might address me alternately as 'sir' or 'ma'am'?" She shook her head. "Then, no, I'm not bothered. Does it affect what it's like to live with you? Just to be practical about it. I don't know much about the everyday life of aspects."

"I wax and wane, a bit. Night tends to stick to me. I don't sleep much… Really, it changes, over the course of the year. It's stronger in winter, when it's dark so much. Summer's easy, almost like being normal, I think."

I shrugged again. "Sounds less eventful than some basic-human roommates I've had."

So I moved in with the goddess — with Arielle, not a goddess, not really, but a woman of night — in May.

Summer evenings were easy. Ari got a duskiness about her as the sun kissed the horizon each night; not a blush or a glow, but something between the two, a quiet liveliness. It was a good time of day to tackle her unruly shadows, as they lengthened. Our back porch looked out westwards, toward sunset. She sat on the deck to watch the sun go down, a glow in her eyes and darkness streaming behind her, while I sat with her, combing shadows out of her hair. Left ungroomed, they coiled up in the bottom of the bath or balled up in corners, leading to stopped drains and stubbed toes and missteps — dark, tricky little dust bunnies. They stuck to her; it was hard for her to separate her shed shadows from her fingers, but easy for me, with my mundane human hands. I liked the task. It had a simple intimacy, and we chatted or sat in sunset quiet as I worked.

Other than shadow-combing, she was particular about touch; I noticed the care she took to avoid bumping into anyone if we were out and about, and she rarely touched me directly, either. But how much would one touch a housemate, anyway?

Not long after the solstice, I asked her about her hair. Not the shadows — those seemed self-evident, an element of her aspect — but its inconstant length. It had been short again when I moved in, grown down to her low back by late May, and then just — *diminished*, down to a pixie-cut length, barely there. At the end of June it was long again, full of shadows easily tangled.

TRANSCENDENT 2

"It's a moon thing," she said. "The shadows get stronger when the moon's dark. It's sort of the same inside, I guess, I feel it more, but you see it in my hair. Less right now, because it's midsummer. There's so much light all the time."

"Will that change? This winter?"

"Yeah, it's a bit more…dramatic."

"Well, god help us if our cycles sync, then, huh?" I chuckled. "Do yours match the moon, just sort of — automatically?"

She shifted uneasily, and I cringed inwardly. I'd fucked up; been too cavalier, too intrusive. And presumptive. I forget sometimes that even people raised female get uncomfortable talking about menstrual cycles, and of course not everyone who reads as "female" has one — I know better than that. Or I should. "I'm sorry, I shouldn't have said anything, if it's uncomfortable for you…"

"No, it's — I'm just, I don't," she gestured vaguely around her belly, "I don't cycle like that. I don't bleed, I'm not built like you."

"To be fair, most people aren't." I grinned wryly. "I am not exactly factory standard." That earned a smile, to my relief. "I'm sorry if it's a sore topic for you, though. It's a personal thing, I shouldn't have asked. Or assumed."

"Oh, it's a source of embarrassment long past… I just don't talk about it much, so everyone just assumes. It was hard, as a teenager, but these days I don't think I miss it."

"You can have mine, if you like. I've often thought I'd give it up happily, to a trans woman or someone else who'd appreciate it."

Ari chuckled. "No, really, I'm fine. Shadows are enough as it is!"

Conversation moved on, and she relaxed again.

Sometimes conversation would happen that way. It had something of a pattern to it: I'd bumble into some unique element of her aspect, some difference, without knowing; she'd explain, nervously at first, then more confidently. I shared what I could about myself, in return; sometimes she'd be the accidentally awkward one. It got easier for us both as time went on. She saw me walk on two legs or three or four or none; she saw me whirling with activity and flattened by fatigue. She heard about ex-boyfriends, ex-girlfriends, ex-queer lovers of all stripes, in triads and quads. She saw me in ties and dresses and heels and faux sideburns. The strange and fluid things about me I had writ large, exaggerated in preemptive self-defense; Ari lived hers close and quiet. Both were paths we'd chosen to keep us safe in a world where we had never quite fit.

We talked about change: both of us seem mercurial to the outside eye, in flux, maybe even unstable. But there's a constancy to each of us, internally — a familiar, intrinsic pattern, albeit a complex one. I don't even *like* change, as a rule. Surprises make me anxious; unexpected alterations to my environment set me on edge. I make my plans in advance, and it takes me ages to learn and remember new things. I was still asking Ari for reminders of our mailing address come July.

We built routines together. She picked up my morning blackberry-sage tea habit; I joined her for sunsets. We read poetry, swapped our favorites. I started noticing the moon. Our conversations and our silences alike grew easier, over the summer months. Brooding dust bunnies and all considered, I'd never had an easier roommate.

One day in early September I came home cheery, humming to myself. The sun was ripe and golden and the trees were just beginning to turn, punctuating the waves of green with little bursts of autumnal color. The living room was dim, though. Ari was balled up in the corner of the couch, looking quietly miserable.

"Hey." I sat down next to her. She barely moved. "You okay?"

"No." Well. Okay. That had been self-evident.

"What's wrong? Want to talk about it?"

There was a long pause — I wanted to reach out to her, stroke her back or offer her some sort of comfort, some companionship. But she did not ever touch, and I wasn't sure if I'd help, or hurt.

Slowly, she spoke. "It'll be worse soon. The winter, it'll be dark this year, I can tell, and I hate the change. So cold."

"But it's not here yet, right?"

"Soon. Equinox in two weeks, and the moon's going dark."

"That's all right... We'll figure it out, okay?"

She hunched further. "You won't want to be here for that. I should just stay away, be alone. Nobody wants the winter-dark." I could hear tears unshed in her voice, and my heart ached.

"We'll cross that bridge when we get there, huh? After all, my lease runs till spring!" It was not a good attempt at levity. "We'll figure it out, okay?" Silence, a tiny nod. "Hey. I don't know, exactly, but you look like you could use a hug. Would you like a hug? No pressure."

She started to move toward me, shifting in place, and then froze, eyes wide. I saw her eyes track my shoulders and my arms, bare — I was taking advantage of late summer while it lasted, enjoying the days of tank tops, sun-kissed skin. I heard a tiny whisper, just barely audible. "I can't."

"That's okay. No pressure, all right? But the offer's good anytime, if you need it."

She shook, a little, sniffling; I could see the tension in her, trying to pull toward and away all at once. I sat back a little distance, to give her space.

"No — please. Stay?"

"Of course." So I sat nearby, quietly, trying to exude a grounded calm. "It's okay, Ari, really it is." A few quiet breaths. "Would you like me to talk to you?" She shook her head, so I just stayed there near her, quiet together.

She shifted again in a few minutes, just the tiniest fraction of movement. I saw it, and read it; my own body has taught me the importance of little, hard-won movements. She'd moved, barely, but moved, a little bit more upright, a little bit nearer, just the adjustment maybe of one or two vertebrae, a twitch of the shoulder. I could hear her breathing shallowly, and swallowing hard.

"I want to," she said, in that tiny whispering voice.

"Yeah?"

"But I *can't*," and she cried, and it took everything in me not to gather her up into my lap and hold her close.

"Why, honey? What's wrong?"

"It'll hurt."

"You? Or me?"

"You — I can't hurt you, I can't hurt anyone, I can't." She sobbed.

"Hey. Hey, deep breaths, all right?" I stroked her hair, mid-long now, and her back through her shirt beneath her hair. Just like shadow-combing. Nothing happened to me, and in a few minutes I felt her relax a little, slowly. She breathed a little more evenly, and I breathed with her. "You're okay. I'm okay, all right? See, nothing bad happened."

"No, it's just — skin to skin."

"What happens? You don't have to tell me, if you don't want."

"It burns. That's what they told me. It burns, and the night comes."

I managed not to raise an eyebrow, but I was powerfully curious. "The night comes?"

"Around us. My night."

"And burns?"

"I don't know, they said it burns. Mustn't touch." She curled tighter, fists tucked close to her chest.

Ari was possibly the least threatening person I'd ever known, but she'd not been well-loved. And my life had left me deeply distrustful of any "they" who would castigate or shame. I weighed my risks. Pain was, after all, not unfamiliar to me. "Can I try? You need a hug."

She shook, stifling sobs, and I stroked her back. She bit her lip and nodded, two tiny, sharp nods — so I reached for her, and gathered her up.

And yes, it *burned*. It was an electric type of pain, like a static shock that persisted, roaming over my arms; maybe a bit like lightning. But it was a cold pain, like that feeling of meltwater that comes when a nerve is misfiring. Chilled, prickling pain, a freezer-burn. I could feel her skin against mine, where her cheek and ear and wrists rested against my own arms and shoulders, but just barely. The touch of her hardly registered, and she seemed to carry no heat. My skin was stippled with goosebumps; my hair stood on end. I shivered, breath hissing, and heard her sob a helpless apology. But I had known worse pain. I held her, tried to make sure I had her safely encircled, before I went numb, so I would hold her, not drop her —

And then the night came.

The living room faded. I worried I was blacking out, at first — but I could still see Ari, cradled in my arms, shadows gently spooling from her. She seemed to sink into me, as if she weren't quite solid. All around her, night blossomed. It wasn't the pitch-black of midnight, but an earlier, gentler time of night, not long after sundown. The ceiling was shrouded with a blanket of indigo, and where the baseboards ought to have been there was just a thin line of pale gold, the last vestiges of daylight. Between gold and indigo was a whole delicious peacock gradient — pale bleached silver, teal, sea-green, cobalt. The floor was carpeted in long, lush shadows. I thought I heard crickets, and I could almost smell the summer-baked earth releasing its heat into the cool sky, could almost feel the soft breezes of evening.

I had not noticed that I was holding my breath. I let it out in a rush. It joined the sighing in the air, the cricket chirps — it became illusory. I could not feel my arms, or my shoulders, spiraled now with shadowstuff. I didn't care.

But my numbed grip slowly slipped, and Ari shifted away, legs draped over my lap but upper body nestled back into the couch. As her touch faded, so did the night, and the cold. I came to blinking into the late afternoon light, my arms and shoulders prickling all over in cascades of shivering pins-and-needles.

TRANSCENDENT 2

Ari held her face in her hands, slowly trying to part her fingers, to look back at me. Muffled, she said, "I'm sorry — are you okay? I just, I'm sorry, I can't help, I shouldn't have let you. I'm sorry."

I shook my head, still clearing dark spots from my vision. Shadows fell from me. My tongue felt heavy. "No, honey." I tried again. "Arielle. That was *beautiful*."

"…really?"

I nodded, slowly.

"And you're — are you okay? You're not angry?"

"I'm okay. It hurt, but. Not *all* that badly, and it was — it was like being there." I tried to shake my fingers out, get the blood moving enough to massage the rest of me back to life. It was slow going, and the reawakening of cold-pinched nerves is never pleasant. "Are you always this cold? How do you keep from freezing?"

"I think so? I don't know. Oh, you're cold — I'll make tea."

We watched the sun set with tea warm in our hands, blankets wrapped snug around us. The sky was perfect and clear, from golden horizon to indigo vault, sprinkled with stars.

After the equinox, night fell earlier and earlier, and earlier still inside our house. She didn't sleep most nights, only napping at midday. Some nights she'd go out, especially the windy ones, the wild ones, and come home around dawn, starry-eyed, shadows writhing. As the days shortened and the air chilled, my body started to constrict into its winter limits. I went out less and less. I walked less, just around the house, and then not at all. Ari would bring me back tales of the evening. She told me about the different ways the nights could feel: the kind that felt wide-open to the void of space, the kind that were closed-in to near claustrophobia. The difference between half- and quarter-moonlight, the taste of the air before dawn, the scent of impending snow. If the night were fine, and I were awake when she came home, sometimes she'd touch me, just briefly, to share the vigor of her aspect as it grew into its winter-dark force.

It hurt — but what didn't?

We spoke a lot about the nature of pain, its many qualities, its roles and significance. We laid out the poetry of it — the beauty, even, for the right pain from the right source. Not just in a kinky way, but the pleasure of the heartache in a favorite novel's tragedy, or loving to the point of bursting. We talked about its ugly sides, yes, those too, but also about the way its character changes, if you have it long enough as a bedfellow. It was a relief, to me, to speak freely. And when I did hurt, she was perhaps more prepared.

TRANSCENDENT 2

She shared fewer nights as the winter drew in; her touch bit too sharply. Sweeping the shadows from her hair became nearly impossible around new moons: the shadows were so fierce, and just being near her scalp left my fingers tingling, inept. I lose dexterity anyway, as winter comes. The cold sinks into my knuckles and freezes their motion. We were both cold, swathed constantly in thermals and armwarmers and fuzzy socks and shawls.

The first truly bad day of winter came for me on a new-moon day. Her new moon, *and* mine; statistics won out, it had been likely enough.

I couldn't get out of bed. I could barely think. I keep pain meds in my nightstand, for just such occasions, but as is often the case in winter's vise-grip, they were little help. My tendons were seized with cold, and my bones ached and shivered, slipping between the taut threads of panicked muscles. My gut wrenched. I felt like I was vibrating, subtly and off-key. I had no room for thought. Ari found me that way, in midafternoon, when she realized I hadn't gone out but hadn't been seen.

"Why didn't you call to me? Or text, if you couldn't shout! I didn't know you were here!"

I mumbled some sort of excuse. The reality is that pain makes it hard to use logic. It makes it hard to make plans, even plans to make things better. And pain is a lonely experience: it makes it hard to reach out.

She frowned at me. "I'll be right back." She vanished, and I could hear puttering from the kitchen, quick crossings of the house. The kettle boiled, and boiled again; the toaster dinged. She came back with a hot water bottle, and a cup of tea, and some toast. "Extra sugar in your tea, and peanut butter for your toast. I bet you haven't eaten today, have you?"

No, of course I had not. And I could not sit up. I tried, and whimpered, and curled back up again, pulling the hot water bottle close. Ari left.

I sank into further despair, and loneliness, and embarrassment at my own ineptitude — how many people had my pain driven away? But she came back. Beneath her winter layers she'd put on a pair of gloves, dark velvet, ones I'd never seen. She'd pulled her hair back — enormously unruly, shadow-rampant, new-moon hair — into a stark, tight-bundled knot. "I should be safe enough, now. I'll help you sit up so you can eat, okay?"

And she slid one wool-and-velvet arm beneath my shoulders, slowly, slowly rocked me to her chest, and rolled me far enough to pillow-prop me, supported at knees and back and elbows, just like I would have done. Not a single shadow fell against my skin.

TRANSCENDENT 2

Winter marched on, and with a little care, we marched with it. We turned up the heating, made cookies, drank oceans of tea. I tried to teach her how to knit; shadows inevitably tangled up with her yarn, to her consternation and our mutual chuckles. I thought we were getting the hang of winter — we had churned through its first two moons, and my first snow-linked flares. The sun dazzled on the snowbanks, and the cottage was well-sited for natural light. The house glowed bright. We stayed warm, and kept our spirits up.

As the days darkened, Ari drifted further into her aspect. Sometime in December she stopped sleeping altogether, and faded around the edges. I don't mean that metaphorically. She faded, like the light couldn't quite touch her. If she stood in silhouette against a window at night, she'd be missing entirely. At the height of midday, in snow-glare, she seemed pale and drawn; she could barely focus. But she came alive at night, in the long hours of darkness that just made me want to hibernate. It seemed like a positive thing for her at first. She had energy in her, crackling, though cold. She burned through projects. The house was clean. I envied her energy; winter is a lull time for me.

But it wore on her, and as we sank further into December, I began to worry. Night-aspect she may be, but she still lived in a mostly-human body, and that body couldn't keep up. She was exhausted, but her body roared at her through the night and kept her up shakily through the day. She barely ate; she shivered, constantly, couldn't get warm despite her layers. "Just gotta make it through the solstice," she mumbled to me, when I asked after her. I had to coax her to sit still enough to wrangle her hair, but I couldn't stay ahead of it, even so. Shadows littered the floor.

Neither of us had family worth celebrating with, so we spent our winter holidays together. It seemed to make sense to observe the solstice. I cooked us a meal, with what help Ari could give. We sat up through the night together, a fire burning in the grate: light would return. In lieu of gifts, we treated ourselves to chocolate and winter-expensive fresh fruit. I breathed a sigh of relief when the sun finally, finally rose. The light was insubstantial, ethereally bare, and Ari's face was a study in chiaroscuro: a few light-grazed planes sharp against dark hollows. Nonetheless, relief.

But solstice ran straight into a waning moon. Ari's winter-dark didn't ebb. She had always been slim and was now painfully thin; the nights were eating away at her. Unprotected bony prominences bruised as she knocked into door frames and cabinets, rendered as clumsy as I would be on my feet, at this time of year. If

I spoke to her she answered slowly, after a long pause, as if from far away. The velvet voice was now ragged, raven-hoarse.

The day before the new moon would rise, I moved through the silent house alone but for the sound of my wheels. The few extra moments of sun earned back since the solstice didn't do much to offset the overall environment of grays. The snow was dingy, and the sky bleak. Ari was nowhere to be seen. I hoped she'd finally found her way into a nap, but as the sun sank, I still didn't hear her stir — and she hadn't slept in sundown hours for weeks and weeks.

I had been in her room only once, maybe twice. She liked it dark, and private. Her door was often shut. I knocked at it, carefully; no response. I was worried enough to try the handle. I found it unlocked, so I cracked the door, just a hair. Darkness billowed out in a wave. It pushed me back, and I grabbed my wheels to fight against it. It rushed like a tide, a great outpouring of night. I couldn't see in, at all.

"Ari?"

The dark air settled still and cold, puddling around me like the draft from under a door. I could feel the chill tug at my bones and clench around my heart; I almost thought her window must be open, letting in the frigid night air. It had that sharp smell of cold about it, too. I heard nothing.

I felt my way in, trying to remember the layout of her room — bookcase to the right, a desk somewhere, left maybe?, bed under the window at the far side. I found her chair, empty. There were clothes across the floor. I felt each thing carefully as I moved, tried not to roll over anything, hoping she wasn't collapsed below me. I called again, a little louder, a little more worried. "Ari? Are you in here?" She *must* be — the night was so concentrated.

I couldn't see, still, but I could hear: just a little sound, a small sound, shallow. Breathing. With difficulty, but there. I followed it till I ran into her bed, and I walked my fingers across her mattress, looking for her.

She was so cold. My fingers numbed, and I thought for a moment I must have laid my hand on her skin, but no, the texture was wrong, nubbled. A blanket, or a sweater, with a long bony limb inside, an arm's length from the edge of the bed — probably curled up against the wall, beneath the windowsill. She liked edges, and corners.

I levered myself up and out of my chair onto her bed, feeling for her. "Ari? Ari, I'm here. Can you hear me?" I found her, identified hip and shoulder, head with its tangled mass of hair. Somewhere there should be blankets; I found them. I curled around her, tucking her little bird-boned body to mine, pulling blankets around us, talking the whole time, trying to keep my voice calm. She didn't stir. I could feel her breathing, just barely, against my chest — and she was so cold. She shook like a leaf. To accidentally graze her skin, this cold in this darkness, made nearly no sensory change; I was lost, lost and numb, just as she was. We were so cold, and it was so dark, so dark and so cold. No moon. No stars. No sun. Lost. Lost, winter-dark.

I startled — had I been dozing? I was too cold even to shiver. We had to get warm. I couldn't lift her to move her, and I wasn't sure it would do anything, anyway; her dark stuck to her. And the heating was on: it was working fine in the rest of the house. It just wasn't enough, here. What had they taught me in first aid, so many years ago, for hypothermia? It seemed so far away. So hard to remember: bright and smiling, trips to the woods, summer hikes. Dark, now. Cold. Hypothermia: right. You had to heat the core. Get the cold things away.

"Ari," and my voice was raven-ragged now too, cold-constricted. I coughed. "Ari, I don't know if you can hear me. I'm going to touch you, okay? See if I can get us warm." It might have been a stupid plan, but it was my only plan. I tried to flex my cold-stiff fingers and found them seized, had to tug claw-handed at the layers between us. I shifted most of my own layers — everything over my core — wriggling awkwardly, wincing at the cold. Hers were harder; I had to lift her a bit, rock, tug, trying to make sense of what I couldn't see with hands that barely felt. I pulled anything else I could reach, be it blanket or towel or clothes, over the two of us. I did what I could, and when I couldn't shift anything more, I braced myself, and spooned up to her.

Where her back touched my belly, it *burned*. I choked and whimpered, trying not to spasm, trying keep my calm. I could feel a deeper cold spread through me, seizing my limbs, spearing them with icy shards. The pain burst in my bones. I was pinioned and perforated with cold; I could barely breathe. I numbed slowly, frozen, deadened. Any night I saw was indistinguishable from what already surrounded us. I could do nothing but hold her, in silence, for a while; I might have dozed off again, I'm not sure. When I could, I talked to her, teeth chattering, brain as frozen as the rest of me.

Aeons passed.

Her trembling stopped. I didn't realize immediately. Everything hurt, a deep cold ache, nerves burning, but I could feel most of me again, and could feel her stillness. I panicked, first, thinking I'd lost her, but she was still breathing. "Good," I said. I hoped. "Good. Still here with me?"

I must have slept a little, then, because when I next opened my eyes, I could tell I had done so. There was light. Not much, hardly anything, but there was light; it wasn't from the window, just a general sort of diffuse, barely-there glow. Watery, colorless. I looked at Ari. I could see the shapes of her, just barely, dim static against the darker shadows — not so much like seeing where she was, but seeing spaces where darkness was not.

Next time I opened my eyes, I looked for the light. There was enough of it to try to find a source — it wasn't from any fixture, and there was still no daylight at the window. It seemed to be beneath her, maybe by her belly. It moved as I craned to look over her shoulder, and I realized: it was coming from me. Anywhere my skin touched hers, it seemed to be pricked with the tiniest of lights, the most distant of stars. And I thought I could feel heat, between us, between our skins. Not much, nowhere near blood-heat, but it wasn't nothing.

She stirred in my arms and I opened my eyes again. The room was dawn-grey; I could see now the window shade light-limned, and Ari's sharp, fine features. She blinked slowly, found her hand in mine, my chest at her back, my head at her shoulder. "Wh-what?"

"Shhh. It's okay, Ari, we're okay..."

"But you're — are you?" Her brow furrowed into ridges of light and shadow. "Are you glowing?"

"Uhhh." I looked. "I would seem to be, yes. I thought I imagined it." It looked like the warmer light of true dawn had caught the edges of me. The little star-specks were denser where we touched, but had spread a ways, as well.

"Oh," she said. "That's nice," and she fell back asleep. Her steady breathing lulled me, and I slept, too.

When we woke for real, night still played over the ceiling and tangled our hair, but dawn nestled around us. I hurt, everywhere. I always hurt in the morning, but a night cold and frightened and unmoving hurt all the more. I groaned as I moved. I could feel the efforts of the heating system, through our haphazard cocoon of blankets and laundry, though the room was still unpleasantly cold. Ari, by contrast, felt warm.

"Is it morning?" she asked.

"Yes, or gone morning, already, maybe."

"How long were you here?"

"All night." She looked at me, her face puzzled. I blushed, and tugged layers back over myself. As soon as I broke skin contact, my stars faded away. "You didn't come out at sundown, so I came looking…and you were so dark and cold, I hope I did the right thing."

"How? How are you here? How did you stay?"

"I-I don't know?"

"Thank you," she said, and covered my hand with hers. Shadows swirled, and despite myself I shuddered as a chill swept up my arm. But as her hand moved, tiny stars bloomed and closed in its wake. "I've never had stars, before," she said, sounding shy. "And nobody's ever — gone into the night with me. Like that. Thank you."

She made tea, and I laid a fire, and we warmed up slowly in the weak winter sun.

I stayed with her the next few nights of darkened moon, with a hot water bottle and post-holiday-sale electric blanket for backup. She slept the night through easily. Always, by morning, my touch was dawn-lit. "I don't know," she said. "My aspect has never infiltrated somebody else before; I don't think it's supposed to work like that."

"Who knows? You are a mystery."

"Though nobody ever — nobody else ever tried."

"I'll try everything once, and probably twice, in case the first time was a fluke. You know me."

"I do. And I'm glad."

When the next new moon came, she asked for me. It would be an easier one — the days were slowly lengthening, after all, fraction by fraction. I held her, and we were a comfort to each other. A shy one, a quiet one, and admittedly a somewhat dark and chilly one, but a comfort, nonetheless. The cold and my bones grew no friendlier with each other, but kindling stars in my skin seemed to give me a buffer, a little. Or maybe it was just a placebo effect, helped along by its own beauty and that basic human need for touch — either way, it helped. The next moon I volunteered, starting from the waning quarter, and I stayed.

She kissed me for the first time in March, at the equinox. I had asked her if the night she saw — or felt, or showed, I wasn't sure of the word — with her aspect was always the present night, that current night. She thought it over for a moment.

"I think I can find a night-memory instead? I've never tried. Mostly people don't see them on purpose. Should I try to show you?"

TRANSCENDENT 2

"Sure. How about a nice summer one, maybe? Mild and warm." I was jesting, somewhat.

"All right. I know one that…okay. Ready?" and she leaned over, and in one motion, cupped my cheek and kissed my mouth.

Cold burst on my lips, but not the burning ache of winter-dark; this was a summery cool, just starting to crisp up into autumn, damp and tingling. I recognized the night that stretched across the living room — I'd seen it here, just five months prior. The cobalt sky, the light-limned horizon, the perfect dome of a clear September twilight.

I melted into her kiss — strange, to kiss someone with my eyes wide open, but she opened hers, too, as she felt me lean in, lips parting. I saw her eyes smile, dancing, and then widen in surprise: all across the formless, deep-sea night above us, the stars were coming out.

TRANSCENDENT 2

HER SACRED SPIRIT SOARS

◀ S. Qiouyi Lu ▶

鶼鶼 chien¹chien¹ (Wade–Giles), kimkim (Cantonese Standard)
lit. a pair of interdependent mythical birds, each having one eye and one wing
fig. an inseparable couple

Bodies pressed together, we soar over the mountains of Guilin and come to a stop on a verdant peak. We fold our wings together, the iridescent feather-tips of my wing resting over yours. You bear our weight on your leg; when you tire, I bear our weight on mine. We work our two eyes together.

The river below glitters with a million shades of sunset; small boats drift across its surface, marbling those resplendent colors. A zephyr rustles through the trees and whips up the scents of all the flora and fauna around us. We take flight again, our wings perfectly synchronized, and glide over the water.

The little boats scatter, making way for a larger ship that emerges from around the bend. The sight of this ship feels wrong, a gash in the landscape — whereas the other boats are small bamboo rafts lashed together with hemp rope, this ship is a hulking thing, sleek and angular against the rolling curves of the mountains. It smells of fire, but not a wood fire. Something older, dragged up from the earth, acrid and wrong against the petrichor of the mountains.

One shout, followed by another. Humans burrow up from within the boat; they unlatch a mechanism and aim it at us. We climb higher, but it's too late —

pow! A long, low *whoosh* comes up behind us, and knotted rope entangles us, drags us down from the heavens.

We thrash our wings, kick our legs, but the net holds on tight. We are large among birds, but small among humans. They crowd around us, block out the sunlight, and enclose us in a box. Our hearts flutter together, beating fast, faster, staccatos of panic in our chests. The gaps between the slats offer us the tiniest room to breathe. We crane our necks to see out, but they've draped a black cloth over our crate, hiding us from the world.

We have no sense of time in here. Sometimes, when they remove the cloth, a hint of sunlight streams through; other times, the room is dark. The only constant is the rocking of waves beneath us. They feed us half-spoiled fish scraps and we gobble them down, but it's never enough. We tremble against each other.

As the days pass, we wane together. Anxious, we mutilate our bodies; we've plucked out many of our feathers, the glittering emerald and scarlet strewn about in our crate, feather-threads rumpled askew. Only the pale color of ginkgo trunks stripped bare remains on our chests.

When we finally reach land again and the humans take us out of the ship, the smell of the ocean remains the same as that of the ocean back home, but we only recognize half of the stars in the sky. They've shifted and rotated, resting in a different place against the sea-black of night. The humans take us somewhere where there aren't any trees, transfer us from the crate to a cage. We squawk, our voices hoarse; they rattle our cage, squawk back, and we quiet down.

Their voices echo off the walls and create a forest of chatter that we can't understand. I bury my head into your neck, close my eye, and we're left with just your half of the room. You cock your head and peer at a small group of humans in conversation.

They feed us better fish here. There's no river inside, but the brightness of all the metal fixtures reminds us of water anyway. One day, when the humans let us out of the cage to fly around in a large room, we mistake a shining table for a puddle. We come to a stop on its surface, expecting our feet to sink into cool water and mud. But while the tabletop is cold, it does not yield.

Something aches within us.

The humans seem excited the next time they remove the cloth draped over our cage. They murmur among themselves as they take us to a room we've never been in before. They lay us on our back; we struggle against them, clawing at them, thrashing our wings, but still they clamp down on our legs and necks, strap our wings to our bodies. They retreat. We can still see their shapes around us, but there's something dividing them from us.

Buzzing, louder than a million cicadas screeching together, fills our ears. Leagues of lightning flash, arcing purple-bright over our bodies.

The lightning strikes and tears us apart.

The world goes white.

I wake up alone.

I can bear the weight of two kim, but not of one. I struggle to stand, my wing weighing me down; I balance myself only for a moment before tumbling. I reach out for you, but I can't find you anywhere — you're not by my side, nor do I feel your presence in any other way. I want to crash myself into the cage, throw myself around until I can get out and find you, fill this gaping hole in my heart, but my one wing doesn't cooperate without yours, and my one eye can only see half of what we saw together, and my one leg keeps giving way without your weight to balance us.

You can't be dead. I can't be alive. A single kim doesn't make sense — the humans separated us somehow, but why did I survive? Did I not love you enough?

I inch myself over to the door. I struggle to stand, gather my energy, then throw all my weight into my inevitable fall, hoping that somehow, somehow, I can break past this lock.

I crash into the cage until my entire being bleeds.

(Except, without you, I am not *entire* at all.)

They take me to another room. I glower at them, but my heart hurts, I haven't eaten, and I'm too weak without you to resist. A young human lies on an angled table, eyes closed. Wires cling all over to the human's body like leeches; the human breathes, but barely. I sense little vitality. The humans cover me with leech-wires too, all the while braying amongst themselves.

Lightning flashes and the sight of it again shakes me out of my melancholy, hurls me into a panic; I close my eye and flutter my wing — except I can't move my wing, not anymore.

Everything's whirling and I'm caught in a typhoon, ripped from my body, every thought needle-sharp as it draws across my mind, everything a thousand fires and flashes. I ground myself somewhere else, but the entire landscape shifts. My body feels different. Smells grow and diminish; I hear so much more, and the range of noise overwhelms me. I open my eye — my eyes — and find I can

TRANSCENDENT 2

only see what's before me. So many colors have disappeared. I have to turn my head — I *can* turn my head — to see anything else.

A lump of beige dappled with bright green and scarlet and black lies still on the table beside me, and I think: *A bird.* I am a bird; I was a bird, but the bird is dead and —

And I'm still here. I'm still alive. I am no longer the bird; I am this wingless thing, this four-limbed thing, this human. Somewhere in my memories lies the sensation of flying through the sky, but also visions of other worlds: tall buildings, automobiles that smell just like that ship — *diesel,* my mind supplies, *that smell is burning diesel.* From somewhere within bubbles up a word: *Meisun.* A name. My name.

These memories aren't mine, and yet they are mine. They're distant though, so distant, and recalling them is like trying to grasp the shape of pebbles on the bottom of a murky pond.

"You're conscious," someone says. Before, their words were just sounds, but now I recognize them and understand them.

Or maybe I've always understood them.

"Yes."

"Who are you?"

"I'm —" I hesitate. I'm ready to answer, but I'm not ready to answer. A flurry of memories whips up; I try to catch them one by one, but suddenly I want to retch, and instead I shake my head and let everything settle back down. "I don't know."

"Hmm."

As the person before me takes notes, I steal glances back to the bird body. I know it's me, but I also know that it can't possibly be me.

"Where is the other bird?"

"Other bird?"

I try to tell this person your name, but *kim* don't have names. Why does the emptiness where your name should be hurt so much? I swallow and nod at the bird body.

"You separated us into two. That one is — *was* — me. Where is the other one?"

"Oh. It died after we severed the bond. We've preserved the specimen. This one will also be preserved."

My head spins; I raise a hand up to steady myself. Something glints: a bracelet circles my wrist, and the letters stamped into it read REVIVAL. When they catch me looking at the bracelet, one of them speaks up.

"Your identification. We'll continue to monitor you, and this just shows that you're part of our project."

My stomach churns. This thing is a mockery of a jade bangle. It's silver and dead, nothing like the beautiful greens and browns that I dreamed would encircle my wrist, if only I had the money to purchase a piece. The light flashes off the bracelet again — in my mind's eye, I'm soaring, and I see water gleaming with sunlight.

I furrow my brow.

When have I ever had a need for anything like a jade bangle, or even the right kind of limb to wear one?

As they keep me here, I recall more about myself and the world: It's 1949. We're close to San Francisco, in Berkeley. I've been in California for four years now. Days bleed together, all of them the same: the researchers take my vitals and ask me to recount my memories. Each one is a double-exposure, ghosts overlaid on ghosts; some days, it's all I can do to shake my head and say that I can't speak any more.

Gradually, though, like water wearing down stone, the double visions begin to fade, and I can filter them more easily. My memories start to congeal, bit by bit. When I get to the point where I can recount complete narratives, the researchers breathe out a sigh of relief and prepare me for a meeting that they tell me is very important.

Representatives from the NIH come to tour the facility. Dr. Ackerman, who's worked with me the most, explains to me that "NIH" stands for "National Institute of Health" and that they're the ones who fund their research. He's going to need me to speak to them later. I nod.

After Dr. Ackerman comes back from brunch with the representatives, he guides me from my room to a meeting room. I'm seated in a stiff, high-backed chair in the front; Dr. Ackerman stands beside me. The low, warm hum of a slide projector fills my ears. He drones on and on; I don't fully understand what he's saying, even if I do understand most of the words he's using.

"...electroconvulsive therapy, or ECT, is the last option for treatment-resistant mental illnesses, but retrograde amnesia is still a common adverse side effect... kimkim, or Oriental Lovebirds, are two individual birds who have fused into one; they are part of the mythology of the celestials, but they are indeed real, and even their feathers have potent medicinal uses...energy can neither be created nor destroyed, but only transformed...as we've shown in this first phase,

TRANSCENDENT 2

it is indeed possible to reverse the bond between the two birds and store that energy in cells…."

He switches slides between his words, each *click* punctuating the rapt silence. The panel of unfamiliar faces before me nods and scribbles in their notepads; I struggle to stay awake. Then, I hear my name and look up.

"Meisun here is a unique case — our study also partners with the Revival group at Stanford; our colleagues there have shown that, while energy transfer from living animals into comatose humans can effectively bring them back out of their comas, the inadvertent transfer of animal sensory systems and reflexes leaves an indelible mark on the human, who is often caught in a state of being half-human, half-beast…because Oriental Lovebirds are renowned for their healing prowess, we hypothesized that perhaps the effects of transfer would be lessened; we extend that hypothesis to the ECT study and theorize that smaller doses of energy would cause little to no transfer and also prevent amnesia. We have high hopes, as our hypothesis for the Revival study appears to be correct. Meisun, could you tell our guests a little bit about yourself? You can start with where you're from."

I nod. I've discussed my memories so often with Dr. Ackerman and the others that this is becoming routine.

"I was born in Toisan, and most of my family still lives there. My parents married me to a Kam Saan haak, a merchant who was already here in California. I traveled here in the bottom of a boat." I pause. "I was in a box — no, no, that's not right. It was just very cramped, like being in a box. And then once I got here, I was detained at Angel Island for months."

One of the representatives raises an eyebrow. "And what was that like?" he asks.

"It was — it was lonely. Difficult. I was in a cage — a jail cell. The only thing there to keep me company was the poetry all over the walls, all from other detainees." I frown. I feel like I'm missing someone, that there's a hole in my heart. *You,* I think, but recalling details of you is like trying to cup water in my hands.

The representative nods. Another one looks up and scrutinizes me, his eyes a vibrant green, and I think of forests in the mountains.

"Can you tell us about your husband, your life here?"

I nod. "We had a little shop in Chinatown. Hard work, but we made enough money that I could even send some back home. We never made enough to be rich, though." I smile ruefully. "I didn't think I'd settle down here, but it looked like that was happening. And then — "

TRANSCENDENT 2

My heart skips a beat. I close my eyes, and I remember a sound — *pow!* — and things flying toward me. I tremble, but still I speak.

"Then the riots — people coming in to burn down Chinatown, and then they shot my husband, and they captured me — no, no; they surrounded me and beat me down and I remember everything hurting and then lightning — a storm? — and then there was...." I take in a shuddering breath. "Nothing."

The first representative shakes his head in sympathy. "I'm sorry."

"Thank you."

"Well, Dr. Ackerman," one of the representatives says after a moment, "this is indeed a very promising case, and you present compelling arguments for an ECT trial with Oriental Lovebird energy. We'll get to work on renewing your grant and the Revival group's grant; expect confirmation from us within two weeks."

Dr. Ackerman grins. He looks at me and places a hand on my shoulder. The touch feels unfamiliar, strange.

"Wonderful job, Meisun."

A few people begin to join the facility, all of them with bracelets like mine, but I find that I'm skittish. I dart away from them and spend most of my time in my own room, with its bare walls and sparse furniture, its window facing out toward an expanse of unfamiliar trees. Sometimes, I gaze out and a memory flashes across my mind: a forest from above, like I'm flying, and then I close my eyes and I *am* flying, and you're pressed up beside me, and we're so whole and complete together.

Then the memory fades, and I'm left remembering that the only person beside me had been my husband, who I'd never come to love. Who, if I'd loved, would have been a betrayal of you.

Dr. Ackerman knocks on my door one day and I let him in. He's carrying a few bags; there's someone behind him. I tilt my head quizzically.

"Meisun, meet your new roommate," Dr. Ackerman says.

The woman behind him is about my age: somewhere in her twenties. Her black hair, the same color as mine, flows over her shoulder, but the styled waves are limp. The hospital gown she's wearing renders her formless. She looks tired, empty almost, but when she sees my face, a small smile touches her lips.

"Nei kong Kwongtungwa?" she asks softly. I find myself smiling in return.

TRANSCENDENT 2

"Hai," I reply, and I realize just then how sweet Cantonese is to my ears, how it untangles my tongue and my heart when I no longer have to cottonmouth my way through English.

"I'm Yaulan," she continues in Cantonese. "And you?"

"Meisun."

Dr. Ackerman shakes his head. "You people always sound so angry when you speak," he says. I look at him, puzzled.

"We were just introducing ourselves," I say in English.

"I figured," he replies. Beside him, Yaulan rolls her eyes and mouths *Gweilo*, and I fight to suppress my laugh. "Well, get comfortable with each other; Yaulan is part of the trial and will be staying for a while."

Over the next couple of days, between Yaulan's diagnostics sessions, we talk about our pasts, our families, our lives. I'm still mixing up memories, but Yaulan's patient with me and doesn't seem to find me strange. She talks about her parents, how they had a dumpling-making machine, but then — she breaks eye contact and looks out the window at this point — it was destroyed during the riots, and she and her parents had barely gotten out alive.

"I feel kind of bad for leaving them alone to manage the restaurant — I was working as a server, but now that I'm not there, my mom will probably have to work twice as hard — but, well, this is probably my only chance for treatment, so…"

I catch her eye. "Treatment?"

She's quiet for a long time, and then she finally speaks. "I…I tried to kill myself. Twice. It was stupid, but…. Sometimes I can't stop myself when I start thinking about it and then — " She breaks off and takes a deep, shuddering breath. "I'm sick and this might be my one shot at staying alive."

My heart skips a beat.

"I'm sorry," I say, because I'm not sure what else to say.

She shrugs.

"I just hope it helps."

Y ou return to me in a dream.

We're bird-shaped again, the two of us; we sip dew from leaves, the water crisp and cool against our throats. We kick off the branch and take to flight; the branch springs back and casts dew into the air, throwing glittering points of light into the sky. We coast over the surface of the river; you spot a silver fish gleaming just below the water, and we plunge in. The river fills us with calm, presses against us in a soft embrace. We surface with the fish and land on a branch; we feed each other.

I wake with tears in my eyes. It takes me a moment to remember that I'm human, and by the time I do, the dream has started to slip away from me. Someone should be pressed up against my side, but my waist, my hip, they're empty and unconnected, a curve unfilled.

It's past eleven. I didn't realize I'd slept in so late; when I turn over, I see Yaulan sitting on her bed with her back to me.

And I see you, superimposed on her.

I sit up with a jolt. Yaulan looks back at me, and then it's only her, and she gives me a tiny little smile.

"I was afraid you'd never wake up," she says in Cantonese. My heart's beating a galloping rhythm against my chest and my mouth feels dry.

"You're…" I say, then swallow. "Did something…did something happen?"

"Well, I had my first ECT session," Yaulan says. "It was…strange. I'm not sure if I feel better, but at least I don't feel worse."

I feel it: our bond, our energy, torn away from both you and me. I recoil, and Yaulan frowns.

"Is something wrong?"

"It's nothing," I say, my hands trembling. "I just — had an odd dream, and…"

And you were in it, only that's not true. It wasn't her; it was you.

Yaulan leaves for more interviews and testing. I sit on my bed alone; I take a few deep breaths, and suddenly everything fades and I'm left feeling lightheaded and confused over having such a strange reaction to Yaulan. The tide of nausea ebbs, and I let out a sigh.

When I look up, I find that the room feels too big without Yaulan in it too.

I've begun therapy with a psychologist, Dr. Roberts. He tells me that I must fight off the bird memories when they intrude, but I still find it difficult to do so. It feels so real in the moment, so compelling, that I want to cling to them and try to salvage some of that feeling of being whole with you. But when I tell Dr. Roberts this, he shakes his head and tells me that I must let go of these memories, or I'll be a human forever haunted by experiences that I didn't truly have.

I'm not sure how I feel about that. I don't think I want to let go of those memories and forget that they ever happened, that you ever existed. I just want to get to a point where I can think about them and they don't send me into a ruminating spiral, one that leaves me wasting hours as I'm caught in my own conflicting thoughts.

Yaulan's struggling, too. I see her smiling more these days, but sometimes she still looks hollow, still hunches over and refuses to talk to me. Then there are the times when she's just come back from ECT and I almost can't bear to look at her; the energy emanating off of her, sparking energy in me, makes me remember you and again I'm recalling Guilin, recalling Toisan, and I'm lost in my memories again.

On Saturdays, though, I don't have to go to Dr. Roberts, and Yaulan doesn't have to go to ECT; we can do activities or go out on supervised excursions together. Nurse Florence takes us to a café. I've never liked coffee and find the taste of it too bitter against my tongue, too harsh even with cream and sugar, but Yaulan drinks her coffee black and savors every sip of it. Seeing the coffee warm her up makes me smile myself.

On another Saturday, Yaulan and I stay inside for an art class. She's much better at making the flowers and birds look like actual flowers and birds. I feel self-conscious about my misshapen figures, but then Yaulan looks at my painting, her eyes glittering with delight.

"Wow, Meisun," she says. "Look at those colors! You're a natural. My colors always feel so flat."

I look between our two paintings, and I guess mine is a little more vivid than hers. I wonder, though, if we could combine our skills, perhaps we'd create a perfect painting.

Nurse Florence also supervises us while we use the kitchen the next Saturday. There are no knives in here, so we can't really cook, but we can still bake and do things that only require mixing. It's the Mid-Autumn Festival and Nurse Florence has never celebrated it before; we show her how to make mooncakes. Without the special molds, our mooncakes come out lopsided. The Chinese characters we write onto their surfaces aren't as pretty as the ones they sell in the store, but the end results are still delicious.

Through every Saturday, I can't help but think how much I like spending time with Yaulan, how well we get along together. Only when Monday rolls around and we have to go back to therapy do I remember the unease in my heart.

Yaulan's told me before that her terrible thoughts come and go, that she considers feeling better temporary, but I'm still not prepared for it when she crashes.

TRANSCENDENT 2

"I'm never going to be better — I'm never going to be free of these thoughts — I was doing so well and then I wasn't; there's no point."

She's slumped in a corner, her hands over her head.

"But that's just the thing," I say, kneeling down beside her, "you *did* get better, so you can — "

"But it's always going to be like this. Always."

I frown.

"You don't know that; none of us know the future."

"I just — " Yaulan starts sobbing, and the sound of it breaks my heart: her breaths hitch, and her words come out wavering; there's so much pain laced through every syllable, so much pain that cuts straight into me. "I wish I didn't have to deal with this. I wish I could just be better. Sometimes I am, but then I start feeling sad again, and I want to kill myself again. I want to throw myself out the window right now, too; I want so bad for all of this to just be over."

My heart skips a beat. I place my hand over hers.

"It's hard. I know, I've seen you; it's so hard," I murmur.

She lets her hand fall from her head. I stroke my thumb in little circles against her skin, and I give her a sad smile.

"But look at you, you want to do these things, but you're not. You're going on living anyway."

She looks up at me, her eyes red-rimmed, but doesn't say anything, only takes in more shuddering breaths.

"Lanlan," I say, using the nickname I've come to call her, "let's just go to sleep, yeah? Let's go to sleep and see how you feel in the morning, okay?"

For a moment, I wonder if she'll be angry, if she thinks I'm treating her like a child. But I'm not; I'm just trying my best to be gentle with her, to calm her down. Finally, she nods.

"Okay."

I help her up. We squeeze together in her bed. She curls up against my chest, still crying, but silently now. Her tears soak through my pajamas and dampen my chest. I stroke her hair and sing a lullaby my mother used to sing to me, tell her some of my favorite stories, tell her to rest for now, to sleep.

Even when her breaths finally even out, I still hold on to her. She's so warm, such a bundle of light; I fear that if I let go, her light will go out. Only when I fall asleep do I let myself relax.

TRANSCENDENT 2

The next day, Yaulan's eyes are puffy from crying. She looks at herself in the mirror, prods at the newfound creases in her eyelids, and makes a face.

"I want my monolids back," she says. "I don't look like myself."

"You look lovely," I say, and Yaulan turns, frowning.

"Are you making fun of me?" she says, putting her hands on her hips. She's trying to play it off as a joke, but I can tell from her tone that she's feeling hurt.

"No, I'm serious!" I say. "Really, you look fine."

She lets her hands fall and sighs, her stance slumped now. A flush rises to her cheeks.

"I feel so silly for…what happened."

I get up and give her a hug. She's tense at first, but then she relaxes into me. I rub her back.

"Sometimes things like that happen," I say. "It's okay."

After a moment, she breaks away from me. She's looking at me like she doesn't believe that I'm real, and for a second, I start doubting myself too, start wondering why she's looking at me like that — but then she speaks and interrupts my thoughts.

"You're really not going to scold me?"

I furrow my brow.

"Why would I scold you?" I ask. "You told me yourself, you're sick. I wouldn't scold you for coughing; why should I be angry with you for your mind's illness?"

She's scrutinizing me, like she's testing me. Then, she smiles at last.

"I really like you, Meisun," she says, and I blush. "Really. I'm glad you're in my life."

Her words linger with me for the rest of the day. I find that I like her too, in a way that feels both familiar and terrifying. It's a swelling in my chest and suddenly I remember you. Would you be upset? We had bonded for life, after all. But what happens when your life is over, yet mine goes on?

I'm still feeling anxious when I walk into Dr. Roberts's office later that day.

"Is there anything on your mind?" he says. "You seem distracted."

"I…" I pause. "I keep thinking about — about my partner. The other bird. About how we were supposed to live and die together, but I'm still alive. If I were to be with someone else — would that be okay?"

"You aren't a bird, Meisun," Dr. Roberts says, and anger flares in my chest.

"But I am," I retort. Then, I doubt myself and add, "Or, I was."

Her Sacred Spirit Soars

"Then you aren't a bird *anymore*," Dr. Roberts says, his voice level, and suddenly something shifts within me. "You're human now, and you live with humans now, all right?"

Part of me resents him, but part of me considers what he says.

I *am* human.

And maybe humans love differently.

This Saturday, Yaulan and I go out to the beach under Nurse Florence's supervision. It's a beautiful day, with cirrus clouds pulled loose across the gentle blue sky; we pack lunches and bring a picnic basket. Yaulan wears her favorite deep blue cheongsam, and I wear a white one. She teases me for being so modest, my cheongsam looser against my body, and I stick out my tongue at her.

I tell her and Nurse Florence stories about Toisan in between bites of our sandwiches. Nurse Florence nods, acknowledging my words, while Yaulan listens wide-eyed; she's never been to China before.

"Maybe we can visit Toisan together someday," she says.

"I'd like that," I reply.

We explore the beach, climb into the caves, and I'd regret wearing my white cheongsam if not for the fact that I'm having far too much fun. We climb back out onto the sand. Yaulan picks up one shell, and I pick up another; I scour the sand for an unbroken shell, one with that perfect mother-of-pearl sheen.

When I look up, Yaulan's already several paces ahead. The setting sun turns her into a silhouette; the wind whips at her hair and the skirt of her cheongsam as she walks barefoot in the sand. She holds her arms out, like she's balancing herself on an invisible beam. I see her soaring in my mind's eye, and suddenly my heart aches.

She'll never be you, but she's not meant to. She had no part in them taking away our bond, and if our bond helped her so, was that such a bad thing? Besides, she's human, and so am I; we're not meant to be joined together like kim-kim. Love for humans means flying side-by-side in the same direction, two separate beings working together.

I catch up to Yaulan and grasp her hand. She turns, surprised, and a grin spreads across her face. It's the most beautiful sight I've ever witnessed, but even so, sadness still lingers in her eyes, in the way she holds herself.

But that's okay. I'm not expecting magic, for us to live happily ever after. All I want is to be beside her and hope for the best.

I lean in and kiss her forehead, and in that moment I think, *I love you.*

TRANSCENDENT 2

CONTRIBUTORS

CHARLIE JANE ANDERS is the author of the Nebula Award- and Crawford Award-winning novel *All the Birds in the Sky* (Tor Books). She has also won a Lambda Literary Award for her transgender work *Choir Boy*. Anders has had fiction published in *Strange Horizons, Tor.com* and *McSweeney's* and her non-fiction has appeared in *Salon, The Wall Street Journal*, and *Mother Jones*.

GWEN BENAWAY is of Anishinaabe and Métis descent. She is the author of the poetry collections *Ceremonies for the Dead* and *Passage*. An emerging Two-Spirited Trans poet, she has been described as the spiritual love child of Tomson Highway and Anne Sexton. She has been the recipient of the inaugural Speaker's Award for a Young Author and in 2016 she received a Dayne Ogilvie Honour of Distinction for Emerging Queer Authors from the Writer's Trust of Canada. Her work has been published and anthologized internationally. She and her many vintage dresses can be found on Instagram @gwenbenaway.

VAJRA CHANDRASEKERA lives in Colombo, Sri Lanka. His work has appeared in *Clarkesworld, Lightspeed*, and *Strange Horizons*, among others. He blogs occasionally at vajra.me and can be found on Twitter at @_vajra.

HOLLY HEISEY launched their writing career in sixth grade when they wrote their class play, a medieval fantasy. It was love at first dragon. Since then, their short fiction has appeared in *Intergalactic Medicine Show*, *The Doomsday Chronicles*, *Clockwork Phoenix 5*, and *Transcendent: The Year's Best Transgender Speculative Fiction*, and has been translated into German and Estonian. A freelance designer by day, Holly lives in Arizona with Larry and Moe, their two pet cacti, and they are currently at work on a science fantasy epic.

JULIAN K. JARBOE is a writer and sound designer living in Salem, Massachusetts. In 2016 they and their partner were artists-in-residence for a special "Science Fiction and the Human Condition" themed residency at the Bemis Center for Contemporary Art in Omaha, Nebraska. Their work can be found on their website, toomanyfeelings.com, and they tweet @JulianKJarboe.

KEFFY R.M. KEHRLI is a science fiction and fantasy writer, editor, and podcaster currently located on Long Island, NY, where he is working toward a PhD in Genetics. His short fiction has appeared in magazines such as *Lightspeed*, *Apex*, and *Uncanny*, as well as in anthologies such as *Clockwork Phoenix 5*. In 2015, he launched GlitterShip, a podcast that presents audio versions of LGBTQ science fiction and fantasy short stories. You can find more about him at keffy.com or @Keffy on Twitter.

S. QIOUYI LU is a writer, artist, editor, and narrator; their writing has appeared in *Uncanny* and *Strange Horizons*, among other venues. In their spare time, they enjoy destroying speculative fiction as a dread member of the Queer Asian SFFH Illuminati. Find out more at s.qiouyi.lu or follow them on Twitter at @sqiouyilu.

BRIT MANDELO is a writer, critic, and editor whose primary fields of interest are speculative fiction and queer literature, especially when the two coincide. They have two books out, *Beyond Binary: Genderqueer and Sexually Fluid Speculative Fiction* and *We Wuz Pushed: On Joanna Russ and Radical Truth-telling*, and in the past have edited for publications like *Strange Horizons*. Other work has been featured in magazines such as *Stone Telling*, *Clarkesworld*, *Apex*, and *Ideomancer*. They also write regularly for *Tor.com* and have several long-running column series there, including Queering SFF, a mix of criticism, editorials, and reviews on QUILTBAG speculative fiction.

Toby MacNutt is a multidisciplinary artist and educator, with a passion for social justice and community work. MacNutt is based in Burlington, VT. Their poetry has recently appeared in places like *Through the Gate*, *Goblin Fruit*, *inkscrawl*, and *The Future Fire*. They are working on being the best, sparkliest mutant they can be. You can find them online at tobymacnutt.com.

An Owomoyela is a web application developer by profession and a writer by vocation, lives in the San Francisco Bay Area, weaves chain maille, and laughs often at *XKCD*. Se's fiction has been published in *Clarkesworld*, *Fantasy*, and *Lightspeed*, among many print and online magazines, Se's website, an.owomoyela.net, offers more details.

A. Merc Rustad is a queer transmasculine non-binary writer and filmmaker who likes dinosaurs, robots, monsters, and cookies. Their fiction has appeared in nifty places like *Lightspeed*, *Cicada*, *Uncanny*, *Fireside*, *Apex*, and many others. Rustad's work has been featured in *The Best American Science Fiction and Fantasy* several times. Rustad's first collection, *So You Want to be a Robot*, released from Lethe Press.

RoAnna Sylver writes unusually hopeful dystopian stories about marginalized heroes actually surviving, triumphing, and rocking really hard. RoAnna is also a singer, blogger, voice actor and artist who lives with family and a small snorking dog, and probably spends too much time playing videogames. The next amazing adventure RoAnna would like is a nap in a pile of bunnies.

Sonya Taaffe is a Massachusetts-based author of short fiction and poetry. She grew up in Arlington and Lexington, MA, and graduated from Brandeis University, where she received a BA and MA in Classical Studies. She also received an MA in Classical Studies from Yale University. Taaffe's poem "Matlacihuatl's Gift" won the Rhysling Award.

A hybrid cyborg and Philadelphia native, M Téllez writes and performs speculative fiction about bodies/objectification, intimacy/class, neighborhood/land/community, and the violence in relying on binaries to order the world. A founding member of METROPOLARITY sci-fi collective, M is frustrated/pissed with institutional distinction, empire and white supremacy, and fixed rather than fluid treatment of language and identity. They consider the spoken and written word handy and inexpensive tools for deconstructing oppressive world-ordering narratives.

JEANNE THORNTON is the author of *The Dream of Doctor Bantam* (a Lambda Literary Award finalist) and *The Black Emerald*, as well as the co-publisher of Instar Books and a sometimes cartoonist. She lives in Brooklyn. More information is available at http://fictioncircus.com/Jeanne.

GILLIAN YBABEZ was born and lives in South Texas. She writes sci-fi and fantasy stories with women and LGBT characters. She has previously been published in *An Anthology of Fiction by Trans Women of Color*. Her first ebook, *Love and Comets and Other Stories*, collects short stories from her website and is available on Gumroad and Amazon. All of her fiction can be found on her website Gillian-Ybabez.com.

ABOUT THE EDITOR

Bogi Takács (e/em/eir/emself or they pronouns) is a Hungarian Jewish agender trans person and a resident alien in the United States. E writes, edits and reviews speculative fiction, nonfiction and poetry. You can find eir work in *Clarkesworld, Lightspeed, Strange Horizons* and *Uncanny*, among other places; e also had a story reprinted in the previous *Transcendent* anthology, edited by K.M. Szpara. Bogi lives in Kansas with eir cheerful neuroatypical family. You can find Bogi online at prezzey.net or read eir book reviews at bogireadstheworld.com, or eir QUILTBAG space opera webserial at iwunen.net. Bogi is @bogiperson on Twitter, Instagram and Patreon.

PUBLICATION CREDITS

CPSIA information can be obtained
at www.ICGtesting.com
Printed in the USA
LVHW03s0209150618
580751LV00003B/539/P